SUMMER love

marysue g. hobika

The cover art was created by Lee Rowland. For more information please visit her website at www.peartreespace.com

Editing services provided by Jenn Sommersby Young. Contact her at www.somberbee.wix.com/jennsommersbyediting

Find out more about the author and upcoming books at www.onehiplitchick.com

Dedication

I dedicate this book to my beta readers, Sasha Kinsler, Callie Coffey, Abbie Hobika, Lisa Azzara, and Kelly Mooney. I would especially like to extend a great big thank you to Brian Pullyblank for his time and energy in helping me make this book sound legit, giving it the edge that real teens possess. This book would not have been possible without all of you.

Chapter One

Carly

"Glad that's over," Becca said. We walked across the school parking lot to her car, having just finished our last final. We had plans to spend the day together.

"Yeah. The stress was getting to me. Waiting on test results is gonna suck," I said. Good grades were a priority, so I put a lot of pressure on myself to do well.

Becca rolled her eyes. "I'm sure you did great, like always. You worry too damn much." Becca never worried about anything. We were opposites, which was one of the reasons we were perfect best friends. We balanced each other.

"I can't believe we're going to be seniors in the fall." It would soon be our last year of high school.

"I know, but that's months away. Right now it's time to get our summer on! From this moment on, I'm making a rule: no more talking about school. It's summer! Time to relax. Got it?"

"Got it." Becca always knew how to lighten my mood. I had a tendency to take things too seriously. She had a certain aura about her that, to be honest, I wish I had more of. I wish I had the courage to go beyond my comfort zone and break the goody-two-shoes stigma that had plagued me for too long.

We climbed into her car, and within seconds she pulled

out of the school parking lot, tires squealing against the black pavement. We cruised down the road, windows down, the blaring rap music drawing unneeded attention to Becca and me by default, and headed for the country club pool.

"Mark my words," Becca said, pulling into an empty parking spot. "This is going to be the best summer to date. What did Mr. Johnson talk about in social studies—Custer's Last Stand? This is our last stand—our last true summer of freedom before we have to start planning the rest of our lives." I could feel the determination in her voice, see the flash of excitement in her eyes. Becca was ready to drop a nuclear bomb on summer. She continued, "This summer can be summarized in two words: tans and cans."

"What?" I said.

"Tans and cans," she explained as we made our way to the pool area. "We're going to bronze, hence the tan, while checking out the asses of all the boys who walk by. Tans and cans. You know what they say about summer love? It's right around the corner and in our case, right here at the pool." I laughed. I had no idea where Becca came up with this stuff. Before we knew it, schools were going to be offering Spanish, French, and Becca. I swore she had her own language.

I doubted I'd be able to land any "cans," let alone find the courage to talk to any of the boys we encountered. I was more like the audience at a play. I paid my money to see the show rather than star in it. Becca, however, was the lead. I liked to admire the hotties from the safe distance of my lounge chair, hiding behind my oversized, ten-dollar sunglasses. I didn't have the gift of gab. Whenever I spoke to the opposite sex, my body went rigid and I couldn't form a coherent sentence. I became a tongue-twisted idiot. However, I wouldn't put it past Becca to seek out a man-can and work her magic.

I had to admit, I kind of liked the idea of making these two months we wouldn't forget. "You're on, sister. Let's make this one for the history books, starting right now."

"That's my girl," Becca exclaimed. She looped her arm

through mine, scanned the pool deck for the best possible views and rays, and headed in the direction of two open lounge chairs.

We found our epicenter just as Gillian and her clone, Marlena, staked their claims. "Sorry, bitches, these chairs belong to us," Gillian said.

"Oh, really? Says who? Because it looks like we're sitting here," Becca said, throwing her bag onto one chair while simultaneously plopping down on the other. She pushed her sunglasses down and glared over the top, daring Gillian to make a move.

"Actually, we," she pointed a perfectly manicured finger between her and Marlena, "were going to sit here, so get your ass up." Gillian thought being the richest girl at school entitled her to get whatever she wanted.

"Well, that's too bad, because we're not moving," said Becca, refusing to be bullied. She stared at me, willing me to claim the other chair. Whenever I was faced with conflict, I failed to come through. I tried to make my feet move, but they were frozen to the spot. I hated confrontation. What did I do? Nothing, as usual.

Then, as quickly as a swirling Gulf Coast hurricane, I was seated next to Becca. I yelped as she pulled me down onto the lounge chair that her bag had been reserving. I could tell by the way her fingernails dug into my arm that she was pissed at me for having no backbone.

Becca plastered on a condescending smile. "Now, if you don't mind, you're blocking my sun." Dismissing Gillian and her sidekick, Becca pulled a magazine from her bag.

Gillian's face was as red as a ripe cherry and a whole lot of pissed-off energy radiated from her. She stood there for several seconds, tapping her foot. Realizing we weren't going to move, she gave in. "You might have won this round, Rebecca, but this is far from over," she huffed. Becca hated when people called her by her full name and Gillian knew it. "I'm going to make your summer hell, bitches. Mark my words." She spun on her heel and walked off, Marlena trailing behind her like a lost puppy.

I trembled. Gillian would somehow, someway, make good on her threat. She always did. Last year Sarah Newcomer was dating John Hanson, a boy Gillian liked. Gillian demanded Sarah break up with him, but she refused to acquiesce. Soon a vicious rumor spread around school that Sarah had herpes. Kids whispered behind Sarah's back and vandalized her locker. We all knew it was a lie and that Gillian was behind it, but Sarah's reputation was ruined. John dumped her a few days later. Gillian was powerful, mean, and ruthless. I had managed to escape her wrath so far, but it didn't look good for my future. I glanced at Becca to see if she was worried. She sat reading her magazine, looking like she couldn't care less.

Once they were out of earshot, Becca turned to me and said, "Really, Car? How could you just stand there while I was saving these two chairs for us? Some of us don't have the luxury of spaghetti sauce coursing through our veins; some of us actually need prime tanning space to make our skin shimmer." I was part Italian with dark features, while Becca was fair-skinned with blue eyes and platinum hair. "And besides, you couldn't pay me a million dollars to move for those whores."

I sputtered an excuse. "Sorry. I froze. Gillian scares me. She reminds me of Regina George from *Mean Girls*, ready to socially obliterate her next victims: us."

Becca softened. "She always looks like that. Nasty bitch."

"Yeah, but I wish I were able to stand up for myself. I want to speak my mind, like you do. Tell them where they can stick it. The words always get caught in my throat. I wish I could be more outgoing. You never worry what anyone else thinks. You say exactly what's on your mind. And you don't let girls like Gillian and Marlena intimidate you."

"You're perfect just the way you are. And that's why you've got me. I've got your back." She reached over and patted my arm.

"I know. But if I'm going to have your back, I've got to grow some thicker skin." Was this me, Carly, saying all of this?

Becca laughed. "I think you mean balls. You've got to grow some balls."

"What?" I laughed.

"B ... A ... L ... L ... S! Not thicker skin—you need BALLS!"

I laughed harder.

Becca wouldn't let it go. "Say it, Carly. Say that you need to grow a set."

I blushed. There was no way I could ever talk like that. Looking over at Becca, I saw that she was serious.

"Come on, Car, say it."

Now was as good a chance as any to break the mold. I wanted to stop worrying about what everyone else thought of me and speak my mind.

"If you don't hurry up, summer will be over. Just fucking say it, Car!"

Gathering my courage, I took a deep breath. "I'm ready to grow some balls," I said, just above a whisper.

"What? I couldn't hear you? Speak up." Becca cupped her ear.

"I said, I'm ready to grow some balls!" As luck would have it, the moment I uttered those words, a mother and her two young boys walked by. She threw me a disgusted look, causing Becca and I to crack up.

"You just passed your first test on how to speak your mind," Becca declared.

"I did?"

"Yes," she said, the corners of her mouth turning upwards encouragingly. "But don't worry, we'll keep working on it. I'm sure that before summer is over, you'll have plenty of opportunities to test your new skill set." Becca's head whipped around to where Gillian and Marlena were making themselves comfortable on two lounge chairs previously occupied by a couple of younger girls, whom they must've scared off. "Because I'm sure those sluts will be back sooner or later," she said.

"Those bitches are going to be trouble." Practice makes perfect. Maybe speaking my mind would be more fun than I ever thought possible.

Becca beamed triumphantly. "Now you're catching on." She pulled out her phone and began typing.

"What are you doing?" I glanced over Becca's shoulder.

"I'm marking my calendar. You cursed, you bad girl, you," she said.

We settled into our chairs. Closing my eyes, I relaxed as the sun soaked into my skin, pushing all thoughts of Gillian out of my mind. The only sounds were kids splashing and Becca flipping the pages of her magazine. Summer was my favorite season.

"Hey, let's take this quiz. It's called 'Which type of guy is for you?'" Becca loved her magazines and would spend hours poring over the latest fashion trends, hairstyles, and makeup tips. The quiz section was her absolute favorite. She pulled a pen out of her bag.

"Sure." I twisted around on the chair. Quizzes were fun, and sometimes educational.

"Okay. Number one: Which personality trait is the most important to you that your guy possesses? The choices are A. Intelligence—no dumb-ass will do for you. You want someone who is smart and going places. B. Kindness—duh? You've already dated jerks. You're ready for a guy who opens the car door for you and treats you with the respect you deserve. C. Humor—you love to crack jokes and you're the life of the party. You need someone who likes to laugh as much as you do. D. Honesty—you like a straight shooter. You want to know that what comes out of his mouth is the truth. Honesty leads to trust and that means everything to you." She looked up from the magazine, biting the end of the pen. "So ... which do you think is the most important?"

"That's a tough one. I'd like a smart guy who is kind, fun, and honest."

Becca laughed. "You can only pick one."

"Okay. Let's see. If I have to choose only one, then I'll pick D, honesty. I need a guy I can trust." I didn't have any real experience in the relationship department, but I couldn't see myself with a liar or cheater. I'd seen the hurt way too many times when other girls talked about how their boyfriends cheated on them, and I couldn't imagine anything worse. Becca marked my answer in the magazine. "What about you?"

"This is an easy one for me. I pick humor. I need a guy who is fun and likes to have a good time." A typical Becca answer.

"Okay, number two. What would be your ideal outfit for him to wear? A. Jeans and a T-shirt—a casual yet traditional sexy look. B. Board shorts—you like the beach look and showing skin is never a bad thing. C. A polo shirt and khakis—you like the Ivy League, prep-school look. D. Ripped baggy jeans, a hoodie, and tattoo—you're down with the fresh, hip-hop/skater look."

Becca and I answered at the same time. "Board shorts." We laughed because we don't see eye to eye on many things, but visually undressing the boys at the pool had always been one of our favorite pastimes. That said, I could go for a guy with tattoos.

She continued reading the questions, keeping track of our answers. Sometimes we agreed, but other times, we had very different opinions. Becca was more of a risk-taker, while I was quiet and reserved. For some reason, though, I felt different today. Liberated. Maybe it was due to making a vow to challenge myself to attack life with an out-of-the-box approach.

Finally, we were down to the last question. "Number ten: When he kisses you for the first time, you hope he: A. Doesn't slobber all over you—you don't want to feel as if you're being licked to death by a dog."

"That's nasty." I grimaced.

She laughed and continued. "B. Holds you close—you want to feel his heart beating next to yours, inhale his scent, and fall slowly into the depths of his eyes. C. Brushed his teeth—personal hygiene is a top priority for you. D. Doesn't forget to tease you with his tongue—you love it when a guy knows how to French kiss."

"I choose B. I want him to hold me tight in his arms." I sighed as I pictured my dream guy crushing me against his muscled chest.

Becca giggled. "You are such a romantic. Still holding out hope for Mr. Perfect, huh, Car?"

"Yes, yes, I am. What about you?" I asked, but before Becca could even open her mouth to respond, I answered for her. "Let me guess ... D. You want a guy who is a good kisser!"

We laughed. We knew each other so well. She scribbled down our answers and tallied our points. "You scored 24. I got 30." She flipped to the page with the explanations. "Ironically, that puts us in the same category. Our type is 'A Modern Guy.' A guy who isn't overly sappy or indifferent, but is honest and true. He likes to do fun things—movies and concerts every weekend. He's confident and his body language and clothes say so. He'll like you for who you are and not what you look like."

"Does it say where we can find this guy?" I laughed, pointing at the magazine. "Because I'm pretty sure I've never seen this type around here."

Becca made a big deal out of scanning the next several pages, "No, unfortunately, it doesn't say anything about that. This is the last time I buy this shitty magazine," she teased.

"I wonder if he," I nodded at a guy who looked to be around our age, "is a modern guy?"

We watched in awe as a tall muscular figure with sandy-blond hair walked over to the lifeguard chair and replaced the girl who'd been keeping watch. He must be one of the new lifeguards hired for summer. Even with his eyes and his face partially hidden behind sunglasses, it was obvious he was extremely good-looking. He was clean-cut and lightly bronzed.

"One can hope," Becca said with a devilish grin. "Time for your next lesson in being assertive, Carly."

"Oh no. Let's not go overboard."

But Becca rarely listened. She stood and ran her fingers through her long blond hair. "I'm not going to make you do anything, silly. Just sit back and enjoy. Watch and learn, my little disciple."

Becca walked with a purpose over to the lifeguard and struck up a conversation. I never understood how she could do that—I didn't have the guts. I pretended to read the magazine she'd left behind, not wanting to look like a loser sitting here by myself. Lifting my eyes over the top of the magazine, I watched Becca turn on the charm. Once I even saw her reach her hand out and playfully hit him. I couldn't hear their conversation, but I didn't need to. I could tell they were hitting it off. Their facial expressions and body language said it all. Most guys found Becca's beauty irresistible. I wouldn't be at all surprised if she'd scored a date with him, just like she'd set out to do.

It felt like an eternity before she came back. "Wow. If you thought he looked good from all the way over here, you should see him up close. He's gorgeous—totally could be a model. And he has the most amazing blue eyes," she gushed. "The things I would like to do to him." She smacked her lips like she'd just taken a bite of birthday cake.

I laughed. Becca was always enthusiastic when she first met a guy. It wasn't until several dates later that she would get bored, claiming all boys were the same—all they ever thought about was sex. Becca wasn't shy when it came to boys, and I knew she enjoyed fooling around as much as they did, but she complained that the boys she dated never wanted to do anything else. Sooner or later, she'd get fed up and dump them.

Becca's new "flavor of the day" glanced our way and waved. Becca waved back. I looked over at Gillian and Marlena and saw their scowls at the exchange. Normally I'd be scared by the look on their faces, but screw that. Becca and I had just won another round, and it felt good.

"You aren't going to believe this," Becca said.

"Did he ask you out?"

"Yes," she smirked, "but that wasn't what I was going to say. Turns out you know his brother." I raised my eyebrows, encouraging her to explain further. "His brother is sort of a friend of yours." Becca air-quoted with her fingers around the word *friend.*

I narrowed my eyes at the hot lifeguard. He'd taken off his sunglasses to lather sunscreen on his face, and I could see why Becca had said his eyes were amazing. They were a brilliant shade of blue, the exact color of the Bahamian water in the Bahamas where my dad took us every year during Thanksgiving break. I sucked in a breath. I would recognize that unique color anywhere. "That's Gavin's older brother?" I turned to face her, not hiding my disbelief.

"Yes," she grinned.

"Is his name Nathan?"

"How'd you guess? They look nothing alike."

I sat staring in amazement, mentally comparing the two brothers. At first glance, Becca was right. They looked nothing alike. Nathan had short, sandy-colored hair with streaks of blond, no doubt due to the time he spent outdoors, and his skin was lightly tanned. He wore an easy smile, making him appear friendly. Gavin was the complete opposite. His hair was dark, almost black, and his skin olive. His appearance matched his brooding personality. Despite their obvious differences, there were similarities that went beyond their matching blue eyes. Same height, similar builds, except Nathan was bulkier. I was willing to bet that Gavin had the same rock-hard abs hiding underneath the dark T-shirts he was so fond of wearing—said abs looked pretty good on Nathan in his lifeguard uniform.

"Did Gavin ever tell you how hot his older brother was?" Becca asked, like an excited child on Christmas.

"Um, no," I laughed. That was the last thing I could ever imagine Gavin, or any other guy, saying.

"Come on, he must've said something about his brother. I mean, just look at him." Becca stared off in his direction.

Talking about himself or his family was not something Gavin ever did. It amazed me that after being lab partners with Gavin for a whole year and him coming over to study a few times, I still knew very little about him. He'd been a new student in the fall, transferring from an all-boys' Catholic high school. It was clear he didn't want to be at Crownwood High, but he had shared with me it was necessary because his parents were divorced, and paying tuition was no longer an option. I never questioned him further because it was obvious by the set of his jaw that the subject was off-limits. We only ever talked about the lab we were working on, or the material we were studying.

"Please, Car, give me something to work with." She turned and looked at me over the top of her sunglasses, bottom lip in full pout.

I laughed. "Does that look actually work on boys? Is that how you get them to do your bidding?"

"Guilty as charged." She continued to pester me for details until I finally caved. I knew Becca wouldn't stop until I told her something, even if I had to make it up.

"Let's see." I closed my eyes and thought back to the week before our final exam. Gavin came over to study and was in a particularly dark mood, so I made a joke about him not biking over like he usually did. Unfortunately, the joke didn't go over well and he seemed angry about my teasing. He gave a brief response and said his brother Nathan dropped him off and would pick him up later. Until then I hadn't even known he had an older brother. The remainder of the study session was tense. When he left, I tried to figure out what had set him off. I wasn't sure what I'd done wrong, but I felt like I should apologize for something. I glanced over at Becca, still waiting for an answer. I cleared my throat. "He said that his brother had just gotten home from college."

"Did he say which college?"

"He didn't."

"What else did he say?"

"Nothing. This is Gavin we're talking about, remember? We talk about chemistry, not our personal lives."

"Chemistry, huh?" Becca smirked.

I recognized that look and knew I wasn't going to like what Becca had in mind. I cut her off before she could suggest anything. "No. Don't even think about it."

"What?" she said, sounding innocent.

"I'm not going to double with you. No way. No how. Don't even ask."

Becca threw up her hands. "Okay, I won't."

"And don't forget we told Drew we'd hang out. Lucas is throwing a big party to celebrate." Drew was my twin and Lucas was his best friend. We' d run into them on our way out of the exam, and they'd reminded us about the party.

"Yeah, but that's not until later. Things won't even begin until after eleven." Becca settled into her chair. "You have to admit that Gavin is hot, in a dark and dangerous sort of way." Her words were true, and like most girls at school, I harbored a secret crush on him. He was smart and hot as hell. But something warned me that getting involved with Gavin could lead to heartache. Plus, he never hinted that he wanted to be anything other than friends.

Chapter Two

Gavin

"I still think this is a bad idea." I ran my hands through my shaggy hair. Now that I no longer went to a Catholic school, I had let it grow out. We waited outside the restaurant for the girls to arrive. They were late, which was typical, and it added to the uneasy feeling in the pit of my stomach. I glared at Nate, wishing I hadn't let him talk me into this.

"It's not a bad idea. It's a great idea," Nate said, making me want to punch him in the gut. His happy-go-lucky attitude got under my skin. "What else would you be doing right now?"

I didn't respond. The truth was I'd be lounging on my bed with my ear buds in while I worked on my drawings. Same as every other Friday night for the past year. As lame as that sounded, it was what I enjoyed. Ever since my parents' divorce, I'd become a different guy. My life had been turned upside down. I'd spent months partying and getting drunk. Now I stayed locked away in my room. In an instant I went from being happy and secure, to hardened and cynical. The worst part was I had a hard time trusting people. I began to question everything and everyone. I broke up with my girlfriend because I doubted her. Every time she said she was with one of her friends, I thought she was lying. It drove me crazy. And since it didn't really matter because all relationships ended, I broke it off and vowed not to get close to anyone again.

"Exactly." He took a deep breath and sighed. "I don't get you, bro. You should be excited. It's not every day that a hot girl agrees to go out with you. And I know she's smoking hot because she was rocking it in her string bikini at the pool today. You should have seen her—all curves." He licked his lips, and this time I gave in to my urge with a straight body shot.

"What the hell was that for?" Nate rubbed his midsection.

I hit him harder than I'd originally intended. I didn't like the fact that he'd seen Carly wearing only a bathing suit. And it sounded like it was a skimpy one at that. But I knew Nate, and he was a total douche bag when it came to women. He would give a girl the token eye-fuck and comment on her ass and physical attributes without thinking twice. He only cared about good looks and hot sex. Carly was too good to be seen as mere eye candy.

He watched me and threw his hands in the air. "I get it," he said. "Don't worry, dude—she's all yours. She's hot and all, but Becca is more my style. You know, I'm into blonds. I could just see myself lying next to Becca, that silky hair fanned across my pillow, and something tells me she'd be more than happy to oblige. You should've seen the way she flirted with me. I'm really glad I was sitting down."

I felt minutely better that Carly wasn't his type. I didn't want her getting hurt.

"And look at you," he waved his arm at my clothes—cargo shorts and a navy blue T-shirt, which was as dressed up as I got these days. "You clean up good. Not as good as me, but still good." Nathan smoothed out his shirt. He never could give a compliment without turning it around and mentioning himself.

"Carly and I are just friends," I said, making my intentions clear. Just because I didn't like the idea of Nathan checking her out didn't mean I wanted her to be my girl. I don't do relationships anymore. From what I'd seen and experienced, they were nothing but trouble. If this double-date thing had been with anyone else, I never would've agreed. But Carly was different than the other girls at school. She was sweet and innocent. Trustworthy. We had worked side by side all year long, and she never got in my business or asked a lot of questions. She gave me the space I needed. In a way, we had become friends. And I couldn't deny that she was beautiful.

"Well, now's your chance to be more than just friends," encouraged Nate. "I really don't get you, man. Whatever your problem is, snap out of it." He whacked me on the back. "Here they come. Don't ruin my chance of getting with Becca just because you don't know a good thing when it's headed right toward you." He flashed me a warning look and then focused on the girls, turning on his charm full force.

I felt like the wind had been knocked out of me as I watched Carly approach. I'd always thought she was hot, but tonight she blew my mind. She wore a sundress, her long, dark hair falling in waves around her shoulders. She looked exotic with her dark features and glowing skin, literally taking my breath away. I wondered if I brushed my fingertips lightly across her bare skin, would it feel as soft as it looked? Something inside me changed the moment I laid eyes on her. Maybe Nate was right. Maybe I should snap out of my funk and man up. All I knew at this point was that the drawings could wait. I was happy standing here, staring at Carly. I couldn't form a single thought beyond this moment.

Thankfully, Nate nudged me hard in the ribs, breaking my trance. *What is wrong with me? I can't have these dangerous thoughts about Carly. I don't need any complications in my life right now, and Carly would definitely be a complication.* My stomach churned, as my uncertainty about the night ahead of us grew.

"Hi, Nathan," exclaimed Becca, rushing up and hugging my brother as if they'd known each other forever.

"Hey, sexy," he said, swinging her around.

Smoothing her hands down her dress, she said, "I want to formally introduce you to my best friend. Nathan, this is Carly.

Carly, Nathan." I was surprised to feel a twinge of jealousy as I watched them exchange hellos. I wasn't the only one who noticed how beautiful Carly looked tonight. I was sure everyone did.

"Hi, Gavin," Becca said.

"Becca," I nodded. We didn't shake hands. I had mine stuffed in my front pockets and Becca had her arm looped through Nate's.

"You and Carly already know each other, right?" she said.

"Hey, Carly," I said, trying to act cool. I didn't want her to see the effect she had on me or for that matter, read more into this date than there needed to be. Silently, I repeated my mantra: "Relationships are nothing but trouble. Relationships are nothing but trouble."

"Hey," Carly said, revealing perfectly straight white teeth. Her face looked even more beautiful. *This is going to be difficult.*

Becca immediately began firing off questions. From what little I knew of her, she loved to talk. "You first met in chem, right?"

"Yup," I answered.

"We were lab partners," added Carly.

"I'm curious," said Becca. "How *did* you end up working together? Did the teacher assign partners or did you get to choose?"

Carly responded, keeping it short. "We picked our own."

It was part of Carly's sweet personality not to point out what an ass I'd been that day. I'd been stuck wishing I were back at my old school and I took it out on Carly. She walked into the room late, and everyone else was already paired up. A couple of girls had asked me to work with them, but I turned them down. I was hoping there'd be an odd number of students so the teacher would have to let me work alone. And my plan was working great until Carly walked in. When she introduced herself, I thought she said her name was Girly (it sounded a lot like Carly) and I gave her a hard time about it. To this day I sometimes called her Girly to tease her, although she doesn't usually appreciate my humor.

"Sounds like fate," said Becca, winking. Carly blushed at her friend's not-so-subtle hint. Without a moment's pause she continued, "I can't figure out why you take chem anyway. It's not a requirement. I know I'm never going to need it. I'm moving to New York when I graduate to work my way into the fashion magazine world."

"You'll fit in perfectly," Nate said, gazing over at Becca. I could easily picture these two as a couple. They were both overly concerned with their appearance.

"How do you think you did on your exams?" I asked Carly. Normally I didn't initiate conversations. She knew I wasn't a big talker, but I couldn't just stand there and not say anything. I didn't want her to think I was still that jerk from the first day of class, or the jerk from the last time we studied together.

"I think I did okay," she answered. I was sure she'd done better than okay. She was the smartest girl in the class. "How about you?"

"Same," I shrugged. "It wasn't as hard as I thought it was going to be. Studying with you helped." The hint of a smile formed on my lips. *This is wrong. I should be discouraging her.* I reminded myself that I didn't want a girlfriend.

"Who are you kidding?" she laughed, hitting me on the arm. A warm tingle surged where her hand had been. I felt her breath on my neck as she leaned closer and whispered, "You're the one who helped me, but don't worry, I won't tell anyone. I know you don't want it getting out that you're smart." *Wow, I really need to be careful, or I am going to break my number-one rule.*

It wasn't that I cared if people knew I was smart—I just didn't like drawing unnecessary attention to myself by raising my hand in class. I wasn't at all surprised that Carly called me on it. She was perceptive.

"Hey, let's go put our names in at the hostess station," interrupted Becca.

"Already did," said Nate. "We got here a few minutes early. They said it would be about forty minutes, but that was at least fifteen minutes ago."

"Excellent. I'm starving," said Becca. We made our way closer to the hostess station to wait to be called. "I know you mentioned you went to college, but I didn't get the chance to ask you which one?"

"It's kind of a long story. Last year I was at Dartmouth, but since I still have no idea what I want to study, it doesn't make any sense to spend all that money if I don't know what I want to do. I'm staying here for the next year and taking classes at the community college until I figure it out." He shrugged his shoulders. "In the meantime, I'll be spending the summer as a lifeguard by day and a musician by night."

"You're in a band?" Becca's eyes lit up. *Why are girls always so impressed by boys in a band?*

"Sort of," he said. "A few buddies and I have been jamming for a couple years and this summer we want to take it up a notch and enter the Summer Jam Contest." Carly leaned in closer to Nate, seeming to take an interest in what he was saying. I felt that jealous stab again.

"That sounds amazing," gushed Becca. "What's the band's name?"

"We don't have one yet. Can't come up with anything we all agree on."

"I'm sure you'll think of something."

Nate frowned. "What we really need is another band member, preferably someone who can sing. You have no idea how many people have tried out and not one of them can carry a tune."

"Carly can sing. She has an amazing voice," Becca offered up instantly.

Carly drew in a breath, her face flushing.

I knew it was true. I'd heard her sing. Sometimes she sang or hummed while we studied. I didn't think she realized she was doing it; it was just a part of who she was. It was as if the music lived inside her and couldn't be contained.

"I'm sure she can, but the thing is, it's a boy band," smirked Nate.

"What's wrong with having a girl in your band? Maybe she's just what you need," replied Becca, sounding offended.

Carly looked panicked, but Becca and Nate, oblivious to her discomfort, continued to talk as if she weren't standing right next to them. Each one tried to convince the other that Carly would or wouldn't be a good fit.

"I don't think so," he shook his head. "The guys wouldn't like it."

"Why don't you let them decide?" Becca challenged. She turned to Carly, finally including her in the discussion. "What do you think, Car? You've always wanted to be in a band. This could be your chance." Carly remained wide-eyed. "You can totally do this. Remember what you said earlier? This can be another chance for you to test your new skill set." I had no idea what Becca was talking about, but Carly blushed a deep shade of red. She opened her mouth to speak but fell silent.

Before I could think twice, words tumbled out of my mouth. Carly looked so upset that I rushed to agree with Nate. "You don't want to sing for those guys." I felt relieved to be able to do this one thing for Carly. It was obvious that she didn't want to hurt her best friend's feelings, especially after Becca had nagged Nate to give her a shot.

"I don't? What if I want to audition?" she said quietly.

Normally I didn't give a shit about other people's problems. But seeing Carly all dressed up tonight changed me. "I don't think you know what you'd be up against. Trust me, I know these guys, Girly, and you don't ... Some of them are real douche bags. They'll eat you alive if you go through with it." It wasn't completely true. The guys weren't all bad, but Carly was so sweet that I couldn't picture her fitting in with Nate's group. I wanted to prevent her from getting hurt.

Unfortunately, my comments had the opposite effect of what I'd intended. Instead of discouraging her, they seemed to have spurred her on. Turning to Nate, she said, "Let them know we'll be there after dinner.

"You go, Car," said Becca.

"I'm only agreeing to let you audition because I got a little side bet going with Becca," Nate winked at his date, "that I want to win." He pulled out his phone and sent a text.

I silently fumed, trying to figure out how things had gotten so twisted around. Nate told the girls all about the band while we waited for the hostess to show us to our table. I didn't join in the conversation, not wanting anything else I said to be misinterpreted.

The tension between Carly and I was still thick when we took our seats. Becca and Nathan hit it off, but Carly barely spoke. Small talk was out of the question. I knew I should've kept my mouth shut. Nothing good ever came out of putting yourself out there. Tonight was proof of that. Carly didn't understand that I'd only been trying to protect her. When the check came, I was more than ready to put this fucking night behind me.

Nate had driven to the restaurant, so I climbed in to go home, while the girls followed in Becca's BMW. I was going to have Nate drop me off on the way. Listening to him talk about how stoked he was to win his bet with Becca because he was sure there was no way the guys were going to go for a chick in the band, caused me to have a change of heart. I wanted one more chance to talk Carly out of auditioning before it was too late. I held out hope that I could still keep her from getting hurt.

We arrived at Ed's, and Nate rapped his knuckles in a rhythmic beat on the garage's side door. Hearing shouts, Nate walked in, holding hands with Becca. Carly followed behind. I remained several steps back from the group, working on what to say.

"Hey, guys, I brought my brother and a couple friends," he yelled over Ed's banging on the drums. I hadn't been to one of his rehearsals since last summer, but aside from Ed swapping his clean-cut look for spiky hair and an earring, everyone was just as I remembered.

"Long time, no see," Ed said, pointing his drumstick in my direction.

"Yeah, been busy." I quickly made my rounds, bullshitted

with the guys, and put on my "happy to be here" face.

As soon as things quieted down, and after seeing Nate with his tongue halfway down Becca's throat, Ed spoke up. "Is this the emergency, Nate? You wanted to introduce us to your new girlfriend?"

Nate laughed. "Ed ... Connor ... Brady... this is Becca," he wrapped his arm possessively around her shoulder, "and this is Carly." As he pointed at her where she stood by the door, she stepped forward. I moved next to her. "She's the reason I called. She's the emergency."

"You're not making any sense, bro," said Ed.

"She's here to audition for the band."

My eyes scanned the room, assessing the situation. No one was taking Nate seriously.

As if to prove my point, Ed chuckled. "We're a boy band." Slowly and deliberately, he roamed his eyes over Carly, lingering on her chest too long for my liking.

My gut tightened and I struggled with the truth that I wanted to punch him in the face. *What is going on with me tonight? First, I got upset when Nate gave Carly the once over, and then I go out of my way to try and protect her, and now I'm pissed as hell at Ed for looking at her like he's imagining her naked.*

Ed grinned wickedly, "If you hadn't noticed, she's a chick."

"No shit. But I'm here to win a bet." He squeezed Becca's shoulder. "I told her that I didn't think her friend would be a good fit, but she insisted I give her a chance. So here we are."

"What's that?" asked Brady, joining in the conversation. He was pointing at the case in Carly's hand.

"It's my violin," she answered. She stopped by her house to grab it.

"This isn't the orchestra," he laughed. I winced. This was what I was afraid of. Carly was too nice for these guys.

"It's a fiddle, then," she replied with attitude. "I've been fooling around with some new sounds. I thought I'd give it a try."

"This ain't no country band, either," snickered Brady. Connor and Ed laughed too.

My hands clenched at my sides. I opened my mouth to say something in Carly's defense when, as if reading my mind, she shot me a glare. Maybe she did know I was only trying to help. She probably thought she could handle this on her own. "You don't have to do this, you know," I leaned over and whispered in her ear, trying one last time to get her to change her mind.

"Yes, I do," she said. It felt like her eyes were begging me to understand and support her.

I wanted to, but in the end I couldn't watch her get hurt. Refusing to argue with her anymore, knowing it wouldn't make a difference, I conceded. "Okay, but I'm outta here."

I saw her face fall before her eyes turned cold. I didn't wait for her to respond but turned and left. As I was closing the door, Nate said, "Well, since we're already here, I think we should at least listen to her sing. What do you guys say?"

I had made it as far as the end of the driveway when sounds of the band hit my ears. I had every intention of leaving but realized I couldn't. My feet wouldn't let me. Instead, I paced back and forth in the driveway.

The band played and I held my breath, waiting to hear Carly's voice. I thought maybe she'd lost her nerve. I was ready to rush in and rescue her, even if she didn't want me to, when, like magic, she began to sing. The notes that came out of her mouth were full and sensuous, changing the band's sound completely. It was harmonious, free flowing, and full.

I'd heard the band last summer, and even though they were good, something had always been missing. That something was Carly. Her voice fit and molded perfectly with Nate's, and I felt another tinge of jealousy. Their sound filtered through the cracks and walls of the garage and into the night air. For a second, I forgot how to breathe. I found myself slinking back into the garage as the song came to an end. I felt empty and lost when she hit the last note, and every cell in my body craved more. I'd been wrong. So very wrong.

Everyone in the garage was silent, as if the music had cast

a spell on them. All of a sudden, led by Ed, claps and cheers echoed. Carly looked elated until her gaze landed on me. I read in her eyes that she thought I was a jerk for not believing in her, and I couldn't blame her. I was a jerk.

"Damn!" shouted Ed. "That gave me goose bumps." He hugged himself, rubbing his hands over his arms.

"I told you Carly could sing," Becca said, directing her words toward Nate.

"She's great, but it doesn't mean she's right for this band. We," Nate pointed at all the guys, "would all have to agree."

"She's good," said Connor, nodding his head. "The two of you sound amazing together. I can't believe I'm going to say this, but I like the new sound. It totally rocks. What do you think, Brady?"

"I think there's no place for her in this band," he frowned.

"Yeah, but dude, Nate sounded way better just now than he ever did by himself. You have to know that," argued Ed. Nate flipped him off. "Sorry, man, I'm just telling the truth. Aren't you the one who called this emergency meeting?"

"Yeah, but you don't have to throw me under the bus," he joked, making Ed and Connor laugh.

Watching these guys go back and forth made me realize I'd missed hanging with my boys. Maybe I'd make an effort to reconnect with a few of my old friends like Connor. We went way back. We'd been in a lot of the same classes at St. Paul's. He was Ed's neighbor and had been a member of the band from the beginning. I didn't know a lot about music, but I did know that Connor was extremely talented. Whenever we'd kick it out at his house, he was always listening to music or fooling around on his keyboard. I think he wrote his first song in the fifth grade. The lyrics were awful, but it was far better than anything I could ever write. Seeing the band and especially Connor for the first time in ages was nice.

"What can you play on the violin you brought?" asked Connor.

"I've been experimenting," said Carly.

"Right," he said. "Let's take it from the top. Only this time, don't sing—play your violin instead. Okay?"

"Yeah, let's hear it," Ed said, clanging the cymbal.

"Okay," Carly responded, carefully taking the violin from its case. I could tell that it was more than just an instrument to her. Her face bore the same look that I got when I pulled out one of my drawings. She tucked the violin under her chin and held the bow in her right hand. She looked calm, serene. She nodded, signaling that she was ready.

Ed gave the cue and they began playing a song from the radio. Once again, I held my breath. I'd never heard her play before and I didn't know what to expect. Seeing her play reaffirmed for me, and hopefully the guys, that she belonged. Her eyes were closed in concentration and her body moved fluidly as the music flowed around her. She tapped her foot to the beat and the bow glided across the strings. At first, I thought it wasn't going to work; it wasn't quite right. But Carly must've realized it too, because suddenly her sound changed, taking the melody in an entirely new and different direction. Trust me when I say, it worked. The violin meshed perfectly into the band's preexisting sound.

It almost seemed as if Carly's addition allowed the band to create its own unique genre. It reminded me of a Saturday night mixed-tape version you heard DJs sling at clubs. A mash-up of sorts that the radio version lacked. Surprisingly, my own foot tapped to the beat. And I wasn't the only one enjoying the music. Becca had started to dance. She held her hand out and signaled me to join her, but I shook my head with an emphatic no. No fucking way was I going to embarrass myself. And any dance moves I attempted would mean I'd have to take my eyes off Carly, which I didn't want to do. Even though she'd been ignoring me ever since I walked back in.

When the sound faded, Connor was the first to speak. "My vote is YES! This broad is sick!"

On the other hand, Brady emphatically stated, "My vote is still no."

"Really?" Ed said, sounding surprised.

"Really. I'm sticking to my original statement. I don't

think a chick belongs in this band. It's a mistake."

"Sorry, bro," Ed said. "I disagree. We're better with her. My vote is yes." Ed struck the cymbal as if his name had just been called during an encore.

"Nate, you can't seriously think this is a good idea. You'd have to share the spotlight," argued Brady.

Nate's forehead crinkled. "The truth is, I love her sound. A lot. And I don't mind sharing the spotlight if it means we're better. I know we don't sound perfect, but with practice, I think we could turn a few heads and definitely make some noise. It might even be enough to win the Summer Jam. This will set us apart from all the others. It's different, fresh. Besides, her hotness will take the focus off Brady's ugliness. Therefore, my vote is YES." Nathan laughed. Brady looked like he was ready to shove Nate's microphone so far down his throat, it'd be impossible to remove.

Nate's rude comment didn't sit well with me. Brady didn't need another reason to dislike Carly. I was going to be pissed if Brady took his anger out on her. Sometimes Nate didn't know when to shut the hell up.

"That's three against one," Ed said. "She's in."

Brady scowled. "This isn't going to work." I saw him give Carly a dirty look, and I felt my body tense. "And when it doesn't, just remember who voted no against having her join the group," Brady said as he departed the garage.

Nate ignored Brady and directed his attention at Carly, smiling. "Don't worry about that asshole. He's never been a fan of change," Nate said. "So, what do you think?"

Instead of answering his question, she asked one of her own. "What names are you considering for the band?" Her question made me smirk.

Everyone yelled at once.

She laughed. Once the guys had quieted down, she said, "I can see why you can't come to an agreement." She still hadn't accepted Nate's offer to join them.

"Remember, you're the one who gave the okay to call this meeting tonight," reminded Nate. He'd look like an ass if she didn't want to join.

Carly took a deep breath and grinned. "I'll accept your offer on one condition. We name the band 'Karma.' Karma's what brought me here, and karma's going to help us kick ass at the Summer Jam." Did I just hear Carly swear? Were my ears playing tricks on me?

"I like it," said Ed. "A chick who ain't afraid to speak her mind." As the ringing of the cymbal subsided, in walked Brady who apparently had been listening the whole time outside.

"I think it's a fucking stupid name," he said. By this point I was ready to shut this piece of shit up and show him the proper way to act around a girl. There was something menacing in Brady's tone. Carly looked like she wanted to cry.

Connor made a joke to lighten things up. "It sounds a hell of a lot better than Ed's Garage Band."

"Hey, there's nothing wrong with that," Ed said.

Connor interrupted. "I know, Ed, I'm trying to make a point to our good friend Brady here. Don't get your panties in a twist."

"Will everyone shut up the fuck up for a second?" Nate demanded. "Carly, just because Brady's being a prick doesn't mean the rest of us don't like the name. Do you want to be the newest member of Karma or not?"

"Well, when you put it that way ... I'm in!" she exclaimed.

Everyone, but Brady cheered. Nate had held out his hand for Carly to shake, a contractual gesture, but instead of returning the shake, she hugged him and kissed his cheek. My blood boiled as I watched her boobs press against his chest and what I was sure was the tender feel of her lips. When Carly finally broke free of Nate's grasp, she made her way around the garage, giving each band member a quick squeeze, even Brady, who looked completely uncomfortable by her closeness and didn't even pretend to hug her back. Jealousy stabbed me again. *Why do I care if she hugs every guy in the room, while purposely ignoring me?*

I turned and left. I doubted Carly noticed I was gone.

Chapter Three

Carly

"I'm home," I called out, walking through the back door late Saturday afternoon. I hadn't seen my twin brother since our last exam let out on Friday morning, and I couldn't wait to share my good news with him. Becca had slept over, but it was late when we got home, and Drew had been out celebrating the official beginning of summer with his own friends. My hope was to catch him this morning, but Becca had rushed us out the door to go shopping. Apparently she needed an even skimpier bikini.

I knew Drew was home now because the car we shared was in the driveway. I headed to the family room, certain I'd find him glued to SportsCenter.

"Hey, Car, what's up?" Drew said, smiling when he saw me. Being the good little brother he was, he sat up and made room on the couch for me. "Sit." He patted the now-empty spot next to him. I plopped down and put my feet on the ottoman next to his Shaquille O'Neal-looking hooves.

"Where's Dad?" I'd noticed he wasn't in his office when I walked by. He traveled a lot for his job, but I knew he was in town because I'd seen him this morning. He'd been excited to learn I was now in a band. I was sure Drew's reaction would be similar.

"He had some errands to run. Where've you been hiding out? You missed a great party last night at Lucas's. It was crazy. Needless to say, I had to pop some Advil when I got home. But hey, you know my motto: work hard, play hard. It seemed fitting, considering we're going to be seniors. Can you believe it? Fucking seniors!" He smirked. "I was really hoping you and Becca would stop by." I knew it wasn't his doting sister he wanted to see—he was hoping to catch a glimpse of Becca. But I played along.

"Yeah, sorry about that. I meant to text you. We were going to come and then we got sidetracked. It's kind of a long story." I still couldn't wrap my head around everything that happened last night.

"Sidetracked?" he repeated, raising an eyebrow.

"Yes, and you're not going to believe me," I warned.

"Try me," he said. He turned to face me, showing an actual interest in what I had to say. Without hesitation, I started in.

"I'm the newest member of the band Karma."

"Huh?" he said, his expression puzzled.

"I went on a double date, thinking that it was going to end early enough to make it to the party, but then one thing led to another and I ended up auditioning in someone's garage. The other band members liked the new sound I created, so they asked me to join. And now I am the newest member of Karma." My explanation didn't sound as polished as I'd hoped, and I didn't bother mentioning who I'd been on the date with. Drew always scowled whenever I told him Becca was dating someone new, and I didn't feel like talking about what a dick Gavin had been. Drew and I were close, but he didn't need to know everything. I was pretty sure he didn't tell me everything, either.

"You're not making any sense. Start at the beginning. Who did you go on the double date with? Becca?" There was the scowl.

"Yes, with Becca."

"And who else?"

"Gavin."

"Gavin, huh?" He winked and rested his head back against the couch.

"What?"

"I've seen how he looks at you."

I choked out a laugh. "Gavin gives me the same cold, disinterested look that he gives everyone."

"Whatever," Drew shrugged, letting it go. "Who was Becca's date?"

"Gavin's older brother, Nathan."

He sat up straight. "Gavin has an older brother?" Drew's eyebrows shot up.

"Yup."

"What's he like?" This was typical Drew stuff. Wanting to know what kind of guy Becca was dating so he could somehow mimic or at least compare himself to them. I always thought it was sweet that he worried about her, but as we got older, I wasn't sure whether he worried about her like he worried about me, his sister, or whether he worried about her because he wanted to get with her.

"He's nothing like Gavin."

"Meaning what, exactly?"

I knew Becca dated a lot of disreputable guys, but sometimes Drew took his big brother act a little too far, hence my contemplation of his real intentions. Wanting to tease him, I said, "He's blond with blue eyes and nice abs." It was true, but normally I didn't talk about things like that with my brother.

Drew sputtered, "When did you see his abs?" His face was red and his frown deepened.

"He's a lifeguard at the country club. That's where we met him."

"I don't like this guy."

"You've never even met him," I said, smiling. "Anyway, what I really meant was that Nathan isn't quiet and moody like Gavin." I thought about the strange mood Gavin had been in last night, but quickly shook it off. "He's friendly and outgoing.

He plays guitar and is the lead singer in the band, or he was, until last night." I beamed, remembering how much better his voice sounded coupled with mine.

Drew's frown finally disappeared and was replaced with a grin. "You actually sang in front of other people? I thought you were too embarrassed," he gently teased.

"I know, right? I can't explain it. The band just felt right."

"Are you sure it was just the band, and not something else? Or rather, someone else, who made it feel just right?"

"What? No!" I exclaimed, turning red as I realized what he meant. I was not interested in Gavin, but my fire engine red cheeks screamed *guilty*.

"You can't fool me little sis—"

"I'm not your *little* sister. I'm your *big* sister." Drew and I went back and forth on this all the time. He insisted on calling me his little sister, even though I was born four minutes before him. He did it on purpose. He knew I hated it when he called me that.

"Like I've told you a million times, size and strength take precedence here, so that makes you my little sister." He leaned over and squeezed me. I swore he was trying to squeeze the life right out of me, but I held firm. It was true; Drew towered over me. He was at least a half a foot taller than I was and had big, broad shoulders. However, I liked knowing that even though he was bigger, I was older, which was why I wasn't a fan of his nickname.

"As I was saying before you so rudely interrupted—" I stuck my middle finger up, catching him off guard, "it's obvious you like him." Drew grinned mischievously.

"Who?" Drew had gotten me so sideways, I'd forgotten what we were talking about.

"Gavin. And don't even try to deny it. It's written all over your face whenever he's around. You can't fool me. I'm your twin, remember." He sat back on the couch and folded his hands behind his head.

"I don't like Gavin," I protested loudly. "And even if I did, which I don't," I rushed to explain, "he isn't in to me." Drew was still smirking. I took a deep breath and confessed. "Actually, he was an ass last night."

"More so than usual?" he chuckled.

"Yes. He kept trying to talk me out of auditioning, claiming all the guys in the band were jerks."

"And were they?"

"Well," I paused, not wanting to admit that Gavin had been right. Brady had said things I was sure his grandmother wouldn't approve of. "Most of the guys were actually pretty nice. Ed's funny and I love his spiky hair, and Connor seems to really like the violin. And of course, Nathan was down with the whole idea in the end," I said, giving the whole experience a positive spin.

"I feel a but coming. Out with it." Drew stared at me.

"Fine." I blew the loose hairs out of my face. "There was this one guy, Brady, who didn't like me very much. He actually seemed offended that I was a girl. He voted not to let me in the band, and even stormed out of the garage at one point."

"What? Yeah, he sounds like a dick!" Drew stiffened. "Let me know if he causes you any trouble. If you need me to take care of him for you, I will. Or better yet, I'm sure Gavin would be more than happy to put him in his place."

I laughed. "I doubt it. Gavin was acting weird all night. Besides, he was there when all this was going down."

"Well, I still think you should cut the kid some slack. Maybe he didn't want you to audition because he knows you're shy and he was worried about you performing in front of strangers. Maybe he was trying to protect you."

Huh? I'd not thought of that. "Why didn't he say that, then?"

"He's a guy. We aren't the best with words."

"Yeah, but I felt like it was more than that, like he didn't believe in me." I omitted the fact that I was truly hurt when he'd walked out before I even sang a note. I had wanted him there. I sang my best just to prove to him how wrong he'd been.

"He believes in you. Trust me, I'm a guy. I know these

things. And even though there is no excuse for him being a dick, don't be too hard on him. I think he really likes you. So, you're in a band, huh?"

"Yup," I beamed, barely able to contain my excitement.

"Cool. When can I come listen?"

"Monday night?"

"Great. I'll be there."

Drew and I spent the rest of the day hanging out. Our dad returned from his errands and joined us. We watched movies and ordered pizza. It was a great way to wind down after a long week.

"Thanks for letting me crash your movie marathon. It was entertaining. I leave again on Monday. I'll be gone for two days. Let's go out to dinner tomorrow night to celebrate you finishing another year of high school."

"I'm in," said Drew. He was always in when it involved food.

"Okay," I agreed.

"Night. See you both tomorrow." My dad stood and went to bed.

"One more?" Asked Drew, scanning through the list of free movies.

"Sure." I snuggled deeper into the couch, falling asleep before the credits rolled.

***

Drew and I picked Gino D's for our celebration dinner. He wasn't into getting dressed up and this place had the best wood-fired pizza in town.

"Seniors, huh?" my dad said, after we placed our order.

"Yup," replied Drew.

"It's hard to believe. It feels like just yesterday Mom and I were putting you on the school bus for the first time."

"Don't get all emotional on us, Dad," Drew huffed.

"Fine. Have you two narrowed down which colleges you want to apply to?"

Drew was quick to answer. He'd had his future planned out for as long as I could remember. "Syracuse University, of course." All he ever talked about was being an Orangeman and rooming with Lucas.

"Excellent," my dad said. "What about you, Car? Do you still want to go the Eastman School of Music?"

"Yes," I replied. I wanted to follow in my mom's footsteps. She had gotten her degree from there.

"I'm sure you'll both get in, as long as you keep up the good work and don't blow off too many classes your senior year."

I looked at my dad in shock. I couldn't believe he just said that.

"What? I was senior once too, remember? I know all the tricks because I probably invented them. I didn't settle down until I met your mother. And then I was a changed man. I would've done anything for her. She'd be so proud of the both of you."

My dad didn't mention my mom a lot. Not because he didn't still love her, but because it was too painful for him even though she'd been gone ten years now. My mom had been the love of his life. And she was stolen from him, and us, when she was hit by a drunk driver and killed instantly. I could see the sadness in his eyes. My dad had done the best he could after she died. He wasn't much of a cook, but he took care of us in all the ways that counted. Trying to love us enough for two parents.

Our food arrived and we began to eat, finishing almost every bite.

"That was delicious," said my dad, wiping his face with his napkin. "Good choice."

"It sure hit the spot," said Drew, patting his stomach.

"I'm stuffed," I said.

"I'll be going out of town again tomorrow morning. I'll be back late Wednesday night. Drew you're the man of the house while I'm gone. Take care of your sister. I hate leaving you guys all the time, but I don't have much of a choice. Duty calls.

You're old enough now to stay by yourselves. You'll both be going off to college next year at this time." My dad took a new job last year that required him to travel, and he trusted us to stay home alone. He called to check in all the time and refused to be gone on the weekends.

"Got it, Dad," said Drew.

I nodded.

"And no wild parties while I'm gone."

"Dad, I'm hurt you think I'd do that," said Drew. He placed his hand over his heart in mock pain.

"Please," said my dad. "Remember, I was a teen once too."

***

When I woke up Monday morning, I had a million and one notes running though my head. I hadn't picked up my violin—or fiddle—since the audition Friday night. I was anxious to test out some of the new rhythms I'd been mentally working on.

I walked over to the corner of the room where I'd left my fiddle, took it out of the case, lovingly rubbed its side, and placed it under my chin. I was a little nervous and the thought even crossed my mind that I was in way over my head. The Summer Jam always drew a huge crowd. Would I be able to perform like I had in Ed's garage? I closed my eyes and concentrated. Playing always calmed me and transformed me. It allowed me to become someone else. When I played, I was no longer the shy, quiet girl nobody turned a head for. Instead, I became the girl who made people stop what they were doing and listen, mesmerized by the beautiful music. Music gave me power.

I practiced until my back ached and my fingers cramped. Feeling confident once more, I put it away.

I went downstairs to see if I could find anything edible for breakfast. My dad was always either out of town or working, so I usually did the grocery shopping. I'd been so busy studying for exams that I hadn't been to the store in at least a week. The chances I'd find anything were slim.

I met Drew on his way out of the kitchen. "You sounded awesome. Tonight's the big night, right? I get to come and watch?"

"Yup."

"Cool." He ran his fingers through his light brown hair. He did that whenever he had something else he wanted to say. I waited patiently for him to continue. "I'm proud of you. And I know Mom would be too. You sound just like her, you know." He tugged on my dark brown hair. "And you look just like her too."

"Thanks, Drew," I said, giving him a quick hug. He always knew exactly what to say to make me feel better. I desperately wanted to believe my mom would've been proud. She was a professional musician, playing cello in the local philharmonic and giving private lessons on the side. She also had an amazing voice. I remember her singing us to sleep when we were little.

"How about I buy you breakfast to celebrate? It's not like there's anything here to eat." He pointed over his shoulder at the kitchen. "I already raided the pantry and all I could find was an empty box of Lucky Charms."

"I wonder how that got in there?" I said, laughing. We both knew he was the only one who ate sugary cereal.

"No idea," he chuckled. "I was thinking after breakfast, we should get groceries. We're out of everything and I'm craving Doritos, which you always forget to buy."

"I don't forget."

"Yeah, well, I can't survive strictly on fruits and vegetables. I need a well-balanced diet of junk food too."

I laughed. It was impossible to tell by looking at him that my twin ate any junk food at all. I could've easily pointed out the fact that he could go to the store whenever he wanted and that he didn't have to always rely on me to do the shopping, but since we'd already agreed to go after breakfast, I didn't bother. Water under the bridge.

Ten minutes later we were in the car. "Where to?" I asked.

"I don't have a lot of money," he said, simultaneously

pulling out his wallet and sorting through a crinkled mess of one-dollar bills. "Nine bucks. McDonald's?" he said.

"No way," I responded. "Your strip club money is still enough to buy us both a coffee and bagel from Tom Tom's."

"Perfect," he said. Drew backed out of the driveway and headed in the direction of Tom Tom's, which occupied the same building as the local library.

As we walked through the parking lot to the main entrance, Drew nudged me and kept his voice low. "Hey, isn't that Gavin?"

Oh, great. But Gavin surprised me. He saw us and held the door for me, but quickly trailed me before Drew could enter. Typical guy move.

"Hi, Carly," he said. "Drew."

"Hey, Gavin," Drew said. He turned to me and winked, "I'm starving. I'm going to order. I'll get you the usual, Car—plain bagel with strawberry cream cheese, small coffee? Find me when you're done."

"Thanks," I said, through clenched teeth. I was going to kill him for setting me up like this.

Gavin and I stood awkwardly as we watched Drew disappear into the line. I really didn't have anything to say. I was still pissed.

Gavin was the first to speak. "I'm glad I ran into you." I raised my eyebrows in disbelief. He cleared his throat. "I've been meaning to call you, but I didn't want to have this conversation over the phone, so yeah, I'm glad you're here."

"What do you want?" There was no way I was going to make this easy for him. I was learning to speak my mind, and something about Gavin made it easier.

"I wanted to apologize for the other night. I don't know how things got so twisted around. I ... I just didn't want to see you get hurt. I'm sorry I acted like a dickhead. I think you've got an amazing voice. I've heard you sing when we were studying." *Did Gavin just blush?* "I didn't think my brother and his friends would be smart enough to recognize how talented you are. Sometimes they can't see beyond their own big heads. I was only trying to look out for you." It made me think of the explanation Drew had given for Gavin's strange behavior. He wasn't off the hook yet, but a small smile tugged at my lips. "I also wanted to tell you that you totally blew me away. I had no idea you could play the violin with such elegance."

"Fiddle," I corrected him, smiling wider.

Gavin smiled too. He was incredibly handsome when he wasn't brooding. "I had no idea you could play the fiddle like that. I have to admit, you looked pretty hot doing it. Dare I say, sexy?" Now it was my turn to blush. I wasn't sure Gavin knew exactly what he'd just said or if he was simply caught in the moment, but he quickly added, "The band sounds much better with you in it."

"Thanks," I nodded. I was still too shocked by his compliment about being hot and sexy to say anything more.

"Are we okay, Girly?" he asked, pushing his dark hair out of his eyes. And that's how you ruin the moment, I thought.

"Yes, we're okay. As long as you remember not to call me Girly."

"Got it," he nodded, and his shaggy hair fell into his eyes again. He pointed toward the library. "I hate to do this, but I gotta bail. One of my jobs this summer is tutoring and my first appointment starts in a couple of minutes." He looked at his watch.

"Oh, okay." I was surprised by how disappointed I felt that he had to rush off.

"See you around," he waved, entering the library without a backward glance.

Chapter Four

Gavin

I felt lighter after seeing Carly. I was glad she accepted my apology. Throwing in the bit about her looking sexy as she played, probably helped. I wasn't planning on saying it, and it surprised me to hear it come out of my mouth. However, I still wasn't looking for a relationship, and to prove my point I didn't look back as I entered the library.

A half an hour later, my first tutoring session was over. I had time before my next one began, so I sat down at the computer to research colleges. I wanted to study pre-med. My dream had always been to go to Cornell, but it only took a minute to realize that wasn't happening. It cost way too much money. My dad offered to pay, but we weren't on speaking terms. I wouldn't take his money. I wouldn't take money from my mom either. I didn't want to burden her. This was my problem. I could take out a loan, or go to a local college and live at home to save money, or go to a state school. I researched a few options. Narrowing down my list, I made appointments on-line to visit them.

My phone buzzed, signaling a text message. It was Connor. He asked if I wanted to do something. At first I typed an excuse why I couldn't, but then changed my mind before hitting send. It had been good to see him. I missed hanging with my boys. Getting out would be good for me. I made plans to swing by once I wrapped things up here.

My second tutor session lasted a half an hour. I packed my stuff and headed to Connor's.

"Hey, what's up?" Connor asked, opening the door and moving aside.

"Not much." I followed him to the basement where he had a TV. We sat on opposites ends of the couch.

"I was glad you showed up at Ed's the other night. I was beginning to worry you'd died from food poisoning. I've heard the cafeteria food at Crownwood High is disgusting. It's good to know you survived."

"I'm surviving, all right."

"It looked to me like you've been doing fine. Carly's a friend of yours?"

"Why?" There was an edge to my voice. Did he call me over here so I could give him inside information on Carly? Was he interested in her? I tensed. Maybe coming over was a bad idea.

"Just wondering."

"Yeah, we're friends," I answered, trying not to think the worst, but not offering much of a response.

"She sure can sing." Connor's eyes filled with admiration.

"Yeah." If Connor kept this up, I was outta here. I didn't come here to talk about Carly.

"Do you want to play Xbox?"

"Sure." I breathed a sigh of relief. I guess he only wanted to hang out after all.

We played Xbox for over an hour. We joked around as if it had only been days, not months, since we last hung out. Hanging with Connor was exactly what I needed. It was cool how guys could just pick up where they left off without the need to question things. I'd missed this last year, while I was locked away in my room. I hadn't bothered to make any real friends last year at Crownwood High. I hadn't wanted to put in any effort. I didn't see the point. Those closest to you only hurt and disappointed you.

"Damn, all this gaming is making me hungry. Let's go see what we can find," said Connor.

We raced up the stairs, shoving and pushing each other. We searched the cupboards and the fridge, but we couldn't find anything to eat except for healthy shit.

Connor grabbed his keys. "Come on, let's get some slices. I need real food."

My wallet had money from tutoring, and even though I was saving for a car, I didn't think a slice of pizza would dip into my savings too much. "Awesome. I'm starving."

A few minutes later we pulled into Giovanni's Pizzeria. They had an all-day special. Two slices and a large soda for $4.00. We sat down to eat.

"How'd you like Crownwood High? Is it as bad as everyone says?"

"No." All the boys who went to St. Paul's joked about how bad we thought public schools were. Most of us had been going to private schools our whole lives and that left us prejudged against the rest of the population. We thought the classes at the public schools were overcrowded and teachers had to dumb things down. Having experienced it, it wasn't bad at all.

"I bet you like going to school with chicks again. Going to school with only boys is kinda boring."

"Yeah, but girls talk too much." I thought back to the girls who followed me around the first couple of weeks of school, asking me all sorts of questions. Eventually when I continued to give them the cold shoulder, they gave up and left me alone. However, groups of giggling girls filled the hallway all year long and they drove me crazy.

"You're right, my sister never shuts up."

I laughed. I knew Connor's little sister, Courtney. She was in middle school and she never let up. Whenever I'd hung out at his house she'd pester us, asking us what we were doing and if she could join us. I wondered where she was today. His house had seemed quiet.

"Still, you had to have hit it once or twice," said Connor,

not letting the subject drop.

"Nay. Girls are too much work. I don't have the time. I worked all last year."

"My mom said she saw you at Trader Joe's. She has a thing for organic shit."

"Lots of people do."

A group of bubbly girls entered just as we were finishing. Connor asked me if I knew any of them.

"I know 'em."

"Introduce me. The redhead is hot."

"I can't. I know who they are, but I don't *know* them." I emphasized the word "know."

Connor looked at me in disbelief. "Really? You have hot girls like that in your classes and you don't even try to ask them out. Shit, dude. You feeling okay? I remember when you followed Harper around and wouldn't give up until she agreed to go out with you."

"Times have changed. I guess I'm more into getting good grades and working to save money for college than getting laid." After I broke up with Harper, I spent the following two months getting drunk and banging random chicks. That got old. Now I stayed as far away from girls as possible. They were trouble I didn't need. Look what happened with Carly.

"Hmm." Connor studied me. He knew about my parents' divorce, everyone did, but I'd never confided in him or anyone else. His parents were still happily married, so he couldn't understand what it was like to wake up one day and discover everything your parents ever told you was a lie.

We threw out our trash and left.

"Where to now?" Connor asked, climbing into his car. "We can go back to my place. I don't have anything until band practice at seven."

"Alright." I had no plans for the rest of the day. I didn't have to work, since I tutored.

"Excellent." Connor fiddled with the radio, searching for a song. Finally he found one he liked. "Tonight will be our third rehearsal with Carly. She has loads of talent. She's going to be famous some day. What she does on her fiddle is hot as hell." My blood boiled. I didn't like where this conversation was headed. Connor shifted in his seat. "Do you know if she has a boyfriend?"

"Not that I know of." My body went rigid.

"I'm surprised you're not going after her, dude. She's smart, talented, and drop-dead gorgeous."

"Look, can we not talk about Carly. I already told you we're just friends."

"Sure. But just so we're clear, you wouldn't mind then if I ask her out? She's cool and I'd like to get to know her better."

Suddenly I was pissed. I did mind. I minded a lot. She wasn't my girl, but I really hated the thought of seeing her with anyone else. Even a nice guy like Connor. What did this mean? I couldn't tell him not to ask her out. I had no claim on her.

"Have at it, bro. But I just remembered, I can't hang out. I forgot there's something I gotta do. Drop me off at home." My answer came out clipped and borderline angry.

Connor gave me a strange look. "Sure. Whatever you say, man."

Chapter Five

Carly

Nine o'clock in the morning on a Saturday was early for any high schooler, but I hardly noticed the time. I'd been going to orchestra rehearsals on Saturday mornings for as long as I could remember. It was all I knew. I was first chair, first violin. It was a prestigious position that I took seriously, and it required a lot of hours of practice in order to maintain. Someone was always vying for my spot.

As rehearsal began and I pulled the bow across the strings, my thoughts drifted. Playing always cleared my mind and brought me peace, which was why I was surprised to discover my thoughts kept coming back around to a certain handsome, yet annoyingly broody, male. Why did Gavin act interested in me one minute, and then standoffish the next? What was his story? It would help me understand him better, if I knew. Was getting to know Gavin, something I wanted? Maybe. The few times he'd let his guard down, I'd glimpsed the real Gavin. He could be sweet when he wanted, like the day in the library when he'd apologized. And he was swankalishious, to borrow a word from Becca's language. Rehearsal lasted an hour and a half. By the end, I'd decided that if ever given the opportunity, I'd like to uncover what secrets Gavin carried around with him.

I packed my violin away, but my day wasn't over. I was the concertmaster for the younger ensemble that would be filing in any minute. This helped pay for part of my tuition. Also it would look good on my application when I applied to music schools. I was hoping to stay right here in town and go to college at the Eastman School of Music. Helping the younger kids was one of my favorite things. I loved their enthusiasm. Teaching children to love music as much as I did was what I wanted to do.

I greeted the students as they came in and took their seats. My role was to lead the warm up and act as a liaison between the performers and the conductor. When the conductor arrived, the orchestra was ready to play. I was always impressed by how much the kids improved each week. Someday I wanted the honor of being the one who lead students on this journey. Their sound filled the concert hall. Each song had a unique color to me. It is similar to people who have synesthesia, seeing each letter of the alphabet as a different color. Songs filled with movement were green, songs with a lot of bass were blue, and my favorite, slow romantic songs were a deep red. The hour flew as I listened to the sweet music.

I waved to several students as they left, and even paused to talk to a few parents. Finally the hall was empty. Only Mr. Kinsler and I were left.

"Do you have a second?" he asked.

"Of course."

"I wanted to know if you've thought any more about your senior recital?"

"I've thought about it, but I haven't nailed down a date yet." A senior recital was concert given by a serious music student, me, in order to share my musical growth and accomplishments with family, friends, and the community. It was also to thank and highlight some of the teachers I'd had. There'd be a small reception to follow. It was a big deal. However, I was hesitant for a lot of reasons. It made me miss my mom. Music was my mom's area of expertise. She would have known what to do, what date to pick, and where to hold the recital. Arranging this on my own was overwhelming. And sad. Not to mention I didn't like performing solos in front of crowds. I wasn't sure if the recital was something I wanted or not.

"Let me know if you need any help planning. I'd be happy to offer you assistance," said Mr. Kinsler. I'd known him a long time and it was kind of him to offer.

"Thanks. I will."

"Good."

I gathered my instrument and left. The day was already half over. Feeling hungry, I went straight home.

"Hey, sweetie," said my dad when I walked through the door. "How was rehearsal?"

"Good." I still hadn't told him that I needed to start planning my senior recital. It wasn't because I was worried what he'd think, I just wasn't sure if I was into it or not.

"Is something wrong?"

"No. I'm just hungry." I opened the fridge and pulled out the ingredients for a sandwich.

"What do you like better, playing in the orchestra or the band?" He looked at me thoughtfully.

I'd been playing with the band for only a week. We practiced Monday through Friday. It seemed impossible to me that I'd chose it over something I'd been doing for the past fourteen years, but when my dad asked me I realized I would. The band had quickly replaced the spot in my heart previously occupied by the orchestra.

"The band," I blushed. I almost felt guilty because I worried what my mom would have thought.

"I knew it."

"You did?"

"Yeah."

"How so?"

"Ever since I got back from my trip on Wednesday, I've noticed a difference in you. You've been walking around this place like you're on cloud nine. I've never seen you so happy. I know you practice a lot, but it seems like you've been practicing even more than usual. And didn't I overhear you tell Becca just yesterday that you couldn't go to the mall with her because you wanted to work on a new piece. And it didn't sound like Chopin."

"I can't explain it, Dad." I searched for the words. "It just fits." My dad was right, I was happy. Karma was good for me. I'd found a place I belonged.

My thoughts wandered to Gavin again. I wondered if he'd fit. Or were we too different? Would he be good for me?

Chapter Six

Gavin

"Hey, Gav, I'm going to band practice. You want to come?" Nate yelled from the bottom of the stairs Monday evening.

He'd asked me earlier if I wanted to tag along, but I was still undecided. I was in the middle of working on a drawing. Also I wasn't sure if it was such a good idea for me to show my face at a band rehearsal. I hadn't spoken to Connor since he asked me if it was okay for him to ask out Carly. Things were strained when he dropped me off at home. I probably owed him an apology, but I didn't feel like giving him one. As far as things with Carly, I hadn't seen her either. I wasn't sure if she'd completely forgiven me for acting like a tool on our date. And for all I knew, Carly and Connor could be a happy couple by now.

"Nah, I'm gonna stay home," I said. My conscience was telling me to play it cool, so that's what I did—just in case Carly was still pissed. I didn't need any more girl drama.

"Suit yourself," he replied. The back door closed and I listened as Nate started his car.

Sighing, I looked down at my sketchbook. I'd been composing and developing a new character, surrounded by light. She had large, dark eyes, long, flowing dark hair, and the face of an angel. The longer I stared at her, the longer I understood why my vision was what it was—I couldn't get Carly out of my head. She was appearing even in my sketches.

"Shit," I said aloud, closing the book and jumping up. The next thing I knew, I was showered and hurriedly threw on the only clean clothes I could find, a light gray T-shirt and jeans. Nate had already left, but it was only a couple of blocks to Ed's house. I could bike there in minutes.

As soon as my foot hit the bottom step, I froze. My heart sank as I recognized a familiar sound. I slowly walked into the family room and as suspected, my mom was sitting on the couch with a box of tissues. She must've come home while I was in the shower. She was supposed to be with Aunt Sue having a girls' day/night out. Obviously, something had gone wrong. I didn't want to admit it, but I had a pretty good idea what.

"Mom, what are you doing home so early? I thought you were going out with Aunt Sue?" I said, sitting next to her on the couch. I hated crying, especially when it was my mom. I never knew what I was supposed to do or say. My stomach twisted up like a pretzel whenever the water works started to fly.

Trying desperately to conceal her emotions, she dabbed at her eyes. "I didn't feel like going to the movie, so I asked her to bring me home. And she did."

"Why? What happened?" I could tell right away that my mom was only telling me part of the truth. She was trying to spare my feelings, but I knew where this conversation was headed.

"Nothing. I just felt like coming home." Tears were still running down her face, and it was making me angry. There was only one thing, or one person, who caused my mom this much pain. My father. I rubbed my palms on my jeans.

Trying to remain calm, I kept my voice free of emotion. "Mom. I know something happened tonight, so why don't you just tell me. It will make both of us feel better." With a shaky hand, I reached out and gently squeezed her shoulder.

My mom placed her hand over mine. "What did I do to

deserve a son like you?" She took a deep breath and her tears subsided. "Aunt Sue took me to dinner at Rick's Steakhouse, a new place that opened up, thinking it would be drama-free. Little did we know that the instant our waitress took our order, in would walk," she paused for a moment to blow her nose, "your father. And of course, he was with Cindy. It was like they were flaunting their newfound happiness right in front of my face. I couldn't stand to sit there another second and look at her pregnant belly. I wanted to come home."

"I'm sorry, Mom," I said, giving her an awkward hug before standing up. My dad was the biggest asshole around and the hostility I felt toward him ... let's just say there was no love lost. The day I found out he was leaving my mom for a woman fifteen years his junior was the day I jumped into my car and purposely totaled it to work off some of my anger. Probably not the most mature thing to do and certainly not the brightest, but at the time, it was all I could come up with to make that piece of shit recognize how pissed off I was. Although the crash left me carless, I was fine to bum rides from friends. It sure beat the hell out of driving a car that he'd bought for me.

To this day, I haven't talked to him. I avoid and screen all of his calls. Forget about the unexpected drop-ins. The instant I see him pull up, I'm out. I don't have a goddamn thing to say to that snake. What kind of man walks out on his wife and family? He's a selfish bastard. He never thought about us and how our lives would change. And I'm not just talking about not being able to afford the tuition at St' Paul's. He offered to keep paying, but there was no way I'd accept a dime from him and I wasn't about to let that burden fall to my mom's shoulders. So, I did the only thing I could. I transferred to the public high school. I'm talking about the bigger picture. My whole worldview changed. There were few things I believe in anymore. If I couldn't trust my own father, whom could I trust? I don't know if he thought I or Nate would be impressed by the fact that he was banging some younger chick, because the truth of it was simple: I hated him.

"It's not your fault." My dad never deserved a woman of my mom's caliber. She was way too good for him. However, the sad thing was, I knew she still loved him. Even after everything he'd put her through.

She changed the subject as fast as she could. "Hey, are you going out? She must be someone special." Leave it to my mom to think that a girl would be involved. Moms have this sort of sixth sense. It fucking scared me.

"No, I just came downstairs to get something to eat," I lied. I didn't want to make my mom feel worse than she already did. The truth was I no longer wanted to go out and be around people. I'd be terrible company. Seeing my mom upset reminded me that a relationship wasn't something I wanted—ever. "I didn't even know you were home."

"Well, don't let me stop your plans." Obviously, she knew I was lying. "I'm going to soak in the tub. That always makes me feel better." My mom pushed off the couch and headed upstairs, sniffling. Halfway up, she turned around, "Good night, Gavin. Go have fun. You deserve to be happy. Any girl would be lucky to have you."

"Night." I continued into the kitchen to prove I'd been heading that way. I wasn't hungry, but I needed something to do. Searching the pantry, I came up empty. On the counter was an open bottle of red wine. Sometimes Mom drank a glass in the evening. On an impulse, I grabbed the open bottle and walked outside onto the back patio.

Half an hour later, I threw the empty bottle into a neighbor's recycling bin. Red wine wasn't my first choice—I was a Jack Daniels kinda guy—but in a pinch, it did the trick. The first two months after I found about my parents' divorce - all I did was drink. Seeing my mom so upset, brought all that shit to the surface again. Drunk and searching for something more, I stumbled down the street.

I heard her rich voice resonating a block away. I quickened my pace, feeling a pull in my chest. Being buzzed gave me courage. I no longer worried what Carly would think when she saw me walk through the garage door.

I stood in Ed's driveway waiting until the song ended. I didn't want to interrupt. I closed my eyes and absorbed the music. As I listened, images flashed through my mind. More scenes to add to my new drawings, which were currently unattended, sitting on my bed where I should've been. It was strange how her voice inspired me. Quietly I pushed open the door.

The first thing I noticed was Nate staring into Carly's eyes. "Great set," he said, nudging her playfully with his elbow. She was a little flushed, but as sexy as ever. I shut the door with more force than necessary.

"What's up, bro ... thought you were kickin' it at the crib, drawing tonight," he said with a coy little laugh. "Regardless, dude, glad you changed your mind." He stepped down from the makeshift stage to give me a high five. I exchanged a quick what-up with the rest of the fellas—slipping in an apology to Connor. I kept my eyes glued to Carly, waiting for her reaction to my presence. She didn't seem surprised or angry. She lifted her hand and waved. It didn't look like her and Connor had become a happy couple after all.

"Me too," I said, snapping back to reality and responding to Nate. "Hey, did you start the party without us?" Nate said.

I shrugged, not wanting to confirm or deny. But you know what they say when you drink? It seeps through your pores like bad cologne. And I forgot to grab a pack of gum.

Nate knew me too well and could tell by my mannerisms that I was a quarter in the bag. "Hey, when we're done here, we're all going down to the lake to party. You coming?" I looked at Carly again, wondering what her plans were. As if reading my mind, Nate said, "Carly and Becca are going. You can ride with us." He paused to pull Becca against him and roughly kiss her neck. She squealed. When he finally pried himself away, Nate continued. "Carly's driving. She's the DD."

Nate turned his attention to Carly. "You don't mind if my brother goes too, do you?" He gave her a pleading look, and I swore she blushed. My stomach clenched.

"I don't mind," she said, glancing at Becca who nodded in

approval. I never understood why girls couldn't make a decision without first checking with their best friend. Guys weren't like that. We did what we wanted regardless of what our friends thought. But I was happy Becca seemed to approve of me, at least for now.

Ed banged on the drums, getting everyone's attention. "Okay, now that we've all jerked off Gavin, can we take it from the top one more time? The sooner we get though this, the sooner we can call it a night. I don't know about anyone else, but I've got a cooler full of beer waiting in the trunk with my name on it." I found it odd that even the girls laughed at Ed, considering his sexual innuendo. And just like, the members of Karma scrambled to their positions like ants. Apparently, Ed wasn't the only one anxious to get the night started.

"We're ready to knock this out," said Connor, looking around. "Give us the beat."

Finding a seat on the couch next to Becca, I sat down and listened to the rest of the rehearsal. It was amazing how they had fine-tuned their new sound in just a week. Personally, I possessed zero musical talent, but I knew good music when I heard it. And Karma was good. The music was fresh and exciting. Carly's and Nathan's voices blended perfectly together. I just kept wishing I were the one up there singing with her.

By the time we arrived at the lake, the party was well underway. Ed pulled his truck next to ours and handed beers to everyone except the two DDs—his girlfriend Peyton, and Carly. I quickly downed mine and crushed the can, tossing it into a nearby garbage can as we made our way down to the rocky beach by the dock. Carly shot me a nervous look and chewed her bottom lip. I noticed she had this tendency, especially when we studied together. It was a telltale sign that she was anxious.

I was about to ask her what was bothering her when she whispered, "I probably won't know anyone here, except for whom we came with. What about you?"

I let out a sigh, realizing that I wasn't the cause of her

sudden uneasiness after all. "Honestly, I'll probably know almost everyone here. A lot of kids from my old school like to come here, hang by the lake, and drink. I used to live for these parties, but that feels like a lifetime ago. I haven't been around much since I switched schools. I'm not really into socializing."

"Really? Could've fooled me," she teased.

"Very funny," I laughed. "But since you won't know anyone and I'm not much of a talker, why don't we hang out?" I bumped her shoulder, the alcohol making me brave.

"Sure. I'd like that."

We joined the rest of our friends and I helped myself to another beer, popping open the top. I loved drinking other people's beer. After a while, when the conversations turned to who had the best ass in school and who'd slept with who, Carly and I separated ourselves from the group and moved farther down the beach. This allowed for a little more privacy to talk. Nate and Becca had also separated themselves, but it didn't look like they were doing much talking. Carly and I glanced over at them and shared a laugh.

"I'm happy you came out tonight," Carly said.

"You are?" My voice sounded surprised. Carly and I were friends, but I always sensed that she simply tolerated me and my mood swings. She had a well-established reputation for being nice to everyone. I never once thought she was interested in me romantically, or that she'd actually be happy to see me.

"I am," she said smiling, proving at least in my eyes that she meant it. *She is beautiful when she smiles. Especially in the moonlight with the lake reflected in her eyes. If I were interested in a girlfriend, which I'm not, I'd want her to be Carly.*

"Why?"

"I didn't really want to come," she admitted. "I don't know anyone and I hate being the third wheel."

"Why are you here, then?"

"Becca and I promised we'd always have each other's back, which includes sometimes doing things I'd rather not."

Her voice sounded strained.

I nodded. If anyone understood not wanting to talk about something, it was me. "That's cool. You're lucky to have each other."

"What about you? Who's got your back?"

I knew it. Here come the in-depth, personal questions. Why can't I just enjoy a beer with a beautiful girl without revealing too much about myself? At this juncture, no one really had my back anymore. I didn't know how to answer so I simply shrugged.

"What about Nathan?" She gestured to where Nate and Becca had stopped making out and were talking with Connor and Brady.

"We used to hang out together all the time. When I was a sophomore and Nate was a senior we came to these parties every weekend. But then things changed. Nate went to college and I transferred schools. We grew apart." Of course, this was only part of the truth; I didn't want to talk about the rest.

"You're here with him tonight," she said. She found him with her eyes standing several feet away with his arm draped across Becca's shoulder. "Well, sort of."

"Yeah, we've been doing more shit together lately." I also didn't add that me being here had more to do with her than me trying to patch things up with Nate. "It's not the same as it is with you and Drew. It's easy to see that you guys are close and enjoy hanging out." I'd seen the way they interacted, witnessed the way they ribbed each other and joked around. At school, they even sat at the same lunch table and had some of the same friends, like Becca and Lucas. For a brother and sister to be that close, in high school, was un-fucking-heard of.

"It's true. Drew and I get along great. He's the best little brother anyone could ever ask for."

I laughed, as did Carly. Her laugh was soft and reminded me of wind chimes. Drew might've been the younger twin, but he certainly wasn't little. He was at least six inches taller than Carly and outweighed her by at least fifty pounds.

"I've always wondered which one of you was older."

Feeling brave, I leaned in slightly and whispered in her ear, "My money was on you." I swore if anyone saw the move I'd just made, they'd think I was reenacting the dock scene from *American Pie*.

When I pulled away from her ear, she looked flustered. Had I just hit her with an unexpected shock-and-awe moment? To my relief, she said, "Why?" Thank God I didn't whisper something else in her ear.

I took my time and chose my words carefully—or at least I thought I did. "You're good at giving directions." What the hell kinda response was that, you dumb-ass?

"What's that supposed to mean?" Her forehead creased.

"It means you're good at telling me which supplies we needed from the lab cupboards, so that I could get them." Jesus, bro, you pulled out the chem class card. Have another drink, douche bag.

She slapped my arm and a warm sensation traveled up my body, startling me. "You think I'm bossy." It was more a statement than a question.

"I didn't say that."

"Yes, you did."

"No, I didn't." Maybe my stupid statements weren't so bad after all. I mean, all of this playful banter was turning me on and Carly seemed to be enjoying our time together. However, I had to tread carefully because of the promise I'd made to myself. To not get involved with any girl, Carly included.

"Fine. You implied it, then."

"It was a compliment." I was being completely serious.

"Was I that bad?"

"No." I shook my head. Carly had no idea that all last year, the only class I looked forward to was the chem lab we had together. Forget the fact that I wanted to grow up and become a doctor and feel important when I put on my very own white lab coat.

In order to keep the conversation flowing, I said, "I thought we made a good team. I didn't mind gathering the supplies while you read through the lab and set everything up.

We aced every lab we turned in. The lowest grade I got was an A-."

She nudged me. "You're right. We did make a good team."

We fell silent, but it wasn't an uncomfortable silence. It never was with Carly. She was the only girl I knew who didn't feel the need to fill every pause with chatter. Perhaps it was because Carly understood that conversations weren't that different from the songs she sang or played. Sometimes you were required to wait through several measures of rest before beginning again.

I sipped my beer and watched her twirl her hair. Carly wasn't the typical sexy girl who walked by in the hall every day at school—she was a special kind of beautiful, the type of beautiful that took your breath away. And at that very moment, I was in desperate need of an oxygen tank. Carly didn't seem to realize how beautiful she was, which was another turn-on. *I am in serious trouble of breaking my own promise.*

She cleared her throat, jolting me out of my trance. "Gavin, there's another reason why I'm glad you showed up tonight."

"There is?" I wasn't sure where she was going with this, but I patiently waited for her to continue.

"I've wanted to apologize."

"For what?" I quickly racked by brain, but couldn't think of anything she'd ever done to warrant an apology.

"For the way I acted on our date the other night. I was rude," she winced. She looked cute when she thought she'd done something wrong. I ran my finger across the top of her nose.

"Girly, don't be sorry. I should've been supportive." This was the first time she hadn't yelled at me for calling her that. Taking it as a positive sign, I rambled on, "I was a total dickhead, and if anything, I owe you another date." The perfect lead-in. "Carly, will you go on a real date with me? And not a double date, because I don't want to share you with anyone." *Okay, I did it. I broke down and asked her out when*

I'm not looking for anything. And anything with Carly would be something. She's not the type of girl who is known for one-night stands.

She smiled, and I thought for sure her answer was going to be yes, but before she could respond, Nathan and Becca joined us. What a cockblock.

"You two having fun?" asked Becca, nudging Carly with her shoulder.

"Yeah," Carly blushed. "And I won't even ask if you and Nathan are having fun, because we could see from here that you were."

Becca giggled.

"I can't believe how many people showed up tonight," Nate said.

"Yeah, but I'm surprised you even noticed because you've been busy ever since we got here," I joked, rousing a giggle from the girls. It felt good to make Carly laugh.

Nate threw his hands in the air. "Guilty as charged. I can't help it if my girl here," he pulled Becca close to him, causing her to shriek, "finds me irresistible."

Becca wrapped her arms around his midsection. "I think the feeling's mutual."

"Okay, enough already. You're making me sick." I pretended to gag.

The four of us continued to talk and joke around, refreshing considering I had no recollection of the last time I'd had "fun." At one point I had to wipe tears off my face from laughing so hard. It reminded me of the good ol' days when Nate and I would go down to the lake and shoot the shit with our girlfriends.

Only Carly wasn't my girlfriend. I hadn't claimed her or given her the title of "my girl." Although hanging out with her tonight made me realize I wanted her to be. I hoped she didn't forget about my proposed date.

"Hey, before you two start laughing your heads off again, I want to introduce you to some friends who just arrived," Nate said. He slowly moved between the two girls and draped one arm around Becca's shoulder and the other around Carly's. "You coming?" He nodded in my direction. "I'm sure the guys would be interested to know that you're still alive."

"Nah, I'm going to grab another cold one." I raised my empty beer can. "I'll be right here when you get back." The guys Nate referred to were more his friends than mine, so I decided to sit this one out.

"Suit yourself."

"You sure?" asked Carly.

"I'm sure."

"Okay," she responded, not trying to get me to change my mind. That was another thing I liked about her. She wasn't pushy like some girls. She accepted me for who I was. I watched as she trailed along with Nate and Becca. She glanced over her shoulder and smiled at me. I looked down at my chest in surprise. At that very moment, like looking up at the scoreboard as the buzzer sounded and realizing you had just scored the winning basket, I felt something. Something for Carly.

The night was going better than I could've imagined, and it was all because of Carly. There was so much more to her than just a beautiful face and a killer voice. She made me feel things I'd never felt before. When she bumped into me while we were talking, my body reacted as if I'd been shocked, a jolt of electricity that started at my toes and traveled to my head, leaving me breathless. I wasn't sure if Carly felt the same way, but I planned to find out as soon as she got back.

Standing alone, I realized I was getting pretty shit-faced, and I really needed to take a piss. With Carly off meeting Nate's old buddies, she'd likely be gone awhile, so I wandered away from the beach over to the trees bordering the parking lot, stumbling and almost losing my balance more than once on the rocks. I found a tree far enough away from the partiers and took a leak. I'd just zipped my pants when someone touched me on the shoulder and released a breath of hot air on the back of my neck.

"Hey, stranger," she cooed. "I was hoping one of these

nights you'd be here."

I recognized the voice. It belonged to Harper, my ex. I hadn't seen her since the end of sophomore year, over a year ago. I slowly turned to face her, uncertain as all hell how this encounter would play out. Running into her could spell trouble for me. She licked her lips and ran her hand across my chest. In our time apart, I had honestly forgotten how beautiful she was with her long blond hair, pretty face, and big green eyes. Her scent brought waves of emotions flooding back.

I stuttered, "You ... you were?"

"I've missed you. School functions and parties haven't been the same without you. I look for you every time we get together with the boys from St. Paul's and I keep hoping you're going to be with them, and finally tonight, you're here." She grabbed my hands in hers. "Remember how I used to come to all of your basketball games? I was your biggest fan, both on and off the court. You said I was your good-luck charm. And don't get me started on the after-game festivities. Remember how much fun we had, especially when we would ..." Before she could finish her thought, I stopped her, but she was very persistent. "My favorite times were when you'd surprise me and show up at my house after practice and we would hang out in my room." She laughed softly. "My parents actually thought we were working on homework."

Her words took me back. I was happy then. Playing ball and hanging with Harper. Things were simple. Her perfume filled my head, but the scent wasn't quite right anymore. I was just beginning to get my life back on track and I didn't want to do anything that would mess things up.

"I've forgiven you, you know, for breaking my heart." She let go of one of my hands to touch the middle of her own chest. My eyes followed her movements.

"Sorry about that," I frowned. Where was Jack Daniels when you needed him? "I didn't mean to hurt you. I just had a lot of shit going on." I broke up with Harper when I found out my dad was cheating on my mom. My trust in everyone had been shattered. And I didn't see the point in relationships when they always seemed to end.

"I know." She lightly brushed her fingers across my jaw line. "That's why I thought we could pick up where we left off." Realizing her intent, I took a step back and hit the tree I had taken a piss on. "Ah, you're so cute," she smiled devilishly.

Seeing Harper again had completely thrown me off my game. My brain was foggy and my words were sluggish. "I'm kind of here with someone," I finally managed. I really didn't want Carly to see me talking to Harper; I was pretty sure she'd get the wrong idea. Harper was all over me. There was a time when we were dating that I wouldn't have minded—I would've welcomed it because that meant getting some ass that day, but I wasn't that guy anymore and Harper and I hadn't been a couple in a long time. I needed to make sure she understood that nothing was going to happen.

"Harper—"

Her seductive ways were challenging my every thought and move. "I don't see anyone," she interrupted, scanning the grounds. "All I see is you, and I wouldn't mind unzipping those pants again," she grinned, pointing her finger directly in my face and touching my lip.

Before I could react, she was on me. She pressed her lips to mine and wrapped her arms around my neck. I wanted to resist, I really did, but I was drunk for the first time in a year and I gave into temptation. I followed her lead. I moved my mouth against her familiar lips and placed my arms around her waist, pulling her snug against me.

Approaching voices interrupted my trance. Suddenly, I jerked away, as if I'd been burned with scalding water. Carly, Nathan, and Becca were headed in my direction. They stopped dead in their tracks. What had I just done? I could see the hurt and anger in Carly's eyes. The same eyes that only a few minutes ago sparkled liked diamonds. Her jaw was set in a hard, firm line. *Fuck!*

"Are you done?" she snapped, fire blazing in her deep brown eyes. "It's time to go."

"Girly, please let me explain—" Girly? What the fuck was wrong with me? I was digging my own grave, one shovelful at a time.

"There is nothing to explain." She stared at me and I suddenly felt cold. I resisted the urge to rub my hands over my bare arms. "We're not together, so you can make out with anyone you want. I don't care what you do. But if you still need a ride home, I'm leaving." She jabbed a finger at my chest. "And don't ever call me Girly again. Got it?" I nodded.

She hadn't taken more than two steps before spinning back around to face me. "And the answer to your earlier question is—no! I don't want to go out on a date with you. Ever."

She walked to her car and I followed, feeling like a scolded puppy returning to his crate with his tail between his legs. Becca's eyes were like daggers, cutting me deeper and deeper with every glance. I knew she wanted to kill me for fucking with her best friend's head and leading her on. Then there was Nate, who looked sympathetic, but I could tell he thought I was the biggest dumb-ass he'd ever met. And sadly, I was. Once again, I'd ruined a perfectly good night with Carly, and this time it didn't look like I'd get a chance to make things right.

Chapter Seven

Carly

Since I'd agreed to be the designated driver, I had little choice but to give Gavin a ride home. I felt like shoving him out the car door as I drove past his house. It would serve him right for being such a jerk—again! But lucky for him, he was sitting in the back next to Nathan.

How could he do this to me? One minute he was flirting, asking me out, and the next he was making out with another girl. I gripped the steering wheel, my knuckles white. The problem was, if I lost focus of how pissed I was, I'd burst into tears, and there was no way I was going to let Gavin see me cry.

You could hear a pin drop the entire ride home. The only sound in the car was Becca frantically searching for a suitable song on the radio. Every song was either about love or heartache. I pushed down on the gas pedal and sped through more than one yellow light. This ride couldn't end soon enough.

Finally, I pulled into their driveway. Gavin said goodbye and climbed out. I stared straight ahead, refusing to acknowledge him. Becca walked Nathan to the front door and returned several minutes later.

"We need to do something fun," she said, closing the car

door. “He’s an asshole and we need to erase him from your mind. I can’t believe he had his tongue halfway down that skank’s throat. I tried to take a swing at her, but Nathan stopped me. I swear, if I ever see her again, I’m gonna kick her ass.” Becca pounded her fist into her hand. I smiled through the tears I’d finally let fall, grateful to have such a loyal friend.

“Thanks. But don’t bother. He’s not worth it.” I backed out of the driveway and headed home, accompanied by The Fray playing in the background.

“You’re right, he’s not. You deserve better,” she declared, emphatically. “I loved the way you told him to piss off. I didn’t think you had it in you. Or wait, I did, considering the summer oath you took to finally speak your mind and to stop letting people walk all over you. I have to take some of the credit here. It’s obvious you’ve been paying attention to my advice. You didn’t seem to have any trouble telling Gavin how you felt.”

Becca was right. I’d told Gavin exactly what I thought of him and it was liberating. “I’ve never been so angry. I didn’t even stop to think about what I was saying; the words just spewed out of my mouth. Something about Gavin made it easy. Maybe it’s because he’s always pushing my buttons.”

I felt Becca’s eyes studying me. “Hmm, and here I thought it was because of me.”

Glancing over, I saw that Becca was wearing an all-knowing grin. “What?” I asked, confused.

“Nothing.” She pulled out her phone. “I was just thinking we should text Drew and see what he and Lucas are up to. It’d be fun to hang out with them. It’s too early to call it a night.”

I was too wound up to go to sleep, and the four of us hadn’t hung out since summer started. I still owed them one for blowing off Lucas’s end-of-the-year bash. My dad was on another trip, so it wouldn’t matter how late we stayed out. “Sure, why not,” I readily agreed.

Soon, I was pulling into my driveway just as the boys were coming out of the house. Drew was dribbling a basketball, while Lucas carried a bottle of Southern Comfort. Lucas, his brown hair buzzed, was as tall as Drew, but leaner.

I climbed out. “What’s that for?” I said, pointing at the bottle.

“Becca said you had a bad night, so we’re going to fix that,” answered Drew, flashing his infamous shit-eating grin.

“With a basketball and a bottle of SoCo?” I hardly understood how playing basketball and getting drunk could solve my problems.

“Damn straight,” shouted Lucas, raising the bottle in the air. I could tell by the tone of his voice that he’d already drunk more than his fair share. It was summer, and my brother and his friend were known partiers. I wasn’t normally a big drinker, but their energy was contagious and I already felt better just being with my friends.

Becca looped her arm through mine. “Come on, guys, what are we waiting for? Let’s get this party started,” She said.

We headed toward the park. It was a short walk from our house, and no one would care that we were there after hours. I laughed the whole way, watching Drew and Lucas act like idiots.

Once inside the fence, we went straight to the basketball courts. We decided to play horse, like we used to do when we were kids, only with a twist. Every time someone got a letter, they had to take a swig. Becca and I didn’t stand a chance of staying sober. Drew and Luke were the top two scorers on the basketball team, which was probably why they kept saying how much fun this was going to be.

I went first, choosing to stand directly in front of the net. My philosophy was simple: the closer, the better. It was an easy shot. I threw the ball and held my breath. It hit the backboard, but missed the rim completely. Drew and Lucas broke out in hysterics.

“Shut up, or I’ll shove this ball up your ass,” threatened Becca.

“Promise?” asked Drew.

Becca gave him a dirty look, and then concentrated on the hoop. She held the ball in both hands and tossed it. She missed by a mile.

Lucas went next, making an impossible shot that Becca and I both missed. Lucas handed us the bottle. Drew sank his first shot and Becca and I took another swig.

The entire game hardly varied. Lucas and Drew made all the baskets, while Becca and I passed the bottle back and forth. I think Becca and I only managed to sink three baskets each. Twenty minutes and five swigs later, I'd forgotten all about Gavin Johnson.

Needing a break, Becca and I sat down on one of the nearby picnic tables. Drew and Luke ran up and down the court playing one-on-one. They were so into their game that I think they failed to notice we'd walked away.

"I'm buzzed," I said, leaning my head on Becca's shoulder.

"Me too, babe."

"Thanks for making me come out tonight, even though I suck at basketball," I said. "It's been fun."

"Yeah, we need to do this again. This is the first night we've hung out with the boys. We can't forget we promised to make this the best summer ever."

"Except for what happened with Gavin," I said bitterly. I guess he wasn't completely out of my mind after all. "It's been a great summer. I'm in a band. You've got a hot boyfriend. And our tans-and-cans mission has been a huge fuckin' success."

We laughed, the alcohol making us silly and loosening my tongue.

"Speaking of cans, I'm staring at one I'd love to sink my teeth into," exclaimed Becca.

"What?" I was confused. I knew that she was talking about someone's ass, but I didn't know if she meant Lucas's or Drew's. I hoped it was Lucas's because otherwise, things might get weird.

"Have I ever told you that I think your brother's really hot?" Becca said. She undressed the boys with her eyes as they traded baskets. Luckily for Becca, Drew did her a favor, took off his shirt, and threw it in the grass. I never thought about him that way because he was my brother. I always thought Becca looked at him as a brother too.

"Gross. You did not just say that!"

Becca laughed even louder this time, drawing the boys' attention.

"Come back out here. We'll play teams," shouted Drew, as he snuck one past Luke and dunked it. He ran over and pulled Becca up. "And I'm not taking no for an answer. You promised we were all going to hang out." She howled with laughter as he threw her over his shoulder in one swift motion. Her earlier words echoed in my head.

The next thing I knew, Lucas had me by the hands and was dragging me to the court. "I've got my teammate," he said.

"I'm too drunk to play basketball," I protested.

"Think of it this way. At least now you have an excuse when you miss," teased Drew.

"Asshole." I really was getting better at speaking my mind.

We played to ten. Drew and Lucas scored all the points but the winning basket. Becca jumped and Drew lifted her in the air so she could lay it in.

"Cheaters!" I exclaimed, and flipped them off, making everyone chuckle.

We wandered over to the picnic table and sat down, talking and joking well into the night. It turned out to be one of the best nights of the summer so far. By the time we left, I could barely keep my eyes open and the bottle of SoCo was gone.

It was almost four in the morning when we finally stumbled through the front door. Becca and I headed straight upstairs to my room and crashed. She almost always stayed over when my dad was gone, especially since it was summer. Lucas was staying too, because no one was sober enough to drive.

The next morning I woke up with a killer headache and a dry mouth. *Why did I drink so much?* I hated this feeling. Being hungover sucked. Then I remembered ... Gavin. I knew he'd been drinking last night, but there was no excuse for what he did. Seeing him kiss another girl, a pretty girl, had really hurt. She had long blond hair and a perfect body, the exact opposite of me. I sighed. If she was Gavin's type, there was no way he'd ever be into me. I punched my pillow.

I was about to roll over and go back to sleep when Becca came bursting into the room carrying a large glass of water, two Tylenol, and crackers. "Here, take these. It will help."

I eyed her suspiciously. "Why don't you look hungover?"

"I took two when I first woke up, and now I feel fine."

I sat up and grabbed the glass with shaky hands and quickly gulped the water. I wasn't sure if my stomach could tolerate the Tylenol and the crackers, but I took them anyway. I doubted I could feel any worse.

"I'll give you another hour to sleep this off. Then we're going to the pool,'" she said as she left my room.

"I'm not going," I shouted after her.

"One hour, that's all you get." Stubborn bitch.

I was too tired to argue. There was no way I was going to show my face at the pool today. I rolled over and went back to sleep.

Unfortunately, Becca made good on her promise, and by early afternoon I was stretched on a lounge chair, hiding under my darkest pair of sunglasses and a large straw cowgirl hat. My headache had dulled, but I was still super thirsty, like I'd gone for a long hike in the desert. Being in the direct sunlight was only making things worse. I'd just closed my eyes to try to sleep when Nathan came over and reminded me that we had band practice later. I wasn't sure my head could handle Ed banging on the drums, but I agreed to be there. It was my own fault that I felt like crap.

Nathan went on break, so Becca followed him to squeeze in some make-out time. Left alone for a few minutes, I sighed and closed my eyes again.

I must have drifted off because the next thing I knew, Becca was talking to me. "I have just the thing," she said, reaching into her bag and pulling out another magazine. "'Top Ten Ways to Get Over a Guy. Number one: do something fun.'" She turned, and I could feel her eyes on me. "Hey, are you listening?"

"No, not really. I was sleeping," I mumbled.

"Well, wake up. You need to listen to this."

I flipped over and sat up. I really had no idea what Becca was talking about, but I was feeling a little better, thanks to my power nap. "Okay, what is it?"

"I found this article that lists the top ten ways to get over a guy, and I thought we should see what it says."

"Why?"

Becca laughed. "Maybe you can fool yourself into believing that you don't have feelings for Gavin, but you can't fool me. I'm your best friend, Car, remember? He hurt you last night. And now we need to find a way for you to get over him." I opened my mouth to reply, but then closed it. She continued, "Number one—it says to do something fun. We can check that off because we did something fun last night. We played basketball with the guys and got drunk."

"Are you sure that counts? Because right now, I'm thinking it wasn't all that fun."

Becca giggled.

"Ouch. Not so loud." I put my hands over my ears. I didn't want my headache coming back.

"Sorry," she whispered. "You had fun and you know it. You didn't think about Gavin once after we got to the park, did you?" I did a few times, but I didn't want to admit it. My heart cracked a little at hearing his name. *Crap. I have it bad.*

I sat up and decided that maybe I should pay closer attention to what Becca was saying, since Gavin made it pretty clear he wasn't interested in me. "What else does it say?"

Becca grinned and continued reading. "'Number two—treat yourself to something you've been wanting. It will put you in a better mood, and let's face it, you deserve it after everything you've been through.'" She waited for a response. "Hello? Carly. What's something you've been wanting?"

I thought for a second. There was a pair of cowgirl boots I'd been coveting ever since our last trip to the mall.

Becca looked at me over her sunglasses. "What is it?" She really did know me.

I answered. "I've had my eye on a pair of Lucchese cowgirl boots, but they're way too expensive. They're at least $300, and I've only saved half of that so far." I thought they'd match the new style of music we'd been playing.

"Consider it done. We're going to the mall when we leave here, and I'm not taking no for an answer. My parents gave me a credit card, and if I want to treat my best friend to a pair of boots to help her get over a guy who's been a complete dickhead, then that's what I'm going to do." She wore a very satisfied grin. There was no arguing with Becca once she'd made up her mind, so I didn't bother.

I continued listening to the checklist, picking up a few more tips, but most of it was common sense. The only one on the list I had a problem with was number ten—which said to find someone new. *What if I don't want to?*

***

I slowly pushed open the door to Ed's garage, hoping that no one would notice my lingering hangover. My headache was gone, but I wasn't sure it would stay that way once Ed started banging the cymbal every time someone made a comment. Normally I found his enthusiasm endearing, but tonight, I was dreading it.

The guys were playing around and tuning their instruments but once I entered the garage, they stopped, turned, and stared. It seemed like they still weren't used to having a girl in the band—or maybe it was my new boots that got their attention.

"Hey, guys," I said. "Sorry I'm late."

"No big deal. Just hurry up and get your cute ass up here," yelled Ed, clanging the cymbal. I tried my best not to wince at the noise.

"We all just got here a couple of minutes ago. Take your time. We thought we would warm up with you on the fiddle, which only seems fitting with the boots you're wearing," Nate said, chuckling with the guys. All but Brady, of course. He scowled. It seemed like he wore a permanent scowl whenever I was around. I guess it was the boots that got their attention.

"Good idea," added Connor.

"Great," I replied. I took the bright purple electric violin, I'd nicknamed purplicious, out of the case and plugged her in. Upon joining the band, I'd borrowed it from Mrs. Wang, my private teacher. It was difficult to picture Mrs. Wang jamming on purplicious, but she felt just right tucked under my chin. Connor played a note and I tuned up. "I'm ready."

Ed tapped out a beat and we all joined in, right on cue. The music flowed through my veins, making me feel like myself again. Playing could cure anything, even a nasty hangover. I closed my eyes as I sunk deeper into the music, feeling it move from my toes and up through my limbs. I loved the new sound of Karma. It was fun, upbeat, and definitely different. Just as the song was coming to an end, Nathan hit a wrong chord and my eyes fluttered open. I looked at him quizzically. He was blushing. It was unlike him, or any one of us for that matter, to falter. Even though we hadn't been playing together long, we always sounded right on key.

We ran through a few more songs before switching gears and focusing on a new piece that Connor had written. The great thing about this particular song was that it took into account all of our talents. It was a work in progress but had serious potential. We were hoping to play it for the Summer Jam next month. We had a shot at winning if we could pull it together in time.

"Wow!" I exclaimed at the end of the set, breathing heavily and wiping a hand across my forehead. Playing the fiddle was a workout. My skin shone with sweat.

"Let's take five," Ed said, with his usual cymbal crash.

Tonight was one of the hottest nights of the summer. Ed opened the refrigerator and threw everyone a bottle of water. He had a decent setup in his garage with a makeshift stage in the center and two old couches with a beat-up coffee table along the wall. His parents must've been saints to put up with all our noise. I plopped down on one of the couches and was soon sandwiched between Nate and Ed.

"Let's switch things up. Give Carly a break from the fiddle and have her sing," said Connor from across the room. He was a talented musician and usually decided which songs we'd practice. I envied his raw talent.

"Okay," I agreed, secretly hoping my voice had recovered from all the screaming and laughing I'd done at the park last night. I turned to Nathan and asked, "You going out with Becca tonight?"

"I don't know. You tell me. Am I?" He nudged my shoulder playfully.

I laughed. Nathan knew that Becca and I told each other everything. She'd gone on and on today about how close she and Nathan were getting and how much she really liked him. She claimed that he wasn't like the high school boys she'd dated in the past. "Yes, yes, you are. But Becca didn't say where you were going."

"It's still up in the air, but we'll probably grab something to eat. I'm always hungry after rehearsals. You could come too?" he offered.

"Thanks, but no." I shook my head. There was no way I was going to be the third wheel. Again.

"Why in the world would she want to tag along on your date? How stupid are you?" laughed Ed.

"I was just trying to be nice."

"I'm sure she has plans of her own," Brady said, jumping into the conversation, his voice hard. It was like he knew I didn't have anything going on tonight and wanted to point out what a loser I was. All four pairs of eyes were looking at me as Brady asked, "So, what are you doing later?"

I knew he wasn't asking me out. Brady made it clear from the beginning that he didn't like me. He wanted me to verify that I really was a loser. My cheeks grew red, and I bit down hard on my bottom lip. "I'm going home," I answered quietly, my headache returning. I could've lied, but I didn't feel the need to pretend to be someone I wasn't.

Truth was, I was looking forward to hanging out on the

couch and watching TV. My dad had returned from a trip that afternoon and we loved watching reruns of *Saturday Night Live* together. It was kind of our thing. But I wasn't going to explain that to Brady. He was too big of a jerk to understand.

"You should come out with us, to the movies," offered Connor. "I'm meeting up with some other friends and their girlfriends after this."

Connor was handsome. He had short, dark blond hair, and large brown eyes—a picture-perfect, Catholic schoolboy, smart and sweet. Even though he didn't have a girlfriend (at least not one I knew of), I didn't want to go. I didn't think it was fair to lead him on. He flirted with me off and on, but I didn't feel that way about him.

"No, thanks, but it's nice of you to offer," I said, letting him down easy.

"You won't be a third wheel, I promise."

I laughed. "Maybe another time."

He nodded.

Ed clapped his hands and yelled, "Break's over. I've got a hot date with Peyton tonight, and she doesn't like it when I'm late."

"You're pussy-whipped," whooped Nathan.

"So what if I am?" chuckled Ed. I'd met his girlfriend. She was very attractive and seemed sweet enough. She was two years younger than he was and was going to be a senior next year at the other high school in town. They'd been together for a couple of years and it was obvious they cared a lot about each other. "Time to get back to work."

We resumed our positions and for the first time since I joined Karma, I couldn't wait for rehearsal to be over. My voice didn't sound scratchy but it wasn't melodic like normal. It sounded stiff and forced. I wasn't feeling it anymore after Brady's comments. I knew I shouldn't let him get to me, and I should just speak my mind and tell him what an ass he was, but sometimes the old me resurfaced. Last night I had no problem telling Gavin off, but Brady was a different story. Old habits could be hard to break. I was just happy to get through all the songs without any major mistakes. I was sure everyone noticed I wasn't on top of my game, but nobody commented. When Ed banged his cymbal for the last time, I breathed a sigh of relief.

***

Rain pattered against my window, waking me up early. I looked at the clock and rolled over. It was only six. Fifteen minutes, thirty minutes, forty-five minutes later, I was still wide-awake. Giving up, I stood and stretched.

I grabbed my violin and began to play. Drew could sleep through anything, and my dad would already be up. He worked from home when he wasn't on the road, and he said my playing helped him concentrate.

I had ensemble in three days. I placed the violin under my chin and set to work. Playing the trickiest part of the piece over and over again. My fingers itched to play the new song Connor had written, and as soon I felt confident that I had almost mastered what I was working on, I switched gears. The combination of notes in Karma's music weren't as difficult to play, but it was faster and still required me to concentrate. I loved the funky beat and practiced for a long time.

Playing reminded me of band practice last night. Brady had made me feel uncomfortable. Nothing I said or did seemed to be the right thing. But I felt better by the time Drew finally picked me up. He'd gotten tied up and showed up late. Connor stayed and talked to me while I waited. His plans to go to the movies fell through. We discovered we had a lot in common. He was the going to be a senior at St. Paul's and wanted to study music in college too. He wasn't interested in teaching like I was, but wanted to concentrate on composition instead. Based on what I'd already seen, I'd told Connor he had a lot of talent. I could see him being a songwriter someday. In a few years, I'd turn on the radio and someone would be singing a song he wrote. If he asked me out again, I might say yes. I liked Connor. He was a good guy. He didn't have a spilt personality, like someone else I knew.

I frowned. Thinking about Gavin hurt. It had only been a couple of days since I saw him kissing another girl. Why did I have to have feelings for someone like him? I knew it could never work out. We were too different. Connor and I were alike.

I stowed my violin and went downstairs. I was hungry for breakfast. I reached the bottom of the stairs and saw my dad working in his office. He wasn't on the phone, so I entered.

"Morning, Dad," I said.

"Morning, Sweetie. I heard you playing. It sounded great." His eyes twinkled. "I also noticed that you spent more time playing something other than Chopin again."

"Yeah," I admitted.

"Can I talk to you for a minute?" I asked.

"Sure, sweetie. Sit down." My dad pointed to the couch, and I sat on the edge. "What's going on?"

"I'm supposed to be planning my senior recital." I looked at him through my eyelashes and continued. "Mr. Kinsler keeps reminding me, and I wondered if you'd help. I don't know if you know what that is, but it's supposed to be a big deal. I need to reserve a place to hold a recital for family and friends with a reception to follow. I'll sing and play violin, which means I need to find an accompanist. I should already have some of this done by now, but I haven't. Then there's all the little things that need to be done too, like making invitations and finding a new dress."

"I remember students inviting your mom to their senior recitals. She even accompanied several of them. She always looked forward to attending and would come home telling me how blessed she felt to have had such wonderful students. I bet you wish she was here now."

I nodded. I didn't trust myself to speak. We remained quiet for a minute. I was thinking that she should still be here.

"I'm happy to help," said my dad, breaking the silence. "Why didn't you ask me sooner?"

"I've been putting it off because I wasn't sure how I felt

about performing in front of so many people. But I'm in a band now. I have to get used to it if I'm going to be famous some day."

"That's my girl."

I hugged my dad. I felt like a huge weight had been lifted off of my shoulders. We planned to look into some places on Friday afternoon, when his calendar was wide open.

Chapter Eight

Gavin

I was busy restocking the trail mix when Julia headed down the aisle. I'd seen her around school a few times, but I didn't know her name until this summer when she started working at Trader Joe's. She was pretty, with light brown hair and hazel eyes, but I wasn't interested. She wasn't my type—she talked way too much. I cringed. I wasn't in the mood for one of her long, drawn-out stories. She just didn't know when to stop. And the worst part was she loved to ask me questions. Questions I didn't want to answer.

"Hi, Gavin. How are you?"

"Fine." I continued restocking the shelf, hoping that if I looked busy she'd leave me alone and go back to doing whatever it was she was supposed to be doing.

"Last night my friends and I went to the new Summer Fun Center. I know it probably sounds lame to you, but we wanted to check it out because a girl we know from school—maybe you know her—Sasha Allen?" I shook my head no. "Well, anyway, her parents own it, so we went. We rode go-carts and then hit balls in the batting cages. We were having fun until my friend Amanda, she's not a softball player like the rest of us, got hit with a ball in the shoulder." *Does this girl ever shut up?* "You should've heard her complain. She pouted until we finally gave in and took her home."

"Is there a point to this story? I'm kind of working here." I pointed at the box I was emptying.

"Yeah, sorry. Did you play baseball at your old school? I know you didn't play last year because I know all the guys on the team, but you look like you could be a player." I felt her eyes linger on me.

"No, I don't play baseball," I responded without looking at her.

"Oh," she sounded upset, but quickly recovered. "It doesn't really matter if you don't. There's a lot to do there besides the batting cages."

"Uh-huh."

Julia continued to talk, but I tuned her out.

My thoughts drifted to Carly. She knew how to communicate without having to fill every second with noise. I sighed deeply. Too bad I epically fucked that up. I was still pissed at myself for being such an idiot the other night. It should've been Carly's full lips pressed against mine. I'd stared at her lips while we talked on the beach, resisting the urge to lick her bottom lip with my tongue. I'd tried to tell Harper that I was there with someone else, but she kept coming on to me. I knew it was wrong, but I was drunk, and regrettably, I caved. I wouldn't blame Carly if she never forgave me. It wasn't like we were together at the party, but we had been hanging out, and up until then, I was sure we were both having a good time.

"So, Gavin, do you want to?"

Has Julia been talking this whole time? I didn't know what she was talking about. "Do what?"

"I asked if you wanted to go to the Summer Fun Center with me tonight." I finally turned to look at her. She was grinning nervously and biting her bottom lip. Carly did that. And she was the only one I wanted to take to the Summer Fun Center, or anywhere for that matter. Too bad she wanted nothing to do with me.

Even though it wasn't Julia's fault, I took it out on her. "Sorry. Can't. Ever." I knew it was rude, but I didn't care. I wasn't exactly known at Crownwood High for being nice.

She turned red, blew out her breath, and sputtered, "You're an asshole, Gavin. My friends warned me about you, but I didn't believe them." She shook her head. "I can see why you don't have any friends." She spun on her heel and walked away.

I went back to restocking the trail mix, feeling guilty for acting like a dick, but thankfully, it was quiet. For once. I finished my shift without any more interruptions and then hurried home.

The back door had barely shut behind me when I heard it, and groaned. I wasn't sure I could handle any more drama today. I rolled my shoulders back and went in search of the source. My mom was sitting on the couch with a half-empty box of tissues, while the rest littered the floor. Tentatively, I approached. "Mom, what's wrong?" *What did Dad do now?*

She turned her face to me. It was red and tear-streaked, as if she'd been at it for a while. "Your father ... and Cindy ... had the baby," she cried, not even trying to put on a brave face. "I'm sorry, Gavin."

"What are you apologizing for? None of this is your fault." I reached my hand out and awkwardly rubbed her shoulder. My mom wiped at her tears and blew her nose.

"Maybe if I'd waited up for him when he got home late from surgery, or maybe if I'd insisted we go out to dinner just the two of us when he had a night off, or if I hadn't been so focused on my own career and had been there for him when he needed me, he never would've left."

"No, Mom, this is Dad's fault. All of it," I said angrily. I didn't like my mom blaming herself for my dad's mistakes. There was no excuse for cheating.

"Hey, don't blame it all on Dad," stated Nate, who was leaning against the doorway. I didn't even know he was home.

I took two steps toward him, and seeing my intent, he pushed off the wall and met me halfway. It would be so easy to take my anger out on Nate. It pissed me off that he took Dad's side in all this. My fists clenched at my sides. How could he think any of this was Mom's fault? I couldn't believe he continued to have a relationship with our father after everything he'd done. The fucking bastard walked out on us.

"Have you ever even given Dad the chance to explain his side of the story? Have you ever bothered to talk to him or return his phone calls?" My jaw tightened. "I didn't think so. How can you be so sure that everything is his fault? You should at least listen to him before you judge. He's still your dad."

At this point, I was close enough that Nate surely could smell the peanut butter on my breath. "Don't tell me what to fucking do."

Nate didn't back down. "And don't forget, bro," he jabbed me in the chest with his index finger, "Hannah—that's her name, by the way—is your half-sister."

"You're a prick!" I shoved Nate, my blood boiling. "And Dad's a cheating bastard."

"Boys," our mom gasped. She hated it when we fought. I knew I was making things worse, but I was too pissed off to care.

"Go ahead, Gavin. Hit me. I know you want to," he boasted, pushing me hard with both hands.

It was true—I was looking for a fight. I was having a shitty day and needed to let off some steam. I pulled my hand back and punched him square in the face. He'd braced himself for my punch and slightly stumbled.

"Is that all you got? Pussy!"

"Stop it! Please!" my mother yelled. She sounded far away, even though she was in the same room. Nate was the only thing on my radar. There was no turning back now. He was bigger and bulkier than me, but I had speed and agility on my side. Also I knew how to pack a punch.

I took another swing and this time made sure I connected. I smoked his ass directly in the jaw and doubled up with a ferocious shot to the kidney. When fist met face, I swore I heard his jaw crack, and I knew for sure he'd be pissing blood for the next week after the body blow. He keeled over and immediately grabbed for his midsection. Blood poured from a split in his lip.

Before I could process what had just happened, my mom leaped from the coach to attend to Nate. Once he regained his composure, he looked me in the eye, and said, "Fuck you, you piece of shit. You're a hypocrite. Why don't you take a look in the mirror sometime? You're too busy hating Dad to see that you're just like him." And with that, he stood and exited the room.

When I looked back at Mom, she was crying even harder, anguish plastered on her face. It reminded me of the look on Carly's face when she saw me kissing Harper. Fuck! Nate was right—I was a hypocrite. I was just like my dad. Technically, Carly and I weren't a couple when it happened, but I'd still hurt her, and that was the last thing I ever wanted to do. And just when I thought Nate and I were restoring our friendship, I went and popped off. My life was once again spiraling out of control and I knew it. So what did I do? I slammed the back door as hard as I could, ignoring my mom's plea to stop, and I left.

I didn't know where I was headed, but I knew I had to get away.

***

Why was it when the shit hit the fan, guys always fell back on old habits? What the hell was wrong with me?

"I was surprised to see your name pop up on my phone," Harper said, just seconds after I'd dialed her number, half in the bag once more. Although I was still in high school, Jack Daniels wasn't that hard to come by—you just needed to know the right people. And lucky for me, I still had a handful of friends I could count on to come through, no questions asked. "After what happened at the lake last week, I didn't expect to hear from you again," she said. "You left me hanging. I should've chased after that dark-haired bitch and taught her a lesson about rolling up on my man."

"She's not a bitch," I said defensively.

"Whatever."

Why I decided to call Harper to come pick me up was a mystery. Impulse dial, maybe? Regardless, I needed an escape. I didn't want to think anymore. Couple Harper with a bottle of Jack and there you go—lost in the abyss. We sat parked in her car on the side of the road just a few blocks from my house. I wasn't sure whether she could tell that I'd been drinking, but if she couldn't, I'd say she needed an eye exam.

"I felt like getting out of the house," I shrugged, like it was no big deal. I didn't want to talk about what had led me to call her. The whole point had been to forget everything.

Smiling, she twisted in the seat to face me. "Does this mean you want to pick up where we left off?" She placed her hand on my arm and I could feel the other hand slowly inching down my leg.

My voice caught in my throat. I didn't know what I wanted anymore. I was tired of thinking. I just wanted to be numb for a while. On the one hand, I was drunk and could easily bang Harper, right here, right now. But on the other, no matter how much I drank or how close Harper's hand was to my man business, I couldn't get Carly out of my head. I felt like a bowl of Rice Krispies. Snap. Crackle. Pop. And snap is exactly what I needed to do. Snap out of this haze before Harper had my pants on the floorboard.

But again, and I know it's cliché, *like father, like son*. Nate was spot on. I was just like my father. A coward. I couldn't bear to look at myself in the mirror because I was scared of what I'd see.

I was so far down Harper's throat, my hand wrapped around her tit, it just didn't matter who I was at this particular moment. We were both breathing heavily at this point, making it impossible to see in or out of the car. It was the second coming of the infamous Titanic scene where Kate Winslet left her handprint on the glass. I wrapped my fingers in her long, silky hair, manipulating her head every which way. It felt as though my body had morphed into a lion and I wanted nothing more than to ravish my prey. I knew I was being rough, but I didn't care. Harper wasn't complaining. She seemed to be as into it as I was. She had her hands under my shirt and by this time had managed to tug my cock out from under my waistband.

At the moment before insertion, my dick fully erect and ready to take aim, she spoke. "Do you want to move to the back seat? There's more room." Her voice was husky and passionate, but something was off. Her voice, instead of luring me closer, acted as a trigger. If she hadn't spoken and just accepted the fact that she had to be on top for once and deal with the cramped confines of the front seat, I would've made the biggest mistake of my life.

I immediately realized what was going on, and with my dick now soft, said, "I'm sorry, Harper. I shouldn't have called you." The look on her face went from Kate Winslet in her steamy *Titanic* scene with Leo to the writhing, possessed girl in *Exorcism of Emily Rose* in an instant.

"What the fuck, Gavin?"

I put my cock back into my pants. "I thought I wanted this," I said, pointing back and forth between the two of us, "but I would be doing it for all the wrong reasons, and I can't do that to you. I had a shitty day and I thought getting drunk, calling you, and fucking, would make me forget everything."

"Asshole!" she screamed and smacked me. She threw on her clothes as fast as she could and jumped back into the driver's seat. "Get the fuck out of my car!" She gripped the steering wheel tightly, her knuckles white. I'd seen the same response from Carly just a few days ago.

"I said I was sorry," I mustered, hoping that would buy me at least another thirty seconds to collect my scattered clothing.

"Sorry?" she cried. A knowing look dawned across her face as she studied me. "I know what this is really about. It's that chick from the lake, isn't it? I saw the way the two of you looked at each other. All desperate and shit. God, Gavin, how could you do this to me? You got my hopes up for nothing."

"Tonight had nothing to do with her," I snapped, closing

my eyes. I took a deep breath. *Or does it?* Either way, it wasn't Harper's fault and I didn't want to take my anger out on her any longer. "I have a new sister. My dad's new wife popped out a kid," I admitted, the words almost clogging my throat.

There was a time, before all the crazy shit happened, when Harper and I told each other everything. She'd been more than just a good fuck. She was the first real girlfriend I'd ever had, and we were together for more than a year. It felt right to tell her, especially after what had just happened. Although I knew things would never, ever, be the same with Harper, I was once again hoping for forgiveness. And to my surprise, she obliged. I must be part cat because there was no way a guy should get as many lives as what I'd gotten lately.

"That sucks, Gavin. I know things haven't been easy for you." Her smile felt genuine. She has witnessed first hand how blindsided I was by my parents' divorce. She had tried to get me to talk about it but I'd refused. I'd pushed her away and instead turned to Jack, hurting her in the process. It was amazing she'd forgiven me. Again.

"Yeah, but it's still no excuse for what I just did."

"You're right." She slapped me again, this time with less force. "So I guess this means we aren't picking things up where we left off?" she teased, a hint of sadness in her voice.

"No," I said, shaking my head. "But thank you, Harper, for opening my eyes, and pants, as bad as that sounds."

She nodded, silent for several seconds, watching me closely. "I still think you stopped because of the chick. I just hope she knows how lucky she is." She leaned over and briefly pressed her lips against mine one last time. Then she started the car and dropped me off at home. I had more apologies to make.

Chapter Nine

Carly

"You ready to go, Car?" My dad said, coming into my room Friday afternoon. I was practicing for ensemble. If I wanted to keep my chair I had to practice.

"Yeah, I'll be right there," I said, carefully putting my violin away.

"I'll meet you downstairs." He turned and walked away.

I quickly changed my shirt and touched up my makeup. We were checking out possible locations to have my senior recital.

"I'm all set," I said, reaching the front hall.

My dad grabbed his keys, and we left.

We checked out three places. Two were churches, and the last place was a café/bar. We stayed to order food.

"Which location did you like the best?" My dad asked while we waited for our meals.

I took a long sip of water. I knew which place I liked the best, but it was also the most expensive. I wiped my face with my napkin and placed it on my lap. It was another stalling technique.

"Well," my dad said, waiting for my reply.

I had to speak my mind. If I couldn't be honest with my father, I was in big trouble. "This place," I said, looking around. It was perfect. Cozy. It didn't open until noon on Sundays, so it could accommodate us in the morning. There was a small stage where karaoke or live bands performed, depending on the night of the week. It also offered a small catering menu. It wasn't your typical place to hold a senior recital, which was why I loved it. I thought it suited me and the music I intended to play. I had some fresh ideas that fit this type of venue better than a church. I could only imagine the surprise on Mr. Kinsler's and Mrs. Wang's face when they opened the invitation.

"It's settled," my dad said, beaming proudly. He didn't try to talk me into reserving one the churches.

"This place costs more money." The churches were essentially free, although it was customary to make a donation.

"Don't worry about it."

"Are you sure?" I asked feeling guilty. I knew my dad already dished out a lot of money for my private lessons. Plus he'd have two kids going to college next year.

"I'm sure. I can see you playing here. It reminds me of the music you've been playing lately. It's great that you're finding your own niche in the music world. Your mom would be so happy for you."

"Thanks, Dad."

We ate our food, and then booked the café for the first Sunday in April, nine months from now.

As soon as we got home I texted Connor to see if he wanted to hang out before band practice. A half an hour later I stood on his doorstep, knocking.

"This is a nice surprise. Come in," said Connor, moving aside to let me pass through.

"Thanks for letting me come over on such short notice."

"No problem. I was just fooling around on my keyboard." I followed Connor to the family room and sat next to him on the couch. "I'm happy you want to hang out."

I swallowed. I didn't want Connor to get the wrong idea. Quickly, I launched into why I was there, "Actually, I have a favor to ask."

"Shoot," he said.

"I've set the date for my senior recital. It's in April. I want to do something unexpected and I was wondering if you'd help me."

If it wasn't what he expected me to say, he didn't act like it. "Love to. What did you have in mind?"

"The majority of the recital would showcase me on violin, but I don't want to do the same classical stuff that everyone always does. That everyone expects. I want to play something with an edge. Like the stuff we play in Karma. Can you help me?"

"Sure," he nodded.

"Also I want to sing, but I'm not sure what."

"Okay, let's go to my room."

I looked at him with surprise. Was Connor hitting on me? "Okay," I said slowly, making it sound more like two words than one.

He chuckled. "I have a keyboard and computer in there. It's where I work."

I felt like an idiot for assuming the worst. "Got it. Lead the way."

Connor's room was huge. His bed and dresser were in one corner of the room and the rest of the space was jammed with equipment. "Make yourself at home." I sat on the edge of his bed, while he sat in a chair behind his keyboard. "Where do you want to start?"

"Can you help me write a song?"

"To play or to sing?"

"To sing."

"Probably. Have you come up with anything yet? A melody? Lyrics?"

"I have a melody, no lyrics. But it's not much," I admitted.

"Let me hear."

I hummed a few bars. "I was thinking it sounded like a good chorus. What do you think?"

"It's a start," Connor said. He sat at his keyboard and played around for a minute, experimenting with different keys. "What about this?" He said, changing the notes, but keeping the rhythm that I'd written. "Your voice has a wide range. We should highlight it. I'll play it again. Try to sing, or hum, along."

I matched the notes with my voice. "I like it," I said.

"Me too."

We continued to work, losing ourselves in the music. "Damn," Connor said. "It's after seven o'clock. We gotta go."

"Wow. Time flew." I checked my phone and saw that we were five minutes late to practice.

"It sure did," said Connor.

"Thanks so much for helping me."

"Don't thank me yet. It's not done. We'll keep working on it."

"Really? You don't mind?"

"Nay, it's fun. I live for this shit. Making music from nothing but notes," said Connor.

I could really see myself with someone like Connor. We shared a passion for music. Then why did my mind drift to Gavin as lyrics swam in my head for the piece we were creating? Luckily, I didn't have time to sort through my feelings at the moment.

We gathered our things and left. It didn't take long to get to Ed's. He lived right next door. Even so, we were the last to arrive.

"What the fuck, dude. Did your car break down?" Joked Nate, as Connor opened the door.

"Ah, I see what took you so long," said Ed, winking. I entered right behind Connor.

"It's not like that," said Connor.

"If you say so," said Ed, tapping on his drum.

Red faced, I took out purplicious and plugged her in. I barely looked in Connor's direction the whole night. I didn't want the guys to think Connor and I were a thing.

Chapter Ten

Gavin

I checked my bank account and I almost had enough to buy a car. At the very least I had enough to start car shopping. And I had a few hours to kill. I found Nate in the family room watching TV.

It's ironic to think that on the same night I almost made the biggest mistake of my life with Harper, I made the best decision of my life and made amends with Nate. When I got home, I gave Nate a sincere apology. I told him he had every right to hate me and compare me to Dad, but that I loved him and wanted to start fresh. I even took a page out of Mom's book and littered his bedroom floor with Kleenex. To Nate's credit, he understood why I'd been so angry, and it felt like we'd finally made it past a major roadblock. Things weren't quite back to normal, but for the first time in over a year, I felt like we might be able to move past all the shit.

"You want to go look at cars with me? I gotta get my own set of wheels soon. I'm sick of always borrowing Mom's car."

"Sure. Let's go. I'll drive," said Nate.

"Very funny."

"I thought so," chuckled Nate.

We went to a used car dealership, and I saw a couple of possibilities. None were as nice as the car I'd totaled but I didn't care. It would be mine. Buying a car symbolized freedom, especially since I would pay for it with my own money. I'd experienced a similar feeling when I'd gotten my tattoo. I'd had to work for it. I liked the sense of accomplishment and self worth that came from working hard to get something I wanted.

"When do you think you'll have enough money?" Nate asked as we got in his car to drive home. For once Nate didn't mention how if I'd just call our father, I'd be able to drive out of the dealership with a brand new car.

"Soon, brother. Soon."

"Good for you."

Nate dropped me off at home. He had band practice, while I went straight upstairs to work on my drawings. I had abandoned the dark-haired angel sketch, scrapping that character all together. My new focus was drawing a dark forest with trees that appeared to come to life when you stared at them long enough.

"Hey, Gav?" I heard Nate shout from the doorway more than two hours later. I pulled out my ear buds. "Yeah?" I hollered back.

"Karma just got its first gig."

"No shit, bro! Congratulations." I stood up and gave Nate a fist bump.

"We're playing at Ed's cousin's annual summer bash. You should come. It's gonna be the shit. I still can't believe it. You should hear us." He paused briefly, as if debating whether to say anything more, but then continued. "Carly is amazing. She has really turned us around."

"How is Carly?" I asked, without thinking. I couldn't get her out of mind, even though I'd tried.

"She's good. But I think she's dating Connor."

"What?" I said, sitting up. Nate had my full attention. I couldn't believe Connor would do that to me. I know I'd told him I didn't mind if he asked her out, but I'd been lying and he knew it. But then again, I had fucked things up when I'd kissed Harper at that damn party right in front of everyone. Would I forever be punished for that act of stupidity?

"They haven't made a public announcement or anything, but they showed up at band practice together one night. They were both smiling and shit. When Ed called them on it, they acted all weird. Almost guilty."

"Fuck!" I yelled. I never should've asked him about her.

Nathan looked sympathetic. "Just in case you want to come, we'll be playing two weeks from Saturday at Ed's cousin's. We go on at 8 p.m."

I replaced my ear buds and returned to my drawing. My pencil snapped under the extreme pressure. "Shit," I shouted, throwing it across the room.

Chapter Eleven

Carly

After countless hours of practice, we'd finally landed our first gig. And to be honest, it felt awesome. We'd be playing at Ed's cousin's annual summer bash in just a few short hours, and I was nervous. I checked and rechecked my bag ten times.

"Let me know when you're ready. I'll give you a lift," Drew yelled from downstairs.

"I'll be down in a minute." I dashed into the bathroom one last time. Staring at my reflection, I decided it wouldn't hurt to touch up my makeup. I outlined my eyes again in a deep purple to help them stand out and reapplied lip-gloss.

Okay. Ready as I'll ever be.

Drew was lounging on the couch and stood when he saw me. He whistled, "Damn, sis. Maybe I better rethink my plans tonight. I don't want anyone to cop a feel on my baby sister."

I invited Drew to the party, but as usual, he had plans with Lucas and the guys to go to a concert. He said he'd be happy to skip it, but I knew that wasn't exactly true. He'd been looking forward to seeing the band perform ever since he bought the tickets back in April. I didn't want to ruin that for him.

"What are you wearing?" he asked.

I had on a short flowing sundress with my new cowgirl

boots. My bangs were braided off to the side, while the rest of my hair hung in waves down my back. It was a fresh look that complemented the music we'd be playing. Becca had helped me pick out the outfit, declaring that the guys would go crazy when they saw me, and that it wouldn't matter if I sang a wrong note because they'd be too distracted by what I was wearing to even care. I could tell by the look on Drew's face that Becca might be on to something.

"Don't you like it?"

"I hate it. Trust me, I'm a dude. I know how guys think. You should change." He stood firm, crossing his arms across his chest.

"It's Becca's dress. She let me borrow it," I said.

"I still hate it."

"Really? Because I remember you telling her she looked great, or was it *bangin'* when she was wore it?"

His face turned red. "That was different."

"No, it's not. Grab your keys 'cause I'm not changing. I'm ready when you are." Speaking my mind was getting easier and easier all the time.

Drew pulled up in front of Ed's house. "Have fun at the concert."

"Car," he said, holding onto my arm.

"Yes ..."

"I'm proud of you. You're different. You're not the shy, quiet violinist anymore. You're a sassy, outspoken fiddler. You're going to do great tonight. I'm sorry I won't be there to see it, but I promise I'll be there cheering you on from the front row when you play later this summer at the Summer Jam. Break a leg." He reached over and gave me a quick squeeze. "Mom would be proud too."

I held back my tears. "Thanks, Drew. You're the best." Even though we sometimes disagreed on things, we always looked out for one another.

I gathered my things and shut the car door. I made it halfway up the driveway when Drew rolled the window down and shouted, "Warn Becca that she and I are going to have a talk about that outfit. And you'd better come clean and tell me if I need to give anyone a serious pounding." Typical Drew. Always trying to get the last word in no matter what, even if he'd just taken Brother of the Year honors with his previous comments.

"Bye, Drew," I said, annoyed.

I continued up the driveway and pushed open the side door. The plan was to rehearse a few songs before carpooling to the party. "Hi," I called out, entering what seemed to be my second home these days.

I immediately noticed Brady sitting on the couch tearing apart the outer wrapper of a Pepsi bottle. "Are we the first ones here?" I put my case down on the coffee table and looked around.

"Looks like it," he responded, without bothering to look up.

"Where's Ed?"

"Don't know," he mumbled. I wasn't sure what I'd ever done to him, but it was clear he'd never warmed to the idea of me being in the band.

Suddenly worried I had the wrong time, I asked, "We were supposed to be here at three to warm up, right?"

"Yup."

I sat down on the edge of the couch opposite Brady. I pulled out my phone to check the time and see if there was a group text that maybe I'd missed. I scrolled through my messages—nothing. Whatever. Everyone else was probably just running late.

"Do you always have to do that?" Brady grumbled.

My face flushed. "Do what?"

"Hum," he said, still not making eye contact.

My face flushed even redder. "Sorry, I didn't realize I was humming. It's a habit."

"Well, stop." Brady was being an ass, and it was making me anxious.

I stood up and opened the fancy fiddle case. Music calmed me, when I was nervous. And I was nervous. Without taking it out, I gently stroked her, feeling the satiny smooth, purple surface beneath my fingertips. She was beautifully crafted, like a fine piece of art. I had yet to perform a solo in front of an audience larger than five or six people. I grimaced. In a couple hours, I would be performing with the band in front of a large crowd. Ed said there'd be at least 200 people at the party tonight. I sighed and carefully took purplicious out of her case. I hoped I could pull this off and make her proud.

"You aren't going to play that thing now, are you?" sneered Brady. I had been deep in thought and had forgotten that he was here.

Trying to ignore him, I settled her under my chin. "I thought I might as well practice until everyone else gets here." *What is his problem?*

"Why bother? It's not like it'll make a difference." His face was contorted in anger.

I took it off my shoulder. "What do you mean?" I spun to face him, remembering the promise I'd made to myself to be more assertive, especially since I'd never done anything to Brady to warrant his hatred.

Brady stood. "You know as well as I do that you shouldn't be in this band. It's a boy band."

My mouth fell open. *Is that why he hates me? Because I'm a girl?*

At that exact moment, the door flung open and in waltzed Nate and Connor laughing. "Hey, guys. Sorry we're late," said Nathan, interrupting our conversation. He seemed to sense something was wrong because he looked from Brady to me, and then back to Brady, shooting him an accusatory look. "What's going on?"

"Nothing," Brady shrugged, still picking at the Pepsi label.

I didn't want the night to start off with drama and I felt comfortable enough in my own skin to handle the Brady situation internally, so I said, "Just getting ready."

Nate's eyes were curious. He looked perplexed, no doubt trying to figure out the elephant in the room, but I ignored him and tuned my fiddle. The moment was quickly forgotten when Ed bounded into the garage and banged loudly on the drum, announcing his arrival. He claimed his unorthodox entrance was practice for when he made it big.

The guys teased me about my dress and boots, which ironically made me feel more relaxed. Once everyone settled in, we decided on the set list. Our debut was going to consist of a two-set performance, six songs each. Not too long, but long enough for everyone to get a feel for who we were. We ran through most of the songs and then we started breaking down the stage.

"Are you sure you're turning it the right way?" Connor asked Ed for the thousandth time.

"I'm sure," he grumbled, trying with little success to remove the last set of bolts holding the stage together.

The plan was to break down the stage and load it into Ed's pickup. It was supposed to take fifteen minutes, but it had already taken almost an hour and it still wasn't completely apart.

"You were able to take it down and put it back together the last time, right?" I asked, biting my lip. I was sure my lip-gloss had worn off long ago.

"Well," said Ed, not sounding confident.

"It's been a while since we took it apart," Nate added.

"That's okay. I'm sure it'll loosen any second now," I said.

"No, it won't," said Brady. "The truth is, we've never taken it apart."

"Oh ..." I looked around and saw that Brady was telling the truth. Leave it to Brady to make me feel like an idiot. It was obvious everyone else knew it had never been disassembled. I was only trying to help by throwing out a few encouraging words and Brady had to act like a dick, again.

"Lay off, man," Nate warned.

"What are you going to do about it?" challenged Brady.

"Hey," shouted Ed, "I finally got it." He pumped his fist in the air.

Nathan glared at Brady. "We'll finish this later."

"Whatever," Brady said, mumbling something under his

breath I couldn't quite hear.

Once the stage was apart, it didn't take long to load it into Ed's truck. Connor and Brady jumped in with Ed, while I caught a ride with Nate. When we arrived, Ed's cousin showed us where to set up. Our stage was in the backyard, facing the pool and patio. Thankfully, it went back together in a few simple steps. However, there wasn't much time to spare.

Ed hadn't been kidding when he said there'd be a lot of people at the party. I looked out at the crowd and my stomach clenched. I frantically scanned the audience for Becca. She was my one true comfort in all this and I knew she'd be there. I wanted to talk to her before we went on, but there wasn't time. I took a deep breath, hoping to steady my nerves. I felt frazzled after rushing around and having to deal with Brady yelling at me.

I barely had time to collect my thoughts when we took our positions on stage. Ed's cousin's voice echoed through the mic as he introduced Karma to the world. Everyone clapped and cheered. And then it happened. The sign I'd been waiting for. Becca's whistle. She was here. I heard the whistle and saw her waving. She was standing in the front row. How could I have missed her earlier? Nevertheless, I kept my eyes locked on her, pretending that we were still in Ed's garage and she was the only non-band member watching. I relaxed a tiny bit.

"Ready? One, two, a one, two, three, four!" Ed tapped, jumpstarting the beat.

Nate and I were singing a duet for our first number. Missing my cue, I joined in late, my voice wavering. Performing in a band was what I'd always dreamed of doing. *I can do this.* And sure enough, I didn't miss my second cue, although my voice still didn't sound as strong as it had when we rehearsed. I breathed a sigh of relief when the song ended.

Before the second song, Ed made a short speech while Nate simultaneously whispered in my ear, "It's okay, relax. You got this."

I nodded. Nathan's words carried away some of the tension lodged in my stomach. I straightened my dress and stood tall. My voice didn't betray me this time. I sounded like myself again—strong and clear.

"That's it," Nate said, smiling during the pause.

"Time to mix it up," Ed ordered. As soon as I heard Ed's voice, I made the mistake of taking my eyes off Becca. By this time, more people had gathered to watch, and I felt as if everyone was staring directly at me. I felt bile rise in my throat, but I pushed it back. "This is a new song we've been working on. Hope ya'll like it as much as we do," Ed said.

It was one of the songs Connor had rewritten and it required purplicious. My hands shook as I positioned her under my chin and held the bow tightly in my other hand. I didn't miss my cue, but I missed a chord. It sounded like a screeching cat. The audience made an audible cringe. I hadn't made such a novice mistake since I was five years old. I could play this in my sleep. *What is wrong with me? Why do I keep messing up?* I closed my eyes. I got through the song without any more mishaps, but the damage was done. The crowd barely clapped and I knew it was my fault. I could feel Brady's I-told-you-so smirk drilling into the back of my head. I didn't need to turn around and look to know I was right.

We finished the set, but the crowd was no longer into it. Even though we ended strong, people didn't seem to notice. Many had already walked away.

"I told you guys she was a liability," Brady said, as soon as we hit the last note.

I turned around and faced the band members, my head down, tears in my eyes. "Sorry, guys. I messed up."

"That's an understatement," snapped Brady.

"I've never performed in front of a group this big. I got nervous." I looked at my feet in my new cowgirl boots, thinking they weren't helping after all.

"You got better with each song," said Connor, attempting to make me feel better.

"Yeah. That's a tough opening crowd," joked Ed.

"It's okay. Just relax this time. That's the nice part about being able to play two sets. We can still win them over," Nate said, rubbing my back.

"I wouldn't be so sure about that," replied Brady.

"What's your problem, Brady? Your shitty attitude isn't helping," Nate shot back between clenched teeth. His hands balled into fists at his sides.

"She sucked, and you know it. The only thing she has going for her is that slutty outfit. She's got you fuckers in a trance!" He shook his head in disgust. My cheeks flamed and tears escaped my eyes.

"I told you to lay off," Nate said, taking a step closer to him.

"Fine," he relented. "But it's either her or me."

Shock registered on all of the guys' faces. I didn't want them to decide between us, but I knew that if I didn't stand up for myself, I'd be giving Brady exactly what he wanted. What were my options? I wasn't afraid to speak my mind anymore, but at the same time I cared too much about Nate, Ed, and Connor to put them in the middle. They deserved better. Predictable Carly.

"It's okay, guys. Brady's right. I sucked tonight. You were better off before I came along. I'm done. I quit."

Nate grabbed my arm to stop me. "He's bluffing. He knows we're good together. You can't quit. You have more talent in your pinky finger than the rest of us do in our entire bodies."

"Hey, speak for yourself, dude. I've got talent," joked Connor. "He's right—you can't quit." He pleaded with his eyes and walked toward me. "You weren't on like you usually are, but you weren't bad, either. You'll be fine during the second set. We can even switch around the songs if there are certain ones you feel more comfortable with. You can do this." Turning around to face Brady, he growled, "And you, cut her some fucking slack. Don't you remember how you bombed at the talent show in ninth grade in front of the entire school? 'Cause I do."

I looked at Brady and saw pure hatred burning in his eyes. I knew he wouldn't change his mind, and I didn't want to be the reason the guys turned on one another; they'd eventually resent me for it. Brushing away tears and putting on a brave face, I said, "My mind's made up." Then I turned, running of the stage before anyone could try to talk me out of it. It hurt to leave purplicious behind, but I knew either Nathan or Connor would grab her.

Not wanting anyone to follow me, I dashed through the hedgerow that outlined the property. My eyes welled with tears and I could barely see where I was going, but I didn't bother to wipe them. I just kept running without looking back, until I broke through the shrubs onto the sidewalk. I would've run for days if I hadn't collided with what felt like a brick wall. All of a sudden, I was tangled up in strong arms.

"Hey, Girly, what's the matter?" said a husky voice. I'd never been so happy to hear that nickname. Only one person on the planet called me that—Gavin. He stroked my hair and soothed my tears.

"Just get me out of here," I sobbed.

Without a word, he took my hand and led me away from the noise and the lights of the party. I sighed with relief as I felt my body relax for the first time all day. He set a quick pace and before I knew it, we were several blocks away. Realizing our distance, he stopped and stared.

Chapter Twelve

Gavin

"Please tell me you're okay," I begged. "Nobody hurt you, did they?" I held her arms out to the side, scanning her body, looking for any signs of a struggle.

"No. Nobody laid a hand on me."

I felt a huge sense of relief knowing she was safe, so what was it? She was clearly upset about something and I wanted—needed—to know what. She sat down on the curb before her legs could give out.

"I'm a failure."

Sitting down next to her, I put my arm around her shoulders. She leaned into me and cried. I felt helpless. Not knowing what else to do, I pulled her closer. I was going to kill whoever did this.

"What are you talking about?" I asked, leaning down and lightly brushing my lips against the top of her head, trying to erase her pain.

"No, it's true," she cried louder, soaking my T-shirt with her tears. I patiently waited for her to calm down. When she finally took a deep breath and recounted the night's events, beginning with Brady's rude comments at the garage, to his then inappropriate comments about her dress and culminating with his ultimatum, it was easy to understand why Carly was so upset. I didn't blame her for walking away and taking the high road out of respect for the other guys. It wasn't right that Brady put them on the spot and forced to choose between members, especially when it was their first real gig. The problem was, I knew the guys, and besides Brady, they understood how talented Carly was and how much being in the band meant to her, not to mention how much better they sounded. My anger had reached its high point.

"What a prick," I snarled. "I won't let him get away with this." I wanted to punch something, preferably Brady's face.

She laughed a little at my outburst. I brushed away the hair stuck in her wet tears.

"I should've listened to you, Gavin. You were right." She sniffled.

My eyebrows drew together. "What are you talking about?"

"You told me not to audition because some of them were jerks. You were right."

Seeing her so upset broke my heart. "Brady's the only douche. The rest of the guys are cool," I sighed. "And I was wrong to tell you not to audition. I've seen you on stage at rehearsals and you belong up there. You're the star of that band and everyone knows it. Brady's just jealous." I stroked a finger along her jaw. "Don't worry. We'll fix this." Her lips formed a smile when I said "we."

"I just want to go home," she sobbed. Hearing her say that affirmed that tonight wouldn't be the best time to get to bring up our situation. That would have to wait. Right now, she needed a friend, someone who would help her forget what just happened.

"I was supposed to ride home with Becca," she said, "but I ran out of there."

"I live a couple of blocks away. We can walk to my house, and then I'll drive you home."

"Thank you," she said, throwing her arms around my neck. I saw this as an opening and gladly returned the gesture, pulling her to my chest. I didn't know why she was thanking me, but I wasn't going to protest. I liked how she felt in my arms. She fit perfectly, soft curves molding to my larger, harder frame. I leaned my head down, tucking her under my chin. She smelled like summer. I could've stayed like this forever. So much for not bringing up our relationship tonight.

I pulled back just enough to look Carly in the eye. "I want to apologize for being a dickhead the night we hung out at the lake." I took a deep breath, searching for the right words. I didn't want to upset her more than she already was. "I have no real excuse—"

"Ssshhh ..." She held her fingers up to my lips, preventing me from continuing. I was stunned. Actually, this gesture really turned me on and made my mind race, thinking about all the things I'd like to do to her right now. Nevertheless, I tried to focus on what she was saying. "Then don't make one. All I need to know is—is she your girlfriend?" She moved her hand away and I let out the breath I'd been holding.

"She *was* my girlfriend, but she hasn't been in over a year."

"Do you wish she was now?"

"No, I don't. What about you? Are you dating Connor?"

"No. We're just friends."

Her answer pleased me, and gave me the courage to say, "I like someone else." I stared into Carly's deep brown eyes so there would be no mistaking who I was referring to. "I'm just not sure if she likes me."

The corners of her mouth turned up slightly. "She might."

"Should I try and convince her?"

"Yes, you should," she said, smiling broadly. Fucking jackpot.

I pulled Carly against me and ran my fingers along her cheek. I placed a gentle hand on either side of her face and kissed her. I wanted it to be a kiss she would remember. I started off slow, showing her I could be kind and gentle. I traced her bottom lip with my tongue like I'd wanted to do since the first day I met her. When she opened her mouth, I pulled her tongue inside and sucked on it. A low moan escaped her lips, and I picked up the pace. I ran my tongue along the tops of her teeth before tasting her mouth. I crushed her lips beneath mine over and over. Heat burned in my gut and spread throughout. I couldn't get enough. By the time I pulled away, her lips were swollen, her breathing rapid.

"Did I convince her?" I leaned my forehead against hers.

"Yeah," she beamed. Anyone who had just witnessed that moment of passion could see her jubilation.

I wanted to kiss her again, but I didn't trust myself. I wouldn't want to stop, and I needed to get her home.

I tucked Carly close against my side and started off in the direction of my house. We walked in comfortable silence. Talking wasn't necessary. The kiss had said enough.

"Mom?" I called, walking through the back door.

"In the family room," she answered. "You're home early."

Holding Carly's hand, I led her through the house. My mom was sitting on the couch curled up with a pediatrics' medical journal, just like she was when I'd left an hour ago. I cleared my throat, "Mom, this is Carly." I waved my hand back and forth. "Carly, this is my mom."

My mom stood and a huge smile spread across her face. I groaned inwardly. *Don't say anything to embarrass me. Don't say anything to embarrass me.*

"I've heard a lot about you. You're Gavin's study partner, right?" she asked, clasping Carly's free hand between both of hers.

"Yes." Carly glanced at me.

"And you're in the band?"

I felt Carly stiffen and squeezed her hand. "I was," she said hesitantly. My mom looked confused.

I didn't want Carly getting upset again, so I got right to the point, hoping my mom wouldn't ask any more questions. "Carly needs a ride home. Is it okay if I borrow your car?" It was times like this I wish I hadn't purposefully smashed mine.

"Of course. My keys are hanging up."

"Thanks, Mom. See you later."

"It was nice to meet you, Mrs. Johnson," said Carly.

"You too, Carly," my mom grinned, returning to the couch and her magazine.

I led Carly back through the house, grabbed the keys, and entered the garage, never once letting go of her hand. I opened the passenger door for her and waited while she got in, shutting it softly behind her. I climbed in and started the engine. Instantly I remembered the last time I was alone in a car with a chick. But this time I wasn't drunk, looking to fuck, or searching for answers. I had all the correct answers sitting beside me and for the first time all summer, I felt a sense of clarity.

Stopping at the end of the driveway, I said, "I'm starving, and I wondered if you'd changed your mind about never wanting to go on a date with me." I looked at her hopefully, feeling like a super-douche by the way I'd just asked her.

"Why, are you thinking about asking me out?" she teased.

"Only if your answer is going to be yes," I said. This chick had my mind running in circles.

"You'd have to promise not to call me Girly anymore," she said, a playful look in her eye.

"What?" I feigned hurt and placed my hand over my heart. "I thought you liked it."

"I don't."

"I'll try not to call you that, but I can't make any promises. I think it's a perfect nickname for you and sometimes it just slips out."

"I can live with that, I guess."

"So, just to be clear, if I asked you out, you'd say yes."

"Yes," She said, making my heart beat a little faster.

"Girly," I began. She looked at me sternly, and I started over. "I mean, Carly, would you like to grab a bite to eat with me?"

She giggled. "Yes."

"Cool." I pulled out onto the street and headed toward the late-night greasy spoon. "Is Charlie's okay?"

"Perfect."

We sat across from one other in a worn-out vinyl booth. I

ordered my usual, a double cheeseburger and fries with a Coke, minus the Jack Daniels of course, which, for once, I didn't need in order to tell Carly how I really felt about her. Carly ordered a turkey club and a water.

A comfortable silence settled around us again. Carly was the first to speak, "Thank you for rescuing me tonight. I don't know what I would've done if you hadn't shown up when you did."

I reached across the table and took her hand. "Don't mention it. I'm just glad I was there." Carly didn't know I was actually headed to the party to beg her forgiveness. When Carly literally ran into me, I embraced it, and I wanted to keep her attention on the conversation at hand. I wanted her to put what had happened tonight behind her. More importantly, I wanted her to let go of what happened at the lake.

It goes without saying that I hadn't forgotten about Brady and the shit he pulled tonight. I'd find out what his deal was soon enough, but for now, I allowed myself to get lost in the moment.

"I'm glad you were there too," she said. She blushed and moved her eyes downward. I thought it was cute the way she got embarrassed so easily.

"It's weird. We were lab partners for a whole year and I feel like I barely know you. You're such a private guy. I bet I couldn't list ten things I know about you," she said, staring intently at our intertwined hands as if they held clues.

I easily knew more than ten things about her (and wouldn't mind finding out a few more), but I didn't list them aloud because I didn't want to make her feel bad. For example, I knew she smelled like summer. She always entered the chemistry lab as the bell was ringing because she had to walk all the way from the music wing, which was located on the opposite side of the school. I knew that she wrote her name in dot letters at the top of every lab, and that she tucked her pencil into her messy bun when she worked. She liked to sing while she studied and she thought no one noticed what a beautiful voice she had. She loved Diet Coke and the color blue. At lunch, she always sat with her brother and a big group of friends who made her laugh. She went to all of her brother's basketball games, even though she didn't play any sports herself. She never talked about her mom, but I knew she missed her a lot.

Suddenly, I had an idea. "Okay. How about we play a game? It's called 'Two Truths and a Lie.' I'll say three things about me, and one of them will be a lie. You'll have to guess which one is the lie. It'll help us get to know each better." Don't ask me where I come up with this shit—at that point, I didn't care how corny I sounded. She nodded, smiling. "Great. I'll go first," I said. I thought for a minute. "I ride my bike everywhere. I have a tattoo that I designed myself. I was a football star at my old school."

"Let's see. I know you ride your bike everywhere, so that's a truth. I've seen the edge of your tattoo, which I think is totally hot, by the way, and something I'd love to see sometime." Whoa! Was she making a pass at me? Clearly she was—her face turned beet red. Without hesitation, she continued. "I'm guessing that you weren't a football star at your old school. Am I right?" Her brown eyes lit up.

"Correct. I've never played football, which was just one of the many disappointments and flaws my father saw in me," I said. Things had changed between us tonight, making it easy to tell Carly things I'd never told anyone. "He wanted both of his sons to follow in his footsteps. However, this frame wasn't built for football."

"Basketball? You were a basketball star?" I nodded. "How come you didn't try out for the team? Our school has a great team." I knew her twin was something of a high school legend on the hardwoods.

I shrugged. "I stopped playing when I switched schools." I didn't explain that joining a team would've meant forming new friendships, which was something I didn't want any part of back then.

"Well, if you change your mind, you could always try out and play your senior year," she said, smiling. She didn't press me to give her a reason for not joining the team, nor did she judge and tell me what a big mistake I had made, which was another thing I admired about Carly. She accepted me for who I was and the choices I made. Go figure. After some of the shitty choices I'd made recently, how could anyone be so accepting?

"Your turn," I said. "And remember, two truths and a lie."

"I'm older than Drew by four minutes. I love watching scary movies." She took in a shaky breath. "I like to play the violin because it reminds me of my mom."

"I know you're older than Drew, and it's a pretty safe guess that playing the violin reminds you of your mom," I said quietly. Carly didn't talk about her mom, but I knew from the pictures I'd seen at her house that her mom had been in the philharmonic. "The lie must be that you like scary movies. How'd I do?"

She nodded, her dark waves bouncing, momentarily mesmerizing me. "Right. I hate scary movies. They give me nightmares for at least a month afterward."

"Why do you watch them?"

"I don't. Whenever Drew picks one to watch, I leave the room and practice my violin. Back when we were in fourth grade, Drew went through this scary movie phase. It seemed like every other night for a year straight, I was locked away in my room with my violin. It was a turning point for me. Practicing was no longer about becoming more proficient but instead, about finding comfort and peace."

I nodded. "Drawing is like that for me."

I rubbed my thumb in circles in the palm of her hand, deciding which secret I wanted to divulge next. She'd been open with me on her last turn and now it was my chance to put myself out there. I didn't think it was really a secret anymore that I had feelings for her. The only reason I hadn't acted sooner was because I was too caught up in the idea that all relationships inevitably ended in disaster. I had trust issues, but they didn't apply to Carly. She was trustworthy. It was time to get back in the game.

"Okay. My turn again." I took a deep breath. I began with a story, wanting to make her laugh before I turned serious. "Once, when I changed into my basketball shorts for practice and joined everyone on the court, all the guys snickered. I asked what was so funny, but no one said anything. Moments later, after running full speed down the court, I turned around and saw a pair of my mom's underwear lying on the floor. I looked at my friends and they burst out laughing. My mom's leopard panties had been stuck to the ass of my shorts the whole time."

"True," she shouted, cracking up.

"True," I admitted.

"I listen to classical music on my iPod. I've wanted to ask you out ever since the day we met but I was too afraid."

She blushed fiercely, but only addressed my first statement. "The lie is that you listen to classical music."

"Correct. Does it bother you that I'm not a big fan?"

"No," she shook her head. "I know it's not on a lot of playlists."

"Do you think it's weird that I've liked you for so long?"

"No. But you had a funny way of showing it."

"I know. Sorry about that," I said. "Guys aren't really as good at this as they make us out to be in the movies."

"Yeah, I think Drew might've mentioned that once or twice." She grinned. I could imagine that having a twin brother gave her a firsthand glimpse into the male psyche. "How come you were afraid?"

"After my parents divorced, I thought that relationships were pointless."

"Do you still believe that?" She chewed on her bottom lip.

"No." I leaned across the table and kissed her to prove it.

The waitress cleared her throat, interrupting any further exploration of Carly's delicious lips. Our food had arrived. We kept the conversation light and stuck to safe topics while we ate. It didn't take us long to clean our plates. Carly had been too nervous to eat earlier in the day, so she was as hungry as I was. When we finished, I threw enough money on the table to cover the bill.

Reaching the car, I opened the door for her, and as she brushed past me to get in, I caught a whiff of her summery scent. I took a deep breath and exhaled slowly. She smelled amazing. I tried to think back to last fall and winter in order to recall what she'd smelled like then ... maybe she smelled like summer year round. Or did her scent change with the seasons? I couldn't remember, and there was no way to ask her without seeming like a creep.

I scurried around to the driver's side. As soon as I was situated behind the wheel, I looked over at Carly. She was sitting up straight, looking out the windshield. "My dad is away on business," she said, "and Drew is crashing at Lucas's house tonight. And I like being home alone at night." She pulled at her bottom lip with her top teeth. "Which is the lie?"

Holy shit, Gavin. I remained calm and internally analyzed her statements. *Is she testing me? Is she trying to tell me something?* I gulped. "You like being home alone at night?" I said, desperately hoping I was correct.

She finally turned to look at me. Fear clouded her eyes, making them look more gray than brown. "Right. I hate it."

I brushed the hair out of my eyes. At this exact moment, I had no idea what to say. I started the car and pulled out of the parking lot. Driving would clear my head. *Is this her way of asking me to stay over?* My heart beat wildly in my chest. I turned the radio on as a distraction.

"Girly, where's your dad?" I asked, carefully broaching the subject.

"Don't call me Girly," she reminded me halfheartedly. "He's in Vegas. Normally he's not gone on the weekends, but he's at a conference and won't be back until Monday."

Silence filled the car. And for the first time, it felt awkward. We didn't talk the rest of the way to her house. The only sound was Carly humming along to the radio.

I parked the car in her driveway. "Do you want me to come in? Make sure everything is okay?" I asked. The house was dark, not a single light on. I didn't blame Carly for not wanting to be alone.

"Do you mind?"

"Of course not." I wasn't scared of a big empty house, but I was afraid of what was happening between us. I didn't know what would happen once we got inside, but I meant what I'd said at the restaurant—I no longer believed that relationships were pointless. I wanted to see this one through.

I followed her inside. She turned on lights as she walked through the house. I made a big deal about checking the closets and under the beds for monsters, making her laugh with my silly comments and exaggerated gestures.

After a thorough check, we ended up back in the kitchen. Leaning up against the counter, she said, "So, do you have to go home right away, or can you hang out for a bit? Maybe, you could ... even ... um ... stay over? I really don't want to be alone, especially after everything that happened tonight." Somehow she managed to look nervous, embarrassed, and sexy all at the same time.

I swallowed. *She really wants me to stay?* This was going to seriously test my self-control because I was sure Carly hadn't meant anything sexual by asking me to stay. I was pretty confident in my ability to pick up on sexual innuendos, and I could tell by the way she kissed me tonight that she had feelings for me, but that I'd have to take my time with her. She was special. Different. She deserved to be treated right. Is patience really a virtue? I was taking a long time to answer.

"If you don't want to, it's okay. I can call Becca. I should probably call her anyway. She must be worried about me. I've been ignoring her phone calls."

I wasn't about to let this opportunity go by. Quickly, I said, "I can stay as long as you want. I just need to send my mom a text so she doesn't worry." I typed her a quick note. I didn't think my mom would approve, so I didn't wait for her response. I turned off my phone and shoved it back into my pocket. It was late and she probably wouldn't get it until the morning anyway. When she did, at least she'd know I was okay, even if she was angry.

"Thanks. Are you sure you won't get in trouble?"

"I'm sure," I lied. My mom was pretty strict about these things, but I didn't care if I got in trouble. It'd be totally worth it. Anyway, I was eighteen and could do pretty much whatever I wanted.

"Okay, because I'd feel bad if you did." It was hard to look away. I moved in closer, placing a hand on the counter on either side of her, trapping her.

"No worries," I said. "What do you usually do when you have to stay home alone?"

Carly laughed nervously. "Not much. I avoid it as much as possible. Usually Becca spends the night. Her parents don't care. Actually, I think they prefer it when she's not home. Sad, huh?" She frowned. "The last time I stayed here alone was over a year ago. It was awful. I tried everything, but I was too scared to sleep. Every little noise made me jump. When the sun finally came up, I crawled into bed and crashed."

"That sounds terrible." I moved my hand to tuck her hair behind her ear.

"It was," she whispered. "That's why I'm so glad that you can stay."

I couldn't take it anymore. Her words turned me on. I crushed my mouth to hers, and she wrapped her hands around my neck. I easily lifted her onto the counter and stepped between her legs. I devoured her mouth, leaving her breathless. I moved onto her neck, taking little bites here and there, conscience of the fact that if I nibbled too hard, I would leave a mark on her flawless skin. This wasn't my first rodeo, but Carly's touch was making me feel things I'd never felt before.

I pulled my lips off her neck and leaned against the counter opposite Carly. Wouldn't you know, the first words that came out of my mouth were, "I can fall asleep anywhere. I sleep in pajamas. Lots of girls have invited me to sleep over when their dads weren't home and their twin brothers were out for the night." Whoever invented this game already deserves a spot in the game Hall of Fame. Obviously Carly knew what I was referring to.

"The first one is the lie," she said.

"Wrong. I can fall asleep just about anywhere, like cars or airplanes."

"You don't wear pajamas?" Her face was as red as a lobster and I imagined she was thinking about what I looked like naked.

"Wrong again. I sleep in pajama pants in the winter and an old pair of basketball shorts in the summer."

"Then I must be the first girl who's ever invited you to sleep over," she said, as I nodded. "Well, it's a first for both of us, then. You're the first boy I've asked."

"I was hoping that was the case," I grinned.

"Actually, you're the only boy I've ever invited over."

"Really?" I asked, incredulously. "You mean to tell me that a former boyfriend never once came over to hang out or watch a movie?"

Red crept up her neck. "I've never had a boyfriend," she confessed. "Boys never pay attention to me. I'm too shy and regular."

My mouth hung open. There was nothing regular about Carly. She was smart, talented, and beautiful. There had to be a reason why guys hadn't asked her out. I knew she didn't have a boyfriend this past year, but I didn't realize she'd never had a boyfriend. I sputtered the only explanation I could think of. "Maybe they're all just scared that Drew will beat the crap out of them if they ask you out."

She laughed. "Drew acts tough, but he's a giant teddy bear."

Teddy bear, my ass. He was taller and broader than I was, and I knew he could easily punch someone's teeth out if he wanted to.

"He let you through the door," she said.

"True that." I really didn't know what to believe, but I knew Drew well enough to know that he was protective of Carly and wouldn't approve of her dating just anybody.

She yawned. "Speaking of pajamas, I'm going to go put

mine on. I'll bring you a pair of Drew's shorts."

I wanted to help Carly down from the counter, but I didn't trust myself. Instead, I shoved my hands deep into my front pockets. "Okay," I finally answered, watching her jump down. I followed her with my eyes as she left the room. I stayed in the kitchen and filled a glass of water, hoping it would cool me off. I had a feeling it was going to be a long night.

She returned a few minutes later wearing pink plaid pajama bottoms and a black T-shirt. I never knew plaid could be so hot. She handed me a pair of Drew's shorts and told me I could change in the bathroom.

We popped in a movie and curled up on the couch. I kept my promise and nothing else happened between us. When she told me she'd never had a boyfriend before, I decided I needed to be extra careful. I didn't want her to think I'd only agreed to stay over to get in her pants. I wanted to take things slow and get it right. Carly was giving me another chance and I refused to fuck it up.

Chapter Thirteen

Carly

"Dude, you have two seconds to get the fuck off my sister!" Drew shouted, startling Gavin and I. Our legs and arms were tangled, and we practically tripped over each other trying to stand. "Hey, are those my shorts?" I thought he was spending the night with Luke.

"Yup," Gavin said calmly.

"I … I … we … fell asleep." My face flushed, making me look guilty.

"You got balls, dude," he smirked. "I like that. Standing up to me even though I come home to find the two of you spooning on the couch, wearing my shorts. I thought you were just friends." He raised his eyebrows.

I guess the movie wasn't that interesting considering Gavin and I had almost immediately fallen asleep. And in all honesty, I was sad things hadn't escalated further. He didn't even attempt to kiss me once we settled in. I sighed. I thought he liked me, but now I wasn't so sure. Maybe he only wanted to be friends. I looked at Gavin with uncertainty.

"We're just friends," Gavin and I answered at the same time.

Drew studied us closely, and I felt like a caged animal. Suddenly, he burst out laughing. "You two kill me. The best part is, neither one of you has a clue." He turned and laughed all the way up the stairs to his room, stopping halfway to remind Gavin that he wanted his shorts back—washed!

"I don't find anything funny," I yelled at the top of my lungs. Drew didn't say respond, and a few seconds later I heard his door close.

"I'm sorry about that. Drew can be an ass."

"It's alright. I should bounce anyway. I have to tutor early in the morning." He paused, and I waited for him to say that what he told Drew wasn't true. That he did want to be more than friends. But he never did. "Tell Drew I'll return his shorts by the end of the week."

"Okay," I said, trying not to show any emotion. Just because Drew was home now, didn't mean I wanted Gavin to leave. Did this mean the kisses we shared hadn't meant anything? What about all the things we'd said to each other? I was hurt by the fact that Gavin pretended the whole night hadn't meant anything to him. I walked to the front door and opened it, hoping I could hold back the tears until he left.

"See ya," he waved, as he made his way to the car.

"Bye, Gavin." *Why do those words seem so final? And what should I do about it?*

Deciding that a shower was the perfect remedy to clear my mind and relax, I went upstairs. Turning the dial to hot, I stepped in. I didn't understand why suddenly, Gavin only wanted to be friends and was in such a rush to get outta here. I felt my heart breaking with each drop of water. I thought he really liked me.

I'd dried off and returned to my room when I heard my cell ringing. I knew by the ring tone that it was Becca. She'd called several times while Gavin and I were at the diner, but I hadn't felt like talking to her yet. I reached to grab it before it went to voicemail. I knew she was going to be pissed at me for ignoring her this long.

Before I could even say hello, she started yelling into the phone, "Thank God you answered! Where are you?"

"Home," I said meekly.

"What? I thought you were lying in a ditch somewhere. Where the hell did you go tonight? Nate told me what happened, and I've been worried sick. You took off and I couldn't find you anywhere. It was like you disappeared. I thought maybe someone kidnapped you, or worse. I've called you a million times, but you haven't answered. What's up with that? I even tried calling Drew to see if he knew where you were, but he didn't answer, either. I was just getting in my car to drive over to your house to see if you were alive. Now that you're home, I'm on my way over to kill you!" I could hear Becca start her car in the background. "You have no idea how upset I've been."

Becca took a breath from her rant and I squeaked out, "I'm alive, okay!" I felt bad for making her worry, but at the same time, I was happy that I had a best friend who cared so much. "I'll explain everything when you get here."

"Damn straight, you will. I'll be there in a minute," she said, hanging up.

As soon as Becca walked through the back door, I filled her in. I told her how Gavin had come to my rescue and how we'd fallen asleep watching a movie. I apologized for not answering her calls, and she forgave me for scaring her half to death. I told her that Gavin had kissed me several times but kept his distance when we settled in to watch the movie. It still remained a mystery how we ended up wrapped in each other's arms.

"You should've hit that, Car," she said. "He's hot as hell. What were you thinking?"

I blushed. The thought had crossed my mind, but I'd been too afraid to make a move. I didn't have any experience with boys and I was embarrassed. Gavin's kisses were proof that he knew what he was doing. When he pulled his lips away, I felt like a puddle lying on the kitchen floor. Maybe my lack of experience frightened him.

"I don't know," I said.

"Well, he's a fucking fool for not ..." Again, I knew what Becca was going to say, so I stopped her.

Nevertheless, her comment made me laugh. Becca always made me feel better about myself.

Drew walked into the kitchen wearing nothing but shorts. He must've been on the prowl for a late-night snack and by the looks of it, he'd just stepped out of the shower himself. His hair was still damp and he smelled like soap. Out of the corner of my eye, I could see Becca's eyes scanning his bare chest. I couldn't believe my best friend just checked out my brother right in front of me. Gross. I remembered the night at the park when she said Drew had a great can and was hot, but I didn't think she meant much by it. I wasn't so sure anymore.

"Hey, Becca, did you hear that I had to break up Carly's little sleepover?" Drew teased. "You might want to ask her about it. I wouldn't want anyone moving in on your best-friend territory."

Becca laughed. "Are trying to cause trouble, Drew? *I'm* the best friend, remember. I already know everything. I know Gavin was here just a little while ago, so shouldn't I be the one asking you how you feel about a boy sleeping with your sister?" Becca looked at Drew, and I noticed that every once in a while, she let her eyes drift down to his abs.

"You should've seen their faces when I walked in and the two of them were spooning on the couch. Priceless. They jumped up so fast I think they set a new world record. They looked guilty as hell, but it was obvious they hadn't done anything."

What made Drew so sure? Had he read something on Gavin's face? Could it be true that Gavin only wanted to be friends and that the kiss didn't mean anything to him?

"How would you feel if Carly hooked up with a badass like Gavin Johnson? We all know he didn't make a lot of friends last year," Becca challenged.

Drew looked at me closely. "I wouldn't have a problem with it," his jaw tightened, "unless he hurt her."

"Good to know." Becca winked at me. Earlier, Becca and I had tossed around the possibility that Gavin suddenly backed off because he was afraid of Drew. Gavin didn't strike me as the type who was afraid of anything, but if that were the case, this would be good news. It seemed Drew wouldn't mind if Gavin and I dated after all.

Drew patted his flat stomach. "I'm hungry. What is there to eat?"

"Not much," I replied, watching Becca to see is she was staring at Drew's abs again, but she wasn't. She'd stood up and was busy poking around in the fridge. I was happy that everyone was acting normal again. I wasn't sure how I'd feel if my best friend started going out with my brother. Part of me thought it would be really great, but mostly I thought it would be weird. I reminded myself that Becca had a boyfriend right now anyway, and she seemed to really like him.

"How about we make waffles with strawberries and whipped cream? It looks like you have everything we need," she said, pulling the contents out.

"Sounds good to me." I got the waffle mix and the waffle iron out of the pantry.

Once the waffles were served, I strategically sat between Becca and Drew, my waffle drenched in syrup and piled high with strawberries and a mountain of whipped cream.

"Hey, save some whipped cream for the rest of us," Becca said, reaching around me to grab the can.

Laughing, she squirted an even bigger mountain of whipped cream onto her creation.

"Can you pass it to me when you're done?" asked Drew, eyeing the ridiculous amount of whipped cream on our plates.

"Sure," she smiled sweetly. She pretended to hand him the can, and then sprayed it in his face instead.

"I'm going to get you for that," he shouted, jumping off his stool and knocking it over. He chased her around the kitchen while she continued to spray him, laughing her head off.

"Car, help me!" she squealed, as Drew made a grab for her.

I ran up behind him and jumped on his back. He missed Becca, but he managed to grab her plate off the counter instead. I knew what he was thinking, and it wasn't a twin thing either.

"I'm about to get even," he cackled. And just as predicted, he scooped up a handful of whipped cream and strawberries from her plate and launched it at Becca's face.

She laughed and stuck out her tongue to lick off what she could reach. "Yum, this is really good."

Drew reached around and easily pulled me off his back. I shrieked but before I could stop him, he had my plate in his hand.

"No, Drew, don't," I begged.

"This is for trying to help your BFF." He grinned wickedly, smashing the plate and its contents in my face.

"Ugh!" I wiped the cream out of my eyes before joining Drew and Becca in the food fight.

By the time the last waffle was thrown, the kitchen was a mess. Whipped cream, maple syrup, strawberries, and waffles smeared every surface. The three of us sat on the floor, laughing and licking our delicious wounds. "This place hasn't looked this bad since we were in middle school and had a food fight with cookie dough," I said.

"I remember that day. If I recall, I won that battle too," he said smugly.

"You didn't win then, and you didn't win now," retorted Becca, picking a strawberry out of Drew's hair and showing it to him. He grabbed it out of her hand and happily shoved it into his mouth.

"The truth is, we're all losers, because now we have to clean the kitchen," I said.

"And I have to shower again," groaned Drew, running his hand through his sticky hair.

By the time we finished sanitizing the place, it was well into the night, which I had originally planned on spending alone with Gavin, but this turned out to be a fun alternative. Finally, with Becca, not Gavin, by my side, I dozed off.

The sun peeked through the curtains in my room, waking me. My alarm clock showed it was already past noon. Becca was sound asleep, so I nudged her awake. After everything that happened last night, I wanted to stay home and hang low, but Becca wouldn't hear of it. She said it was important for me to put on a brave face and carry on, which included spending the afternoon by the pool. The only reason I agreed to go was because she assured me Nathan had the day off. I really wasn't in the mood to face that disaster today. The wounds were too fresh.

As I baked in the sun, I replayed the night's events over and over again in my head. I discovered that I was more upset about learning Gavin liked me and then simultaneously losing him than I was about the situation with the band ... although I was plenty pissed about that too.

"Am I ugly?" I asked Becca, who sat reading a magazine on the towel next to me. "And tell me the truth." Usually I was content with my lot in life—wavy brown hair, brown eyes, average height, but this thing, or lack of a thing, with Gavin had me questioning everything.

Becca sat up, flinging her magazine to the side, and pierced me with a strange look. "Are you on crack? Of course you're not ugly. Have you ever looked in a mirror? You're gorgeous."

"Then why haven't I ever had a boyfriend? And why did Gavin run off last night?" I needed answers and so far nothing I'd come up with made any sense. "Something must be wrong with me."

"Nothing is wrong with you. And I've seen the way Gavin looks at you. He thinks you're hot. All the boys do. They stare at you when you walk down the hall; you just don't notice."

"No, they don't. You're just saying that to make me feel better," I pouted.

"I am not. It's true. Lucas especially can't keep his eyes off your ass. Why do you think Drew's always hitting him on the back of the head whenever you're around?"

"I thought they always did that."

"Nope. It's because he doesn't like Lucas looking at you like that." I drew my eyebrows together. *Lucas stares at my butt?* The thought intrigued me.

I opened my mouth to argue, but Becca continued. "And Lucas isn't the only one who checks you out when you're not looking."

"If that's really true, then why hasn't anyone ever asked me out?" This conversation wasn't making any sense. "Is it because of Drew?" I was sure it wasn't, but I had to ask.

"I'm pretty sure it's not because of Drew."

"Then what is it?" I couldn't imagine what it was about me that guys found so unattractive.

"It's because they think you're unapproachable."

"Unapproachable? What does that even mean?" I pushed my sunglasses onto my head so I could look Becca in the eye. Becca was speaking her own language again.

"I just read about it. It means that guys are afraid to ask you out because they know you'll say no. They're smart enough to realize that you're too good for them. And let's be honest—you are. Most of the guys at school only want to get laid. They aren't interested in having a relationship. Believe me, I know."

"Huh ..." I guess it made sense. "Does Gavin think I'm unapproachable too?"

"I don't think so. He did ask you out, a couple of times. I think he wanted you to know that he wasn't just there just to get into your pants. It's the only explanation that makes any sense." *Could Becca be right?* "You should call and ask him."

"I can't call him," I said, shocked by her suggestion.

"Why not? It's the only way to find out what really happened."

"Yeah, but I'd feel like an idiot."

"So what? What's the worst thing that could happen? Remember, you wanted to learn to speak up this summer, and here's your chance. Call Gavin."

Becca was right. The only way to get to the bottom of things was to call Gavin and talk to him. "Later," I said to appease Becca, not really knowing if I'd actually go through with it.

"I'm not going to stop bugging you about it until you do," Becca smirked, knowing me all too well. "If it helps—I can totally see you two together. You'd make a great couple."

Her words pushed me in what I hoped was the right direction. "Okay, I'll call him tonight, I promise." I slid my sunglasses back where they belonged. "Now I just have to figure out what I'm going to say."

"Be honest, and it'll work out," Becca said, sticking her nose back in the magazine. "If I find any useful advice in here, I'll let you know."

I flipped to my stomach to ensure an even tan when a shadow appeared. I looked up and saw that Gillian and Marlena blocked the sun. I groaned inwardly. The only reason they ever stopped to talk to us was to cause trouble.

"Where's your boyfriend today?" Gillian asked, in a sweet voice that sounded as fake as her blond hair looked.

"Where's yours? Oh, wait. I forgot. You don't have one," Becca replied. I bit the inside of my cheek to keep from laughing.

Gillian blushed slightly, but she let Becca's comment go. She'd obviously set out to make a point. "My older sister and her friends were here the other day and out of the blue, one of her friends just burst into tears."

Becca laughed. "Why do we care that your sister's friend is a crybaby?"

Gillian had a satisfied look on her face and it scared me. I knew we weren't going to like what she had to say. "She was crying because your boyfriend is a player. He broke her heart when she walked in on him at a party having sex with another girl. They had been going out for six months and the whole time, he'd been screwing around with other chicks behind her back. And what's even worse is, afterward, he told everyone that she was a stalker, and that he'd tried to break up with her but she kept following him around. None of what he said was true. He ruined her reputation. This all happened two years ago and she still can't get a date."

"Your sister's friend sounds like a loser. I recommend she find a new one," Becca replied calmly. By the look on Becca's face, I could tell she wanted to strangle Gillian for talking trash about Nate, but she played the game and kept her cool. Gillian was just looking to piss her off. She had promised to get us back for taking her lounge chairs. And like everything that came out of Gillian's mouth, this story was a lie too. It had too familiar of a ring to it to be believable.

"Maybe." Gillian shrugged. "Or maybe you should find a new boyfriend."

"Why would I do that?" she growled angrily, pushing to her feet. "So you can stick your sharp claws into him?" She took a step toward Gillian, forcing her to take a step closer to the pool.

"I don't want him. He's all yours." Gillian threw her hands up in self-defense.

"Make sure you don't forget it." Becca took another step forward.

Finally, Gillian turned and walked away, Marlena attached to her hip. Once she was far enough away to avoid ending up in the water, she called out over her shoulder, "I can't wait to say I told you so."

Becca made a move to follow them but I grabbed her arm and convinced her to sit down. "She's not worth it. She's lying, and you know it."

"Still, what if she's not?" Her forehead creased. "I think I might love him."

***

I was sprawled across my bed with my phone in hand. I'd decided to text Gavin to see if he could come over and talk. I didn't want to have this conversation over the phone. I sighed, stalling. I'd texted Gavin plenty of times. Of course, that was to find out when he wanted to study, but still, this shouldn't be that hard. Last night I'd asked him to sleep over.

Determined, I picked up my phone and typed:

Hi, Gavin. It's Carly.

Gavin responded. *Hey, Girly.*

I giggled nervously. He called me Girly again. Maybe I still had a chance.

Can you come over?

When?

Now.

A few minutes passed and Gavin hadn't texted back. I sat staring at my phone. I picked it up and was about to throw it at the wall when it beeped. Gavin had finally responded.

I'll be there in 5.

Great!

Shoot! What had I been thinking? I wouldn't be ready in five minutes. Rushing around my room, I changed my shirt and brushed my hair. In my haste, I didn't have time to over think things. The doorbell rang and I thought my heart was going to pound right out of my chest. *What if this doesn't work?*

Gavin stood on my porch as handsome as ever, but a cut near the corner of his left eye was held together with sterile strips. That hadn't been there when he left last night. He pushed his hair out of his eyes.

"Are you okay?" I pointed at his bruised face.

"It's no big deal," said Gavin, downplaying whatever had happened. I didn't press further—I got the feeling he didn't want to talk about it. Gavin was a private guy and I respected him for that. I never pressed him for details. He'd tell me in his own time if he wanted to.

"Can we take a walk?" Drew was home and I didn't want him overhearing our conversation. This was going to be difficult enough.

"Sure," he nodded. I walked out and softly closed the door behind me.

At the park, we found a bench and sat down. I turned to Gavin. "I've been going over everything again and again, and I can't figure out where things went wrong. I thought you liked me. I mean, it felt like you did when you kissed me." My cheeks warmed as I remembered how hot his kisses had been. My pulse had raced. I'd never felt anything like that and I wasn't about to give up without finding out the truth. "But then you told Drew you only wanted to be friends and you took off before I could ask you about it."

He looked surprised. "I am into you. Last night when Drew came home, you looked at me like you wanted me to tell him that we were only friends. I'd been ready to yell the truth from the rooftops. I'm not afraid of Drew, or anyone else, and I don't give a shit what they think. I only said that because I thought that's what you wanted me to say; I'd do anything for you. It hurt when I heard you tell Drew at the same time that I did that we were only friends. I thought you'd changed your mind about us."

"I thought you'd changed *your* mind. You didn't kiss me once during the movie." It was easier than I thought to tell Gavin what I felt. Something about him made it easy to speak my mind. I wasn't afraid to be myself.

"I didn't want to pressure you, or make you think I was only there because I wanted to have sex." *Becca was right!*

"I wouldn't have thought that, Gavin. I trust you." I reached out and traced his jaw.

"Does this mean you want to be more than friends, Girly?" he asked, swiftly pulling me onto his lap. I let out a giggle. "Is that a yes?" He tickled me, and I laughed harder. "What? I can't understand you."

"Yes!" I shouted.

"Good. No more games. I'm yours and you're mine," he said, staring into my eyes.

He moved me so that I was facing him, straddling his legs. Burying his hands in my hair, he pulled my head toward him until our lips touched. This time, he didn't start out slow—he kissed me hard and deep, intense pleasure spreading throughout my body. My toes curled and electricity hummed along my skin. My heart pounded so hard that I thought it was going to explode out of my chest. When I opened my eyes, Gavin looked as caught up as I was.

I wrapped my arms around his neck and played with his shaggy hair, running it through my fingers. It was even softer than I'd imagined. It was easy to follow Gavin's lead. My mouth slanted across his and I teased him with the tip of my tongue. I pushed it all the way into his mouth. I felt starved, like I'd never eaten before, and it would be impossible to ever feel fulfilled. I'd always crave more.

Gavin ran his hands down my back and under the bottom of my T-shirt. His thumb gently stroked my bare skin where my waist curved, sending small shivers up and down my body. I no longer cared that we were making out on a public park bench. All I thought about was how good his hands would feel all over my body.

I leaned my head back and Gavin kissed my neck. He slowly traced along my jaw line with his tongue and then kissed his way down. His hair was tangled in my fingers and I pushed him closer. He stopped when he reached my collarbone. Once again, his hot lips were on mine.

My lips felt swollen and bruised when we finally stopped for air.

"Damn, Girly, for someone who's never had a boyfriend before, you sure know how to kiss." He ran his hands through his hair. "I'm gonna lose my mind if you keep doing that thing with your tongue." His voice was rough and full of desire.

"What thing?" I asked innocently. "You mean this?" I kissed him again, and I felt him shake.

"Yeah, that." He stroked my hair. "You're beautiful."

"Thanks. You're not too bad yourself," I teased. I leaned up and gingerly touched the cut on his face. "Does it hurt?" I still had no clue as to what happened. It looked like he'd been in a fight.

"Nah."

I smiled at his handsome face. I still couldn't wrap my head around the fact that he wanted to be with me. Quiet Carly. The shy girl.

We hung out in the park talking in between kisses. Finally, we decided to head back. Drew was having a party and I'd promised him I'd hang out for a while. Gavin agreed to come. He was ready to announce that we were officially a couple.

We walked back hand in hand. A lot of cars lined the side of the road leading up to our house. I quickened my pace. There were cars everywhere. I had no idea Drew had invited this many people. I thought it was just going to be his core buddies—Lucas, Dominic, and Zach. It looked like the entire senior class was inside.

I pushed open the front door and was immediately hit with how loud it was. I hoped Drew had things under control. I walked through the house, taking inventory. His friends were everywhere and beer cans littered every available surface. This would be a huge mess to clean up, especially by the time my dad's plane landed at noon.

Heads turned to stare as we passed through, like everyone was trying to figure out how an unapproachable (to borrow one of Becca's words) girl like me had ended up with a dark, moody guy like Gavin. They didn't know the sweet side of Gavin like I did, the one who let me cry on his shoulder and made me laugh, so I was sure they couldn't understand. We continued through the house, looking for Drew. He had some serious explaining to do.

I found Lucas in the family room drinking a beer. "Hey, do you know where my brother is?" I asked after he'd slammed the contents down his throat.

"He's around here somewhere. I just saw him a few minutes ago." Noticing I was holding Gavin's hand, he exclaimed, "When did you two get together?"

"Today," I said, happy.

"Lucky bastard," Lucas said to Gavin, patting him on the back. Becca had said Lucas was fond of staring at my ass and something told me Gavin wouldn't be as nice about it as Drew was if he ever caught him glancing.

"Thanks," Gavin answered suspiciously.

"Come on. Let's see if we can find where my twin is hiding," I said, I pulling Gavin along behind me.

I stopped dead in my tracks when I spotted Drew out on the back deck surrounded by a bunch of friends. He had one arm around Gillian and the other around Marlena. *What are they doing here?*

"What the fuck is going on?" I shouted. Out of character for me, yes, but tonight was different. I was different. I was learning to speak up and this was a perfect opportunity.

"What's it look like? I'm having a party," Drew said, looking a little wobbly. I had no way of knowing how much he'd had to drink, but it looked like a lot. I felt Gavin stiffen, but he didn't say anything.

"Let me be clearer—what are they doing at my house?" I pointed at Gillian and Marlena. I didn't like them and Drew knew it. It was probably part of Gillian's plan to make my summer hell like she'd promised. She'd already taken a stab at Becca when she'd talked smack about Nathan.

"I invited them."

"You got a problem with us being here?" said Gillian.

"Yeah, I do." It felt good standing up to them. I'd never done it before. Maybe I really had changed. I could handle whatever Gillian dished out this time.

"Why? Are you afraid I'm gonna tell everyone how last year you got your period early and bled through your tight-assed, white skinny jeans? Every idiot knows not to wear white pants when it's getting close to that time of the month. Well, almost every idiot." My face heated. The moment had arrived. Gillian was paying me back. Only this time she wasn't lying and the look on my face proved it. "I found you in the bathroom crying. I went and got my gym clothes for you, so no one would know."

Tears filled my eyes. It was humiliating having her throw that in my face. I couldn't believe I actually trusted her to keep it a secret. I should've known her kindness had been an act. She always waited until her comments had the most impact, like right now to expose what she knew. A lot of people were hanging outside when Gillian made her announcement and all eyes turned on me. I was speechless. Maybe I hadn't changed so much after all. This I couldn't handle. I wanted to flee.

"It's true," said Marlena. "I saw Carly leave school early that day wearing Gillian's clothes."

"You promised not to tell," I whispered as tears slid down my cheeks.

Gillian ignored my plea. "And that's not all either. You should've seen the bathroom. There was enough blood that it looked like she'd had a miscarriage."

The deck had grown quiet. I gasped. I felt like I'd been punched in the stomach. The wind knocked out of me. Gavin squeezed my hand tighter. Of course, her last statement was a complete lie, but it wouldn't matter. Everyone believed what Gillian said like it was the Gospel and I'd already proven her previous comment was true.

Drew's jaw tightened. "What, you think dudes don't know about periods? Shit, we learned all that back in fifth grade health." Turning to Gavin, he said, "You want to help me with this?"

"Gladly," agreed Gavin.

I stood back and watched Drew and Gavin pick the two girls up, tossing them over their shoulders and carrying them outside. The girls kicked and clawed the whole way through the house, screaming obscenities. A few onlookers stopped to stare and I even saw someone take a picture. Served them right if it ended up on someone's online wall. Before getting into her car, Gillian shouted, "You're a fucking bitch, Carly DeWitt. I'm gonna make you pay for this."

Even though it was satisfying to watch the girls be thrown out of the house like the trash they were, I ran upstairs to my room. I was too embarrassed by what Gillian said. I also wished I'd been able to handle my own problems and not leave it to my brother and my boyfriend.

"You okay, Girly?" asked Gavin. He had followed me upstairs.

"Not really."

"I wouldn't worry about what Gillian said."

"That's going to be difficult."

"All everyone is going to remember is her grand exit," said Gavin, lightly stroking my cheek with his thumb.

"Maybe," I said, but I knew Gillian would get even. Her

hurtful comments tonight didn't even scratch the surface of the damage she was capable of causing. And I'd just been moved to the top spot on her *Ruin Someone's Life* list. I was trying to overcome my inability to stand up for myself, but it was moments like this that set me back.

Gavin lay down on top of the bed with me and held me against his chest until I feel asleep, not asking for anything in return. I don't know when he left, but when I awoke the next morning he was gone.

Chapter Fourteen

Gavin

I was on my way to pick up Carly for the romantic evening I had planned down at the lake. I'd worked the past three days, and I hadn't seen her since the night I'd held her close. I was eager to make a good impression. I know it sounded stupid, but I was on a mission. Now that she was giving me another shot, I couldn't fuck it up. I couldn't wait to crush my lips against hers again and hold her tight. It would be hard to continue resisting temptation. However, Carly was different, and I was still holding true to my word about wanting to get this right and not rush anything. Although the red-horned devil on my shoulder kept telling me, "Launch your rocket, let her feel and experience the passion between her legs," I was confident I could keep him at bay. For once, I didn't want my sexual desire to get the best of me and cost me a chance at true happiness. Carly wasn't just a chick to me—she had qualities that stretched beyond the ordinary girl.

"Hey, Girly." Carly climbed into my mom's car, looking as beautiful as ever, red lips shimmering.

"What have I told you about calling me that?"

"I thought you liked it," I said, raising my eyebrow.

"I do kinda like it." She grinned.

Not wanting to wait another moment, I leaned over and

kissed her. At that particular moment, I didn't think we were even going to make it out of the driveway. If, for some reason, she asked me to stand, my flag would've been at full staff. I had my hands in her long, silky dark waves, and she was teasing me with her tongue again. She was driving me fucking crazy. Again, the red-horned devil whispered, "Throw her in the back seat. She wants it and so do you." Shit, at this rate, it was easy to see why Adam and Eve failed miserably and ate the forbidden fruit; the devil is a damn instigator.

Nevertheless, this was important to me. I had to get it right.

"Where are we going?" Carly said.

"It's a surprise."

I hadn't given her many clues besides telling her to wear something comfortable. I glanced over and saw what she was wearing. Perfect, I thought. A sexy, intelligent girl who listens. I'd noticed that she usually wore sundresses, but tonight she had on a pair of white shorts and shirt that really showed off her summer tan. She looked fucking amazing. I smirked because we looked like we belonged together. In honor of our first real date, I put effort into what I wore. Ironically I too was dressed in white. Part of my tattoo was visible. I remembered Carly mentioning something about wanting to see my tattoo because she thought it was hot, so I decided to show it off a little.

I packed a picnic basket filled with a variety of sandwiches and some homemade chocolate-covered strawberries. It wasn't fancy, but she seemed the type of girl who'd appreciate it because I did it myself. I wasn't much of a cook, but I knew how to make a sandwich, and I'd seen my mom make the strawberries plenty of times. I also snagged a bottle of white wine from my mom's not-so-secret stash. My only concern was that Carly might mistake the wine as a sign that I wanted to get her drunk, which wasn't the case. All I wanted to do was add another romantic element to our first date.

I was a little surprised by the nervousness manifesting itself in my sweaty palms as we pulled into the parking lot overlooking the private lake in my neighborhood. It was a good-size lake with a large dock, a small clubhouse, and a playground. My family and I stored a canoe here, just like the majority of our neighbors. I hadn't been down here in a long time, but I thought it'd be a cool place to take Carly. A quiet Wednesday evening, I knew the coast would be clear, once again adding to the romance. This was more a weekend locale for families, children, and the occasional tweens who may or may not have tried to sneak down a few guzzles from stolen bottles of hard liquor.

"Are we in your neighborhood?" she asked, looking out the window.

"Yeah, but I live at the other end. This is Carrington Lake. Anyone who lives in this development can come here and chill. Lots of people use the clubhouse for family reunions and graduation parties. Have you ever been here?" I wasn't sure if Carly was friends with any of the other kids who lived in this neighborhood.

"No, but Becca's neighborhood has something similar."

"Come on, I'll show you around. I brought a picnic, but let's go check out the lake first."

I unlocked our canoe and Carly helped me carry it down to the water's edge. It was a perfectly calm evening. The lake looked like glass. We carefully stepped into the canoe. I paddled out about halfway. And I'm not going to lie, I was flexing the entire time. I even caught Carly stealing a few glances at my toned biceps and tat. The conversation was light. I teased her here and there, and every time Carly laughed, I could sense our connection growing stronger. On the way back, I rowed slower.

After stowing the small boat, I spread out a blanket on the dock along with the picnic. Carly looked like she was about to cry. *Oh no! What did I fuck up now?*

"What's wrong, Girly?" I asked, almost afraid to speak.

"Nothing ... I just ... no one has ever done anything so sweet for me," she said. I was relieved to know that these were happy tears glistening in her eyes.

"Well, get used to it," I said, kissing the tip of her nose.

I was learning more and more about Carly every minute. I learned that she preferred turkey sandwiches on whole grain bread. She loved strawberries, especially ones dipped in chocolate. Last but not least, she loved things made from scratch, just as I had done.

"Everything was delicious," she said, eating the last strawberry.

"I'm glad you liked it."

Chocolate clung to her bottom lip, an invitation for me to lick it clean, which is exactly what I did. Her lips tasted sweet and I knew the rest of her would too. I gently pushed her down onto the blanket until she was lying beneath me. I ran my hands all over her exposed skin, memorizing her soft curves. I kissed her mouth long and hard. She moaned as I trailed my tongue down her midsection. I could feel her hard nipples through the thin fabric of her shirt and it was almost my undoing, but I managed to keep my promise and maintain control. Although I longed to move my tongue across her nipple, unbutton her pants, lick between her thighs, and discover the treasures of her extremely hot, seductive body, I held back. When it happened, it happened, and it would be perfect.

We spent the next hour kissing and talking. This girl had gotten under my skin and I wanted to prove to her how much she meant to me, which I was doing by taking things slow. Carly was more than a quick bang in the back seat to relieve pressure. She was the grand prize.

The sun began to set and we silently watched the beautiful colors spread across the sky. Tomorrow, I'd try to recreate this scene in front of me—Carly wrapped up in my arms watching the sun descend. We stayed until the sun was gone and the last bit of color vanished.

"We should probably go," I whispered. It was a moonless night, the sky dark. Not wanting our date to end, I suggested we head back to my place. My mom wouldn't care if we hung out and watched a movie. Plus, I suddenly had a sudden urge to show Carly something.

When we got to my house my mom was watching TV in the family room. "Hey, Mom."

"Hi, Gavin. Oh, Carly, nice to see you again," my mom said. "Hi, Mrs. Johnson," Carly replied, blushing. She met my mom the night I found her running away from Ed's cousin's party.

"Carly and I are going up to my room. I want to show her something."

"Gavin, you know the rules. No girls allowed upstairs." My mom looked horrified by my statement. *Does she really think I'd try to have sex with Carly while she's in the house and could walk in at any minute?*

"Mom, it's not like that." Out of the side of my mouth, I repeated, "I just want to show Carly something." I pierced her with a look that said *you should know what I'm talking about*, but she just stared at me with a blank face.

"Gavin, just forget it," Carly pleaded, tugging on my hand.

Her beautiful face was striped with confusion and embarrassment. I'd never seen anyone blush such a deep shade of red. She must've been worried that my mom would think she was some sort of slut that I'd brought home. I hadn't stopped to think how my words might make her feel.

"Shit!" I declared, running my hand through my hair. My outburst made my mom gasp; she didn't approve of cursing. "I wanted to show you my drawings, which are in my room. I wanted it to be a surprise. You'll understand when you see them."

Understanding finally dawned on my mom's face. "Oh. Sorry, Gavin, I should've known what you were talking about."

"Can we go upstairs now? Please? I'll keep the door open."

"Sure. And here, take this." She offered her scarf that had been loosely draped around her neck.

I stepped forward and took it from her. "Thanks," I said. Standing behind Carly, I whispered, "I'm gonna cover your eyes with this, okay, Girly?" She nodded. "This way it can still be a surprise." I carefully tied the scarf over her eyes. "Can you see anything?"

"No."

"How many fingers am I holding up?"

"Three."

"I thought you said you couldn't see!"

"I can't."

My mom and I laughed. "I'm only kidding. I had two fingers up."

I carefully led her over to the stairs and then up. She didn't seem scared about not being able to see where she was going. Besides, I'd never let anything bad happen to her. When we reached the top, I stopped.

"Okay," I said. "Now, turn to your right and take six steps." She held on tightly as we made our way down the hall. "I'm going to take the blindfold off now," I whispered.

She opened her eyes. My room was not your typical teenage boy's room. No trophies, no posters of half-naked girls or rock bands. Rather, the walls were divided in half by a chair rail. The bottom half was painted a dark red and the top portion was a giant collage of black and white drawings, some large, others small. The subjects varied.

Carly inched closer. As she wandered about the room perusing my work, I could see the amazement in her eyes. At that exact moment, I wish I had the gift of being able to hear exactly what she was thinking, like Mel Gibson in *What Women Want*. How did Carly like this side of me? I can honestly say that this was the longest I'd ever held my breath.

She finally turned to me, practically speechless. "These are amazing," she said. "When did you do them all?"

I pulled her down onto the bed next to me. "I've been drawing for as long as I can remember. Some of these are pretty old," I said, pointing at the golden retriever I'd drawn as a kid. I was eight or nine when he died. "Others are more recent." A manga drawing of a girl with dark hair who looked a lot like Carly surrounded by beakers and test tubes took center stage. I wondered if she noticed the resemblance. I was sure she did. She didn't say anything about it, but that was probably because she knew it wasn't necessary. "My dad never approved of me spending so much time drawing. When he walked out on us two years ago, I was so pissed off, I painted the walls red and added the corkboard with my drawings just to spite him. At the time, I had no idea how much I'd grow to love it. It's the only place in the whole house that feels like home to me."

"I can see why," she smiled. "You're really talented."

"Thanks."

"Which one's your favorite?"

"Hmm ..." I took my time studying one wall, then another. "That's a tough one, Girly." I stood and circled the room, while Carly waited patiently on the edge of the bed. "This one." I pointed at a drawing of the same manga girl with dark hair, only this time she was being held by a boy who looked a lot like me. The key to the entire drawing was the obvious love that shined in their eyes. It was like they'd been made for each other. By choosing this drawing, I was putting my feelings out there clear as day for Carly to see. I'd decided that this would be the one chance for me to truly reveal how I felt about Carly.

It reminded me of the times when Coach would draw up the last-second play, hoping that his team would execute to perfection and win the game. These drawings were my starting five, and the one I'd pointed out was my star player. In order to be successful you had to execute, and I was really hoping I wouldn't fall flat on my face. Talking about anything, especially my feelings, was not my forte. My heart raced, waiting for her response. I did something I've never done before—shot a prayer upstairs. I always laughed when athletes did that on the court, but for some reason, it felt necessary in this situation.

"Why did you pick this one over all the others?" she asked, her voice raw with emotion.

"I think it's obvious—don't you?"

"Yeah," she whispered, looking at me with the same love-struck eyes as the girl in my drawing. She held her arms open and I closed the distance in one giant step.

I immediately sat back down on the bed and kissed Carly with the same intensity I imagined the boy in my drawing would as he kissed his dark-haired angel. Ours was no ordinary kiss. It was intimate and powerful. If I could draw a kiss like this, it would instantly become the new skin-a-max logo (which I was guilty of watching every now and again, but what guy wasn't?). Carly was doing something to me that I couldn't explain. Nevertheless, I wanted to keep the promise I'd made to myself, so I pulled away.

It was becoming increasingly harder to control my sexual desires. This was especially true because I'd just put all of my feelings on the table with the drawings, and Carly had accepted me. However, the last thing I wanted to do was put her in an uncomfortable position. "I could kiss you all night, but I'm pretty sure my mom will be up in a few minutes to check on us." We sat quietly for a moment waiting for our temperatures to return to normal. "I should take you home now."

I stood and Carly followed me out of the room. My heart was swelling in my chest. Today had been the best day of my life. I accomplished the goal I'd set for myself, to let Carly know how I felt about her without mixing it with sex in order to show her that I was interested in more than a good time. The truth was, I was falling in love with her. Hard. And more importantly, it looked as if she was falling in love with me too.

Chapter Fifteen

Carly

My eyes were focused on the floor as I walked into my lesson with Mrs. Wang, carrying purplicious. It felt like a million pounds. It wasn't my arm that was breaking, it was my heart.

"What is this?" Mrs. Wang asked.

I handed her the borrowed violin without meeting her eyes. It was hard to breathe. "I'm not in the band anymore. I wanted to return it. Thank you."

She waved it off. "Why don't you keep it for awhile? I don't need it right now."

"No thank you." I didn't want the reminder of what could have been. My situation with Karma wasn't going to change. I looked at Mrs. Wang, pain filling my face.

She sighed, "Okay. If you ever need it again, just ask."

I nodded.

I took out my own violin, I'd carried it in my other hand, and the lesson began.

"I know last time we talked about your senior recital and preparing something. Have you given it any more thought? Do you have a piece in mind that you'd like to start working on? Nine months will go by fast."

"About that," I paused. I ran my fingers over the wood on my violin. "I'm not going to have a senior recital after all." I'd choked at Karma's gig. How was I supposed to put together and perform a recital? I couldn't do it. I'd already told my dad to cancel everything.

Surprise registered on Mrs. Wang's face, but she quickly recovered. Her voice was steady when she said, "There is an ancient Chinese proverb called, 'The Red String.' Have you heard of it?"

"I don't think so."

"It goes like this: 'An invisible red thread connects those destined to meet, regardless of time, place, or circumstance. The thread may stretch or tangle, but never break.' The proverb extends to everyone we meet."

I sat quiet, absorbing the words. I wondered if it could apply to purplicious. It was more than a violin to me. She was a friend. "I hope you're right, " I said.

Chapter Sixteen

Gavin

It seemed strange that Carly and I had only been going out a week. It felt like longer, and I didn't mean that in a bad way. I felt close to her in the way couples did when they'd been together a long time. I'd fallen hard and fast. She was at Finkbauer today and was coming over later. I had some loose ends to tie up between now and then. I got ready and headed out.

A few minutes later, I rang Connor's doorbell. I didn't tell him I was coming over. I wanted the element of surprise. I didn't want to give him the chance to think about how he was going to respond to my questions. I'd thought he'd be more honest if he didn't expect me.

"Hey, Gavin," said Connor. "What brings you by?"

"I wanted to talk."

"Come on in," Connor opened the door wider and I followed him inside. His little sister and a group of her friends were watching TV in the family room and his mom was cooking in the kitchen. I followed Connor though the house to the back patio. "We can talk out here."

I didn't waste time with small talk. "I'm dating Carly. I wanted you to know. I'd heard you went out a couple of times."

Connor laughed. "Carly and I are just friends. Nothing

more."

I nodded. Carly had told me the same thing, but I had to be sure. It went back to me having trust issues. "I know the last time we hung out I was a jerk and blew up when you brought up Carly's name. I should've told you then I was interested in her. I didn't because I didn't think I was good enough for her. I still don't, but she wants to give this thing between us a try."

"If you'd spoken up, I would've told you that she had a thing for you. I never had a chance even if I'd wanted one."

"She told you that?"

"No, but she didn't have to. I pay attention. I see the way her face lights up when you're around. But don't hurt her, Gavin. She's one-of-kind."

"I know," I took a deep breath. Hurting Carly was the last thing I wanted to do, which reminded me of the other reason I'd come here. Carly was hurting and I had to fix it. "I want know what happened with Carly. Why isn't she in the band?"

"I'm sure she told you what happened."

"Yeah, but I want your version. What she told me doesn't make any sense," I said.

"None of it makes sense. Brady just went off on her, and she left. Ask Nate."

"I did. I thought maybe you heard or saw something. Why does he hate her so much?"

"I have no idea. But right from the beginning he was against her being in the band. I can't imagine what his problem could be. As far as I know, he never even met Carly until the night she auditioned. And sadly, he never warmed up to her."

"Weird," I said.

"Yeah. Everyone else liked having Carly in the band. She made it fun. And she is super talented. It's not the same without her."

"We gotta change that. If anyone deserves to be in Karma, it's Carly. And I know she misses it."

"Do you have a plan?" Connor asked me.

"Not yet, but I'm working on it."

"Let me know what I can do."

"Thanks, man. I knew I could count on you."

"Absolutely. I'm happy for you and Carly. It's the only good thing to come out of all of this shit."

"Yeah," I agreed.

After clearing the air, I hung out and shot the shit with Connor. We retired to his basement and played Xbox until I had to leave. I wanted to make sure I was home when Carly called.

I was in my room working on the drawing of the angel when Carly texted to see if she could come over. She was back from ensemble. I sent her a quick yes. We were taking things slow, and I couldn't be happier. It was amazing to see the personal progress I'd made. I felt as though I'd come a long way since my drunk dial. Carly made me feel different. I promised myself I wouldn't do anything to screw this up. I wasn't my dad. There was no way I'd ever cheat on Carly, or do anything stupid like that. She was far too important to me. I knew I loved her but didn't have the balls to tell her, at least not yet. I was a firm believer in the old adage that you can't throw a word like *love* around—it needs time to marinate. Even Robert Frost would've been proud of my ability to channel the inner poet. When the time came to confess my love for Carly, I would be confident knowing that love truly was the **L**ong **O**verdue **V**indication of **E**verything.

When the doorbell rang, I raced down the stairs. To my surprise, Nate had already answered the door.

"Here to see Gavin?" he asked, leaning against the doorframe and giving what I perceived to be the casual "eye fuck." Carly was wearing short jean shorts and a blue tank top that hugged her curves. I didn't like anyone checking out my girl, especially my own brother. That was fucked up. I'd already set Lucas straight when I caught him looking at her ass, and I wouldn't have a problem telling Nate, either. I wouldn't call him on it now, though, because I didn't want to embarrass Carly.

Nate and I had already had it out last Sunday, the morning after Carly had been forced to quit Karma. I was pissed that she'd gotten hurt and Nate hadn't done anything to stop it. I couldn't believe he and the other guys hadn't stood up to Brady. Carly had talent and it wasn't her fault that Karma's first gig tanked. Guys were different from girls—we threw punches and moved on. Nate and I had been settling our problems this way for as long as I could remember. Just like when Nate brought up the issue about our father, we fought things out, left a few bruises, and moved on. At this point in time, we were back to being brothers again.

"Yeah," she said. She shifted her weight from one foot to the other.

I walked over to her, putting my arm around her and pulling her to me. She looked uncomfortable. I wasn't sure if it was because Nate was looking at her like he was picturing her naked or if it was because she hadn't seen him since she left the band. I was pretty sure it was the later.

Nate cleared his throat. "I'm glad you're here. I wanted to apologize for what went down with Brady. It was fucking bullshit that we didn't stop you. We never should have let you run off like that. Practice hasn't been the same this week without you. We were hoping that you'd reconsider."

"What about Brady? Did he change his mind?"

"Don't worry. We set Brady straight."

"Do you know why he has it out for me?"

"No," said Nate, quietly. Connor hadn't a clue either when I'd asked him. Seemed like nobody knew what had crawled up Brady's ass. "I promise he won't try to pull something like that again."

"As much as I love playing with you guys, I can't. It's not just because of Brady. Don't forget I bombed on stage. I don't want to put everyone through that again." Her eyes filled with tears and she was shaking. "Thanks anyway."

"I'm gonna keep after you until you change your mind. We need you," said Nate.

The three of us stared at each for a full minute. The

conversation came an en abrupt end.

"What are you guys doing tonight? Hanging out?"

"Yeah," I said.

"Becca and I are going to the movies if you wanna come," Nate said.

The last time we doubled with them, it was a disaster. "Thanks, but no thanks," I answered for the both of us.

"All right," he said, "but let me know if you change your mind." He hurried off to get ready for his date.

"So what do you want to do tonight?" I asked Carly, leaning up against the counter and pulling her between my legs. I'd be lying if I didn't admit that I wanted her to say, "Make love to me, Gavin. That's what I want to do tonight."

As she wrapped her arms around my neck and reached up on her tiptoes, she whispered, "This." She kissed me hard on the lips, causing my body temperature to rise. All thoughts disappeared. Our tongues danced, as we explored each other's mouths. I was blown away when she took things further, sliding her hand down to grab my cock. The shy, quiet girl who couldn't play in front of a crowd vanished. Carly was doing things to me that I couldn't explain. This girl standing in front of me with her hand on my manhood was bold, brave, and sexy. At this point, I was sure there was no turning back.

"I want to do this all night," she sighed. My first thought: "I can't do this all night. I might not be able to last another two minutes." My next thought: "How did I get so lucky?"

Fuck the promise I'd originally made to myself. I was going to give her what she clearly wanted. I concentrated on her warm lips, easily my favorite feature, kissing them until they were swollen. With my hand inching down her leg and my tongue now behind her earlobe, I heard her moan. I undid her shorts and slipped my hand under. I felt the silky smooth skin of her freshly shaved pussy, and I knew it was time. She was wet and ready. With my pointer and middle finger primed for insertion, I heard a voice that stopped me in my tracks.

"Holy shit, bro. What the fuck! I think you two need to get a room, or better yet, take it upstairs to your own," Nate said.

"You son of a bitch!" I yelled, looking for anything I could to throw at him—a knife, perhaps. However, at that moment, Carly took precedent over getting revenge. Red consumed her beautiful face, and I knew she was embarrassed for getting caught. I pulled her close to block Nate's roaming eyes. Nate laughed as he walked out of the kitchen, pissing me off even more. Carly trembled in my arms.

This was my fault. What was I thinking, trying to finger Carly in the kitchen? Imagine if that had been my mother who walked in instead of Nate? I don't even have the words to describe how that conversation would've gone.

I immediately felt remorse. Could I have just ruined everything I'd been working for with Carly? How could I have just given into temptation like that, knowing where I was and what I was doing?

Carly lifted her head, which had been tucked under my neck. "I'm so sorry, Gavin," she said.

"Don't apologize, Girly. This was my fault. I should never have let what just happened get to that stage. Do you hate me?" I asked.

"No, not at all," she said. "Do you think Nate will tell anyone what he saw?" she whispered.

"Probably ... but don't worry, Car, I'll have a talk with him. Come on," I said, kissing her and leaving the room. I needed some space or I was going to take her upstairs like Nate suggested and that wouldn't be cool because my mom was home.

There wasn't a lot to do, so we settled on watching a movie in the family room. Carly laid on one end of the couch, her feet in my lap. My mom walked through several times, but we were a safe distance apart so she didn't catch us doing anything inappropriate. I couldn't get what had happened in the kitchen out of my head. I guess the only thing I could do was wait and see what would happen next.

The movie ended and I shut the TV off, feeling restless once again. There was no way we could end such an up-and-down night like this. "Let's do something. I've got to get out of the house." It was hard having Carly so close, yet so far away. I had no idea what was running through her mind.

"Sure," She agreed.

I stood and grabbed her hand. Calling out to my mom, I told her we were going for a walk and that we'd be back later. I didn't have a plan but headed for the door. Hot air hit us immediately. The sun was down, but the humidity was still high. Sweat beaded on my forehead and Carly looked a little flushed as well. We walked in silence for a couple of blocks, I'm sure both still thinking about what had occurred earlier.

Suddenly an idea popped into my head. I made a quick turn and cut through several backyards, holding my finger to my lips for Carly to remain quiet. She flashed me a curious look. Finally, I stopped in front of a wrought iron fence that surrounded a kidney-shaped pool.

"What are we doing here?" she whispered.

"Swimming," I said.

"Swimming?"

I nodded.

"Do you know these people?"

"No," I shrugged, like it was no big deal.

"I can't swim in that," she pointed at the perfectly landscaped pool.

"Why not?"

"Because we could get in a lot of trouble." She chewed on her bottom lip.

"After what we've already done tonight, I think this should be the least of our worries," I said, hoping she wouldn't take it the wrong way.

"Ha, ha," she said. "Very funny."

"But really, Girly, don't worry. We won't get in any trouble," I stated confidently, leaning over to kiss her.

Carly pushed me away, "Seriously, Gavin. Don't try to distract me." I laughed because there wasn't any anger in her voice. It was light and teasing. "I can't swim in somebody else's pool."

"Look at the pool, Girly. It's begging us to take a swim.

That's what it's there for. The people who live here don't even use it. It's like a toy sitting on a shelf collecting dust, and there's nothing worse than that." I paused to let my words sink in. "Come on, please. It'll be fun." I saw Carly debating what to do. Ever since the beginning of summer, she'd been doing things she never would have before, which included taking risks, evident by her earlier actions. She'd discovered it was fun to break the rules once in a while. And for some reason, that turned me on. There was no way I was letting her back out this time.

"Come on, I'll help you over." Without giving her a chance to argue, I lifted her high enough in the air so that she could place her foot on the top of the four-foot fence and jump down onto the other side. She landed gracefully, and I quickly joined her. We were standing on the inside of the fence, the gleaming pool in front of us.

"Now what?" she giggled.

"We swim."

I quietly kicked off my shoes and pulled my dark T-shirt over my head, tossing it to the side. Carly had never seen me without my shirt on, even though she'd already explored my lower half a little bit, and I worried what she would think of my naked chest. At first, her eyes were wide with surprise. Once the shock wore off, they filled with heat. I slowly approached Carly and took her hands in mine, placing them over my heart.

"I had no idea your tattoo was so huge," she said. "I'd seen the edges of it peek out from under the sleeve of your T-shirts, but I didn't know it ran up your arm and around your chest and back."

"Does it bother you?" I asked. It was a lot to take in. I'd gotten it shortly after my parents' divorce. I wasn't eighteen, but I used a fake ID and the artist didn't question it. I think he let me get away with it as a favor from one artist to another. The tattoo had been another way I'd tried to get back at my dad for leaving us. He'd always been vocal about his hatred of tattoos, even though I'd wanted to get one since I was a kid.

He thought they were for rednecks and punks, and I'd wanted to prove him wrong. This tat was personal. I held my breath waiting for Carly to answer. I couldn't believe how much I wanted her to like it.

"No. I love it," she said, her eyes blazing. "Did it hurt?" she asked.

"Did it ever," I confessed.

"Can I touch it?"

"Of course." I was thinking that she'd already touched something else without asking permission, not that I minded. The thought of her hands upon my body again set my mind in motion. Carly turned me on like no one else ever had. I'd always be hers, and I hoped she'd always want to be mine.

I held my breath while she lightly traced the black ink with her fingertips. She started with the head of the dragon on my chest and made her way down the top portion of my arm where the feet were, and then around back to where the tail spanned across my shoulders. I shivered. I'd never experienced such a rush. When I'd been with Harper, we'd bypass the foreplay and just get down to business.

"It's beautiful," she whispered, her voice laced with emotion. "I can't believe you designed it yourself. Is there a significance behind it?"

"Yeah," I said. "I've I never told anyone why I chose a dragon." This was true. No one knew the meaning behind my ink, but I was glad Carly had asked. I wanted her to know why it was so important to me. "I've always been interested in Japanese culture," I said, "especially art. I drew this particular dragon because it represents freedom and fearlessness. It's symbolic of the way I make decisions. Through the dragon's eyes, I'm free to make choices that make me happy and not my dad, starting with this tattoo. The dragon is powerful and courageous, two attributes I try but don't always succeed to mimic. So there you go—my version of *The Boy with the Dragon Tattoo.*"

"Hmm," she said, using her tongue to retrace her steps back to the front of my body. I had to bite the inside of my cheek to stop from crying out as sensations rippled through me. This girl drove me fucking crazy. She continuously made me feel things I didn't think I was capable of feeling.

We were face to face once more. I decided to *carpe diem* and gently caressed the side of Carly's cheek. I whispered in her ear, "I'm glad you like it." Once again, I found my way to her luscious lips. Then, to my surprise, I was transported back to my kitchen when Carly had unexpectedly grabbed my unit. I felt her fingertips slowly making her way down to the Promised Land. If my balls weren't blue before, they were now. Even though we weren't on the basketball court, I gave her an assist and shed my shorts. Here I was, in the flesh, standing in front of the girl I'd already come to love, wearing nothing but my boxer briefs. It was damn near impossible to hide just how much she turned me on.

Carly followed suit and threw her arms in the air. This was all I needed, the invitation I was waiting patiently to receive. I reached out and pulled the bottom of her tank top over her head, tossing it on the ground with my clothes. I ran my hands down the length of her arms, and this time is was her turn to shiver. Goose bumps surfaced on her silky smooth skin. I made quick work of unbuttoning her shorts and letting them fall to the ground. Seeing her in nothing but a black lacy bra and matching panties drove me insane.

Even though I'd already touched the forbidden fruit earlier, something about the way she looked now changed everything. Carly had the body of a goddess. Yes, her pussy was smooth to the touch and perfectly manicured as I'd found out earlier, but she had been fully clothed before. Now, the tables were turned. She was borderline naked and as the thoughts raced through my mind, I pulled her toward me. I'd almost forgotten where we were, but then remembered that nothing was more romantic than floating in a body of water with a gorgeous girl locked between my legs. Something about the word *wet* made everything seem better. I applied the theory of carpe diem yet again.

I led Carly to the edge of the pool and climbed in. I

reached my arms up and helped her into the water, letting her incredible body slide against mine as I lowered her. She wrapped her arms around my neck and her legs around my waist. I know Carly had seemed ready and willing earlier this evening, but taking things slow was just as much for me now as it was for her. Everything with Carly felt so damn good that I wanted more than just to fuck her; I wanted to make love to her. I'd had sex before, but I knew with Carly, it would be different. She already made me feel things that no other girl had.

"Even if we do get caught, this is totally worth it," she whispered in my ear, her words making it impossible to ignore how good she felt in my arms and how much I wanted her.

My answer was to crush my mouth against hers. Our tongues ran circles around each other, dancing. It felt so good to feel her warm skin pressed against mine. At his point, the pool felt more like a hot tub. I knew she could feel how much I wanted her, evident by the way my pulsating penis pressed against her leg. Her hands clenched onto my back, fingernails slowly digging in. I unhooked her bra and tossed it on the patio. Running my tongue from earlobe to breast, I stopped just short of the nipple. In a counterclockwise motion, I circled her areola with my tongue, which instantly triggered her soft moan.

"You're beautiful," I whispered, hoping my words would keep this incredible evening and embrace going.

I continued my exploration of her body, my tongue and hand serving as the compass, until I finally made my way back to her soft lips. Carly's eyes were shimmering with passion and excitement when I finally pulled away. I was dying to take things further, especially considering my dick was rock solid and I probably couldn't exit the pool anytime soon, but all of a sudden, I asked myself, is this the time or place to make love for the first time? I don't know when I turned into such a pussy, but I wanted our first time together to be special, which didn't consist of getting it on in someone else's pool. I'd been dreaming of this very moment since I first laid eyes on her and not being able to pull the trigger worried me. Was I growing up? Had I actually reached the point of adulthood where these types of decisions actually impacted the rest of my life? Why was I turning into Socrates and philosophizing everything? What the fuck! Why was it so difficult to answer these questions?

The only explanation I could come up with was love. I was truly in love with Carly and had reached the pinnacle of understanding what that word defined. In her ear I whispered, "Let's swim."

Carly slowly untwined her legs from around me, letting her feet drop to the bottom of the pool. Her normally melodic voice was hoarse, but echoed my words. "Let's swim."

I ducked under the water without making a splash and swam to the opposite end. Carly appeared next to me within a few seconds. We swam around as quietly as we could, trying not to attract any attention. The cool water felt refreshing, helping to bring my body temperature back down to normal. Eventually, Carly sat on the pool steps with just her shoulders peeking out of the water.

"I love to swim and always wanted a pool in my backyard. My mom didn't want one because she was afraid that with twins running around, one of us would fall in and drown."

"So you wanted a pool, huh?"

She nodded.

"Me too. Nate and I begged my parents every summer to put one in, but my dad always said they were too much work." I let out a forced laugh. "Funny thing is, he put one in when his new wife asked him to. I haven't seen it, but according to Nate, it probably looks a lot like this one." I looked around at the picture-perfect pool, trying not to let it show how much that hurt.

Carly was the only person I'd ever talked to about my dad walking out on us. In the short time we'd been together, she knew me better than anyone. I was so glad that I hadn't let what happened between my parents prevent me from getting to know Carly. She was the best thing to ever happen to me.

She made me happy and whole again.

She stood, still naked, but with her hands covering her chest (lucky for her, I let her keep her panties on) and came over to where I was leaning against the pool ledge. She made everything all right by giving me exactly what I needed. “I, for one, am glad that neither of us got our pool wish, because we wouldn’t be doing this right now.” She pushed up on her tiptoes and kissed me hard on the mouth, making me forget all about my dad and his broken promises. I welcomed her sudden aggressiveness, and matched it with a hunger of my own. Suddenly, falling in love with Carly was all that mattered. She had done the impossible—changed me.

Chapter Seventeen

Carly

"Hey, girl," I said, opening the passenger door and climbing in on Monday afternoon. "What's with all the honking?" Becca had come to pick me up. We were hanging out at the pool today to work on the tan portion of our summer tans-and-cans mission. As far as the second half of our mission, I hadn't had any interest since Gavin came along. Becca had a boyfriend too, but that hadn't stopped her. She said it was okay to look, just not to touch. I didn't agree.

"Wow, look who woke up with attitude this morning," she said. "The reason we need to get our fine asses to the pool is because I got a new bikini and I can't wait for Nathan to see me in it."

"Of course you can't," I said.

She backed out of the driveway and sped toward the pool. I swore she thought she was Batgirl when she got behind the wheel. The same two chairs we sat in the first day of summer were open. It felt like a bad omen, and I scanned the pool area looking for Gillian and Marlena, but I didn't see them. I shook it off. Instantly spotting Nate on his lifeguard perch, Becca waved like a lunatic. I simply nodded in his direction.

"What did you and Gavin do last night? Nathan said he invited you to the movie. How come you didn't want to go out with us? Did you guys have more exciting plans?" I blushed, and really hoped Nathan hadn't told Becca what he'd seen in the kitchen. Nevertheless, even the thought of what happened, and of course didn't fully happen, made my body temperature rise a few degrees. "Oh my God," she said. "You had sex last night. Or at least went down. Or wait—he went down. Or ..."

I stopped her right there. "Enough, Becca. Nothing happened." The problem was I didn't think she bought it. Something had happened and I hated to admit it, but sooner or later, my BFF would pry it out of me, not to mention that as she spoke, my face turned tomato red.

Becca still wouldn't shut up, so I told her once more. "Nothing happened!" I think I said it loud enough for everyone to hear as I saw a few heads turn and look. I didn't feel comfortable talking about sex, even with my best friend. Although I clearly didn't mind when Gavin explored my body like he had last night.

"Really?" Becca asked.

"Really."

Becca didn't have any qualms about discussing sex. As a matter of fact, it was one of her favorite topics. "Nathan and I did it. I held out for as long as I could, but I wanted to know if college boys were better at it than high school boys. All the boys I'd ever been with got off in like two seconds," she said, rolling her eyes. "I mean, hold your shit together and let me at least fake something and find a little enjoyment out of it. Am I right?"

I ignored her last comment because I didn't have anything to add to it. What happened between Gavin and I last night was the furthest I'd ever gone. Instead I responded to her early statement. "And?"

"Nate is fucking amazing. He gave me multiple orgasms, which no high school boy had ever done. I was so wet, Car. It was amazing," she said, fanning herself with her hand.

"Ugh! Too much information!" I shrieked. I really didn't need that visual.

"What about you? When do you think you and Gavin will

have sex?"

Although Becca had told me about all the boys she'd ever slept with, I didn't want to tell her about Gavin and me. It was too personal. Although he'd started to finger me and seen me almost completely naked, we hadn't gone all the way. I respected Gavin even more now because I'd been ready to give up my virginity to him, and he hadn't taken it. He wanted to wait until the moment was right, making me feel special. Being intimate with Gavin was more than just a means to an end, and telling anyone about it would take away some of the magic.

Interpreting my hesitation for uncertainty, Becca searched in her bag and pulled out a magazine and a pen. "Don't worry, I have just the thing." She quickly flipped to a page and read aloud, "How to know when you're ready to have sex." I blushed. The truth was, it was all I thought about lately. Gavin made my heart race and my skin tingle with the slightest touch. Even though he was my first boyfriend, even I knew the difference between what was real and what wasn't, and what Gavin and I shared was real. That's why I'd decided I was ready to share this with him too.

"There's not a quiz for that," I said, grabbing the magazine out of Becca's hand in disbelief. "Oh my gosh, there is." I shook my head. I was continually amazed by the content in the magazines Becca read.

Grabbing it back, she continued, "Okay, let's see. First question: 'How long have you and your boyfriend been dating?'" She looked at me.

"A little over a week." When I said it out loud it didn't seem possible that I was ready to have sex after dating for only a week. Maybe things were moving too fast. However, it seemed like we'd been together longer.

She looked back at the magazine. "Yeah, but you've known each other a lot longer than that, so that counts for something. I'm checking off five months." Her pen scratched across the page.

"You can't do that."

She held up the magazine and smirked. "Already did. Next question: 'How do you feel when you're together?'"

"Amazing." My cheeks warmed again. Becca grinned and marked the magazine. I needed to be careful with how I answered these questions.

"'Have you discussed birth control?'"

"What?" I said, taken completely off guard.

Becca laughed. "The magazine wants to know if you've discussed birth control. It's question number three." She looked at me over her sunglasses and saw that my mouth was still hanging open. "I'll take that as a no."

"Of course we haven't."

"Are you on the pill?"

"What? No," I said, emphatically.

"It's not a bad idea, you know. I've been on it forever. It helps with my periods. I used to get the worst cramps. Now, my period only lasts two days and it's super light. Plus, I don't ever have to worry about getting pregnant. That is not a scare I need, nor do you. If you and Gavin are getting serious, it wouldn't be a bad idea. I'm happy to go with you to the appointment, if you want." That's why I loved Becca—she told it like it was and was supportive at the same time. However, most girls at school didn't know how to take her, which was why, other than me, her friends were all guys.

"Good to know, but Gavin and I aren't there yet. But please tell me you make guys wear a condom. You have to be careful. Even though the pill protects against pregnancy, it doesn't protect against STDs."

"Damn, girl. You sound just like the presenter from Planned Parenthood that came into our health class last year to talk to us. You should see if they're hiring."

"Haha. Very funny."

"I thought so," said Becca, chuckling.

"Well, it's scary stuff. Don't you remember the gruesome pictures she showed us?"

"Yes. Don't worry, Mother, I made Nathan wear a condom," she said. "I'm not an idiot."

"Okay, good."

Becca continued going through the list of questions. I didn't pay a lot of attention to the answers I gave. The quiz couldn't determine when Gavin and I would be ready to have sex. Only we could. I couldn't imagine when and where it would happen, but what I did know was that when it did, it would be perfect. I wanted to spend every minute I could wrapped in his arms, but there was more to it than how he made me feel physically. I was falling in love with him.

***

It was late and Gavin and I were curled up on the couch in my family room watching a movie when my cell phone started ringing. It was Becca. I was surprised that she was calling—I'd overheard her and Nathan at the pool today making plans to go out with the guys after band practice. It wasn't like her to call me when she was on a date.

I quickly grabbed my phone before it could go to voicemail. "Becca, is everything all right?" I sat up, tense.

"No. Can you give me a ride home? I'm at the lake with Nathan and our DD is drunk. There's no way I'm getting in a car with him, and none of us are sober enough to drive."

"I'll be there as soon as I can," I said.

"Thanks," she sighed, hanging up.

"What happened?" Gavin asked, lightly stroking my arm.

"Becca and your brother need a ride home. Whoever was supposed to drive, is drunk." I chewed my lip.

"I've got my mom's car. Let's go." Gavin stood and gave me his hand. It was warm and strong. I followed him out the door.

It didn't take us long to get there. We pulled into the parking lot and walked down to the lake, following the noise. Right away I spotted Becca standing next to Nathan and all the other guys from the band. Suddenly, the events from the last time I'd seen all of them came rushing back. But I told myself I wasn't that girl anymore. I was here for one reason and one reason only: to make sure Becca got home safely. I didn't have to stress myself out with events of the past. If there was one thing I'd learned this summer, it was to live in the present and enjoy life. For me, I couldn't be happier living in the now, especially with Gavin by my side.

I'd almost made it to the small group of friends when Brady and I locked eyes. Next thing I knew, he was in my face yelling, "What the fuck are you doing here?" He reeked of alcohol, and I took a step back.

Before I could even get out a response, Gavin jumped in, rage distorting his handsome face. "Don't you ever," Gavin shouted, pushing Brady hard in the chest, causing him to stumble backward, "talk to Carly like that again. Do you hear me?" He shoved him again and this time Brady fell. Gavin clenched and unclenched his fists several times. The entire party stared in our direction.

I'd never seen Gavin angry like this. He was always so quiet and appeared emotionally detached. However, I'd always sensed that it was a cover-up. The look in Gavin's blue eyes was dark, and it scared me.

"Let it go, Gavin, " I said, tugging on his hand. "He's not worth it." I really didn't want Gavin getting into trouble because of me.

He shrugged me off. "I'm not finished with him yet. I've been waiting for the chance to find out what his problem is, and now I finally have it." He stepped closer and towered over a clearly drunk Brady, still sprawled on the grass. "I can't let him just get away with what's he's done to you. He's the reason you're not in Karma anymore." I winced. It was true—Brady had been the main cause of me giving up my dream of performing with them and winning the Summer Jam Contest.

Gavin grabbed Brady by the front of his shirt with one hand and made a fist with the other, threatening to hit him if he didn't cooperate. "So, Brady, I want to know what your fucking problem is with my girl?"

I held my breath, waiting to hear what Brady would say. I'd been curious since we first met why he hated me so much.

I'd never done anything to him. Nate went to stand behind Gavin, and Becca came to stand next to me, looping her arm through mine. Everyone else formed a circle around us.

"Brady was the designated driver," she whispered.

Now it was my turn to get angry, and I was pretty sure the look on my face matched Gavin's. I felt the anger build in the pit of my stomach. There was nothing I loathed more than drunk drivers. I left Becca and stepped in front of Gavin who still held Brady's shirt in his hand, waiting for his answer.

"Give me your keys," I demanded, and held out my hand.

"No fucking way, bitch," he said.

I felt Gavin tense behind me, but he didn't move. If he tried to reach around me to hit Brady, he might hurt me in the process, and he'd never do anything to hurt me. I turned and looked at Gavin, placing my hand on his chest. I could feel the anger coursing through his body.

"I've got this," I pleaded. This was between Brady and me, and I had to settle it myself.

Gavin sighed deeply. "Fine. But I'm not moving. If he so much as tries to lay a finger on you, I'm going to kill him." His jaw tightened and I didn't doubt his words.

I faced Brady again. Feeling Gavin right behind me, I gathered my new courage. "You're not driving in your condition. Give me your keys, or I'm calling the cops." I waited several seconds, but Brady didn't make a move. I pulled my phone out of my pocket. "Fine."

I'd started to dial 911 when he yelled, "Go ahead and call the cops. You and your family already ruined my uncle's life."

I stopped before hitting the send button. *What is he talking about?* My breathing became shallow. "What?"

"It's because of you and your family that my uncle's whole life has been ruined. He paid for his mistake by going to jail, but he can't get past it. He refuses to leave the house because he has a panic attack every time he gets in the car. He's terrified he'll hurt someone else."

"Oh my God," I whispered, covering my mouth with my hand, as the pieces of what Brady was saying came together.

My knees started to buckle and Gavin let go of Brady to grab me. "It was your uncle who killed my mom?" I heard everyone gasp. Gavin pulled me into his arms, my back pressing against his hard chest.

"Yes," Brady sobbed in defeat. "He was coming home from a party late one night and lost control of the car, hitting your mom's car head on, killing her." He continued to cry. "He wasn't supposed to be driving that night. He'd called my mom to pick him up, but she couldn't because she was in the emergency room with me. The guy who was supposed to drive was in even worse condition, so my uncle decided that he'd drive. He reasoned that it was only a few miles. They'd be fine." Nobody interrupted as Brady continued. "I was supposed to be sleeping, but instead I was playing Superman in my room, leaping from my dresser onto my bed. I missed and landed awkwardly and broke my leg. My mom got the call from my uncle just as I was going into surgery. Do you know how many times my mom had told me not to play Superman? If only I'd listened, your mom would still be alive, and my uncle would never have gone to jail." Brady had curled into a ball on the ground and was crying even harder.

The sole sound in the park was Brady's sobs. I was only eight years old when my mom was killed; all I knew was that the driver of the car had gone to jail. I was so young when it happened that I never really thought about the driver as a person with a family of his own. All I ever thought about was how much I missed my mom. I missed everything about her—her magical voice, the sound of her cello filling the house, her cheery laugh, and how she smelled like the cinnamon mints she always ate and would let me sneak from the tin in her pocket. I thought of her every day.

No wonder Brady hated me so much; he hated himself. He blamed himself for what happened, even though it wasn't his fault. It was Brady's uncle who ultimately made the decision to get behind the wheel of his car wasted. I couldn't believe Brady almost made the same mistake tonight, putting the lives of my friends and others at risk. That was unforgiveable.

"Brady, give me your keys," I repeated for the last time. He should know better than anyone not to drink and drive.

"I can't."

"You mean you won't?" I was thinking about asking Gavin to beat the crap out of him for me. Even though he'd calmed down, I doubted he'd mind.

"No, I mean, I can't. I don't have them anymore. When I realized I was too drunk to drive, and no one else here was sober enough, either, I threw them in the lake."

A laugh bubbled up and escaped my lips. "You mean, all along you had no intention of driving?"

He looked at me like I was crazy. "What? No!" he shouted. "I'd never drive drunk. My family has already learned that lesson the hard way. I'd never do that to them, or anyone else."

Breaking free of Gavin's embrace, I reached down and hugged Brady. I wanted him to know that he didn't have to blame himself anymore. It was never his fault. As I held on tight, I felt Brady relax and finally release some of the tension he'd been carrying around with him for the past ten years. Tears ran down my face too. Thinking about my mom always made me cry. Helping Brady move past some of his own pain actually helped my heart. I held him until we ran out of tears.

I stood up, wiped my face, and cleared my throat. Some of the partiers had gone back to whatever they'd been doing before the circus had come to town, while everyone else searched for a ride.

"Okay, who needs a ride?" Several people called out all at once. I looked at Gavin and he nodded. "We'll do it in shifts. We can drive three at a time. Once those three are safe, we'll come back and get three more until no one is left."

It took us five trips to transport everyone who needed safe passage home. It was really late and I was physically and emotionally drained when Gavin pulled into my driveway and parked.

I leaned over and looked him in the eyes. "Thank you, for everything. I couldn't have gotten through this night without you."

"You were awesome." He brushed the hair out of my face and tucked it behind my ear. "You were so brave and so sure of yourself, standing up for what you believe in. Your friends are lucky to have you. You're so different from the girl I first met in chemistry." He took a breath. "I'm so sorry about your mom. Her death was tragic and senseless. I didn't know."

"I know. I'm sorry. I should've told you. I thought you might have heard it at school. Everyone pretty much knows about it. It was a long time ago, though. My dad has always protected us from it. He only ever focuses on how much my mom loved us. That's why I don't talk about how she died." I paused, gathering my thoughts. "However, I realized something important tonight. I do need to talk about it. I need to take action so that other innocent people don't suffer the same fate. No one should ever drink and drive. We have that rule in our house. If one of us is in trouble, we call someone to come and get us—no questions asked. That's why Becca called me tonight. It makes sense that Brady would have the same rule in his house too. I'm still not sure if it was necessary for him to throw his keys in the lake," a faint smile broke across my lips, "but I understand why he did it. I know some schools have a SADD chapter, but our school doesn't, and it should. I'm going to see what I need to do to set one up. I can't bring my mom back, but maybe I can save someone else's mom."

Gavin gently ran his fingertips along my jaw. "You're beautiful, Girly," he said.

"Thank you."

Gavin walked me to the door. It was really late and Drew was home, so he didn't come in. Holding my face in his hands, he dipped his head and gently kissed my lips. It was a long, passionate kiss. Tonight had brought us closer together. My heart belonged to Gavin and always would. I breathed a sigh as his mouth trailed down my neck, branding me. He moved his lips back to mine and we shared another earth shattering kiss before he pulled away.

"I'll see you tomorrow," he said, walking to the car.

"Night," I said.

Chapter Eighteen

Gavin

Nate was standing at the kitchen counter, cracking eggs into a bowl when I entered through the back door. Breakfast food was his preferred late-night snack. "Some night, huh?" he commented.

"Yeah, it was fucking crazy."

"Did you know about Carly's mom?" Nate asked.

"No," I said, sitting down at the counter across from where he was cooking.

"You want some? I'm making more than enough."

"Sure." I remembered that the last time Nate offered me eggs was before our dad moved out. Nate and I were best friends then. We used to talk about girls, parties, and school. It was amazing how my parents' divorce changed everything, even though they both promised it wouldn't. Nate and I were getting back on track, but it wasn't like it was back then, and I didn't know if it ever would be.

Nate dumped the eggs on two plates and added two slices of toast to each. He passed one to me and sat down on an empty stool.

"Did you know Brady's uncle was involved and that's why he had it out for Carly?" I asked, returning to our conversation.

"No. I'd been trying to figure out Brady's problem for weeks. All the other guys had liked Carly right from the beginning, but he was always giving her a hard time. There's no way I'd ever see that coming."

"Nobody could. Not even Carly. I think Brady kept that locked up for a long time," I sighed. Tonight, I witnessed firsthand the damage caused by keeping your feelings bottled up inside.

We ate in silence for several minutes, each starring down into our plates. I was the first to speak. "I've been trying to come up with a plan to get Carly to rejoin Karma. Now that Brady isn't a problem anymore, she might go for it."

Carly missed Karma, even though she'd never directly admitted it. It was painful to watch her cut music out of her life on a daily basis, as if the reminder of what happened on stage and the conflict with Brady hurt too much. Her constant humming ceased, which told me she was aching on the inside. I loved her, which meant her pain was my pain. I even noticed that when she rode in the car, she'd switch off the radio. She wasn't interested in asking me about my recent adds to my iPod. Whenever the topic of music came up, sadness crept into her eyes. I would do anything to make that look and those feelings go away.

"I have an idea," Nate said. "Can you bring her over to Ed's garage tomorrow night around seven?"

"Sure."

"Excellent," Nate said, cracking a smile between egg slurps.

Tonight Nate and I reached a milestone. We shared eggs like old times and came up with a plan to get Carly back in the band, putting me in a good mood. I contemplated asking Nate about our new sister. I knew he'd already seen her a couple of times, and I was beginning to get curious about her. I searched for the words, but then I chickened out like a big pussy, deciding I'd had enough excitement for one night.

"Thanks for the eggs, Nate." I slapped him on the back and got up to rinse my plate.

"Dude, what the fuck ... I cooked. You gotta clean my shit up too." He handed me his empty plate. That was the rule—when we sat down together as a family to eat, the cook received a cleanup pass.

Nate stood. "See you tomorrow, bro. Remember, Ed's garage, seven o'clock."

"Got it." I loaded the dishes and washed the frying pan before heading upstairs to crash.

***

Unfortunately, I had to borrow my mom's car again, with the plan to pick Carly up at 6:45 p.m. My goal was to have my own car by the end of the summer. With the money I'd made tutoring and at Trader Joe's, I'd have enough to buy a cheap whip. I was tired of always depending on my mom.

I wasn't supposed to tell Carly where I was taking her, which proved to be difficult. She pestered me as I waited for her to finish getting ready. I wouldn't answer, and she was getting frustrated. When we were set to leave, I pulled her against me, staring into her deep brown eyes. "Do you trust me?"

"Of course I trust you, Gavin."

"Perfect," I replied. "I think it will make you happy." If it didn't, I was fucked. But as they say, there was no shame in trying, and I definitely condone that statement based on my relationship with Carly.

"Okay," she nodded.

"It might be better if you put this on," I said, pulling out a bandanna. If I didn't blindfold her, she'd easily recognize the way to Ed's house.

"It was a good surprise the last time." She turned her back to me and I tied it over her eyes.

Fifteen minutes later we pulled into Ed's driveway. I walked around and opened the car door for her. "Can you guess where we are?" The air was thick with humidity and the sound of a guitar blended with a mass of muffled voices.

"Yes," she said. A smile lit up her face.

"Where?"

"Ed's."

"Yes. Are you okay with that?" I asked, removing the bandanna and looking into her dark brown eyes.

"Are you going to stay?" She was worrying her lip between her teeth again.

"I was planning on it. Unless you don't want me to."

"I want you to stay. I do better when you're by my side."

"Then I'm not going anywhere. Ever."

I grabbed her waist and pulled her close. Pushing her up against the car, I felt the same sexual rush I'd felt both in the kitchen and the pool. She wrapped her arms around my neck, and I momentarily forgot why we were here. Truth be told, I wished we were in my bedroom. I licked her bottom lip that she was always biting, and ran my tongue across the front of her teeth, sliding my tongue in her mouth. She moved her hands down my back, sending heat surges through my body, especially my cock, which I was sure she felt. I honestly didn't care, but remembering we were in Ed's driveway, I decided it was best to separate. If those guys walked out of the garage and saw me standing there with a massive boner, they'd never let me live it down. (Mostly because they'd be jealous.) Not that I really cared if they saw, but I didn't want to embarrass Carly. I must've inherited a sixth sense because not thirty seconds after pulling away, I heard the voices in the garage grow louder.

"You ready, Girly?"

"Yeah," she said. "And afterward, I'm ready for something else." Did my ears deceive me, or was Carly hinting at the fact that she was ready to have sex? Either way, this was her night, and I was glad to play second fiddle at her party.

"Okay, let's do this." I grabbed her hand and led her toward the garage.

"Wait, I don't have my violin." Sudden panic flashed across her face as she tugged on my hand, pulling us in the opposite direction.

I grinned. “Don’t worry. I have it under control.” I walked her back to the trunk, popped it open, and revealed that it was safely tucked inside.

“How’d you do that?” she asked, looking at me like I was a magician.

“Drew,” we answered at the same time.

Drew and I bonded the night I helped him dispose of Gillian and Marlena, so when I needed him to do me this favor, he came through.

She reached in and lovingly grabbed the case. I could see the calm and confidence it brought her. I knew then that everything would be fine.

I tapped on the garage door and pushed it open. A sense of déjà vu washed over me. I quickly pressed the pause button and told myself that tonight wouldn’t be like the last time. I believed in Carly and her talents. There would be no reason to act like a jerk tonight. When we walked in, the garage erupted in cheers. Carly’s face lit up like a Christmas tree. Seeing her reaction already made this night memorable. With that in mind, we still had one obstacle to overcome.

Brady tentatively approached. “Carly, I owe you an apology. I ... I’m sorry ... I was a complete asshole to you. There’s no excuse for how I treated you.” He had a hard time looking Carly in the eyes. She reached out and lightly touched his arm.

“I know.”

He cleared his throat and looked around the room where the guys were obviously waiting for him to say more. “We’d love it if you’d reconsider and join us again. We’ve all missed you. Karma hasn’t been the same without you. You are Karma.”

“Fuck, yeah!” Ed yelled from across the room, punctuating his sentiment with a signature cymbal crash. Carly burst out laughing, and the sweet sound filled the air, erasing any lingering tension. Her laugh was contagious and soon everyone was cracking up.

“Is that a yes?” Nate asked.

The room was still and everyone's focus shifted to Carly. I knew she didn't like this much pressure, but the night hinged on her acceptance of Brady's offer.

"Yes," she beamed.

Connor was the first to run over and gave Carly a quick, friendly squeeze. "Glad you're back. We really did miss you. Quality hasn't been the same since you left."

"I've missed you guys too."

Everyone took a turn giving Carly a hug. I thought maybe I imagined it, but it seemed to me that Nate held on to her a little longer than anyone else, which reminded me of the talk I needed to have with him. The one where I set him straight about keeping his roaming eyes and hands to himself. Carly didn't seem to notice anything weird in his behavior, though, and went to get her fiddle. She walked by me on the way, reaching up on her tiptoes and planting a kiss on my lips.

"You were right. I did like this surprise. Thank you, Gavin."

"You're welcome, Girly." I kissed her on the forehead and then sent her on her way. The guys were anxiously waiting to start their set. Carly rushed around and finally took her position on the makeshift stage next to Nate. I made myself comfortable on one of the worn couches to watch.

"Okay, everyone. Time to get serious," said Ed, clanging the cymbal. That guy and his fucking cymbal. Sometimes I wanted to shove it somewhere else. I didn't know how anyone took Ed serious when he was always doing that. He stopped the cymbal from vibrating and continued. "The Summer Jam Contest is only three weeks away and we've got our work cut out. Everyone ready to rock?"

The unanimous response was yes. They started right in.

They practiced for over two hours. I didn't know what happened the night of the concert because I wasn't there, but tonight, Carly possessed all the confidence in the world. Her voice was strong and beautiful, never once wavering. When she played the violin, or as she liked to call it now, the fiddle, it was as if it were a part of her. I watched the faces of the guys and saw them each fall a little bit in love with Carly. Her music, like her personality, did that to people. She was like a siren, casting a magical spell on those around her. The funny part was, I didn't think she realized the power she had.

After Karma had finished for the night, I drove Carly home. Like any gentlemen would do, and certainly a guy in love, I walked her to the door. What I didn't know was that this wasn't like any other time I'd walked her to the door. This time, her dad was back from his latest business trip and she invited me in to meet him. Nervously, I brushed the hair out of my face. What would he think of me if he found out that I'd spent the night on his couch once with his daughter because she didn't like to be alone when he was out of town? More importantly, what would he think of me if he knew I'd been engaging in sexual endeavors with his daughter?

Carly opened the kitchen door and made her way through the house to the office where her dad was busy on his computer. She knocked lightly on the glass of the French doors and then pushed her way in. Her dad smiled when he looked up and saw her, then frowned when he noticed that she was holding my hand. But I didn't let go. I wanted everyone to know Carly was mine, including her dad.

"Hi, Dad," she said. "There's someone I want you to meet."

Without getting up, her dad studied me. I could feel his sharp disapproval in my gut. I tried to see myself through his eyes. I probably looked like a punk to him with my shaggy hair, torn jeans, and black T-shirt. The edge of my tat was even showing. I didn't look like the clean-cut boy he probably wanted his daughter to date. After what felt like an eternity, but in reality was only a second, he said, "Nice to meet you. I'm Mr. DeWitt."

I reached my hand out to greet him, "I'm Gavin. Nice you meet you," I said.

"So, you're the one dating my daughter?"

"Yes," I replied, brushing the hair out of my eyes again. Even sitting down, he looked like a big dude. I could see where

Drew had inherited his build.

Carly jumped in. "Dad. Gavin and I were lab partners last year." I could tell he was having an internal war, but without hesitation, the corners of his mouth turned up ever so slightly. It was evident that Carly had him under her spell, just like she had me eating out of the palms of her hands.

"I have good news," she beamed.

"You do?" said Mr. DeWitt.

"Yeah. I'm back in the band."

He looked pleased. "That's wonderful. I know you've missed it. It's been too quiet around here."

"Gavin helped me change my mind."

Mr. DeWitt gave me a second look, more thorough this time. "Good," he nodded his head in approval. "Does this also mean you've changed your mind about canceling your senior recital?" He asked Carly.

"Yeah, but it's too late. I'm sure the café is no longer available."

The corners of Mr. DeWitt's mouth turned up. "I never canceled. I held out, hoping you'd change your mind."

Carly hugged her dad. "You're the best."

"I try."

"We're going to hang out and watch a movie. Is that okay?"

He nodded.

"Thanks. Glad you're home." Carly kissed her dad on the head and skipped out of the room, dragging me along with her.

I flopped on the couch next to Carly and let out a sigh. "That was awkward," I said, rubbing the back of my neck.

"My dad is cool. I know he looks intimidating, but he's really a giant cupcake," she said.

I chuckled. I remembered her calling Drew a giant teddy bear. Like father, like son, I guess.

"What is a senior recital? I heard your dad mention it."

She explained what it was. It reminded me of a portfolio that an artist would have. However, I didn't have one, because art wasn't my major. Drawing was my hobby. She also confided that Connor was helping her compose a song and they'd met a couple of times to collaborate.

I stayed just long enough to watch a movie, and made damn sure to keep Carly at a safe distance I thought her dad would approve of. After the movie, she walked me to the back door where we bumped into Drew.

"Hey. How'd it go tonight?" he asked, smirking.

"Great," she smiled, her face radiant. "I know you had something to do with it."

"All I did was sneak your violin into Gavin's car," he said.

"Well, thanks." She hugged him.

"You're welcome."

"What did you do tonight?" she asked.

"Not much. Lucas and I played Xbox. I crushed him."

"Nice," said Gavin.

"Hey, I'm glad you're still here. I wanted to ask you if you were free to play a pickup game at the park tomorrow. We're one short." He'd asked me once or twice before, hinting at the fact that I'd be a great addition to the team next year. Actually, the more I hung out with Drew and his friends, the more I liked the idea, but I still wasn't ready to commit.

"Wish I could, but I can't. I'm tutoring in the morning, and then working an eight-hour shift. Next time?"

"No problem. I'll get you out there one of these days." Drew bumped my fist.

"I should go," I said, turning toward Carly. "It's getting late and I don't want to piss off your dad." This fucking guy was definitely cockblocking me at this point. His mere presence was enough to stop my hands and dick from exploring Carly's body.

"I told you, he's a giant cupcake," Carly repeated.

Seeing the look on my face, Drew said, "Yeah, you should probably go."

I knew he wasn't a cupcake. More like a protective father who would kick my ass up and down the street if I touched or hurt his daughter.

"Drew ..." pouted Carly.

"What? It's true. Don't think for a second that Dad wouldn't have tried to kill him if he'd been the one to find you guys on the couch." Drew laughed, and Carly reached around to slap him.

"Let it go already," she fumed.

"I can't. It's too damn funny." He stood. "I'm calling it a night. Catch you guys tomorrow," Drew said, leaving us alone.

I gave Carly a quick kiss goodnight and then left.

Chapter Nineteen

Carly

Summer was flying by. It was already the last week of July. When I wasn't sunning with Becca at the pool, or hanging out with Gavin, I was practicing with the band. Once again jamming on purplicious. We practiced every night and with only one week remaining until the Summer Jam, we had to be at our best. Actually, we were all confident that we had a shot at winning the whole thing. I didn't want to get ahead of myself, but our sound was different from what everyone else was playing. I was nervous as hell, but I knew I wouldn't crash and burn like the night we performed at the party. I wasn't that girl anymore.

"That's a wrap," shouted Ed, hitting the drum after an amazing session.

We always ended practice by 9:30 sharp. His parents threatened to not let us use the garage if we so much as went a minute past. Ed said the neighbors were beginning to complain. He always joked that someday in the near future, his neighbors would be able to brag to all their friends how they'd once lived next door to a famous drummer.

I finished packing my stuff and pulled out my phone to text Drew. He was picking me up tonight. Usually Gavin did, but his mom needed her car, and he an early morning appointment to visit a college. We made plans to see each other tomorrow instead. I sighed as I carefully put purplicious in its case. I missed Gavin already. Most nights we hung out after rehearsal.

My phone buzzed and I read Drew's text, my anger bubbling. I wanted to throw the phone against the wall. *I'm going to kill him for this.* Something had come up and he wasn't coming to get me. That something probably had a name.

"Hey, Nathan ... do you know if Becca's on her way?" I asked. She wouldn't mind giving me a ride home. I was surprised she wasn't already here. She came to almost all of our rehearsals.

"She's not coming. She just sent me a text saying that she got too much sun at the pool today." I must've reminded her three or four times today to reapply sunscreen. He held up his phone, showing me the picture she'd sent him of her burn.

"Ouch! I kept telling her she'd had enough," I said, stifling a laugh.

Suddenly, my face fell. If Becca wasn't coming, there went my backup plan. I was stranded with no ride home.

"Is everything okay?" Nate asked.

"Yeah," I shrugged. I didn't want to bother him. I'd figure something out. Too bad Connor had already left. I could have asked him for a ride. We could've talked shop. I had a new idea I wanted to run by him.

"Where's Gavin? Isn't he picking you up tonight?" Nate asked.

"No. Your mom needed her car. Drew was supposed to, but he can't make it. I was going to—"

"Walk home?" He raised his eyebrows. "You live miles from here and it's dark."

His over protectiveness was sweet. "No," I reassured him, "I'm going to call Gavin to see if he'd mind if I walked over and hung out until either Drew can pick me, or his mom returns with her car."

"I'll give you a ride. Gavin and I live at the same address, remember?" he said with a laugh.

"Sure, that'd be great. I'll let Gavin know I'm on my way over." I pulled my phone out.

"No, don't do that," Nate said, grabbing my arm. "Surprise him."

"Okay," I said slowly, tucking it back into my pocket, a little confused by Nate's tactics. "Are you sure you don't mind? Did you have plans to go out with the guys tonight?"

"I had plans with Becca, but those fell through. I was just going to go home and chill."

"Okay. Thanks." I grabbed my case and followed Nate to the car.

As soon as I climbed into the passenger seat and closed the door, Nate began talking. "I've been meaning to tell you how happy I am that you're back with the band and how talented I think you are."

"Thanks," I said, feeling my cheeks warm.

"What you do on the fiddle is hot."

Assuming he was just teasing me like he always did, I turned to give a witty comeback, but the look on his face stopped me. He was staring at me like he wanted to be more than friends. I shook my head, thinking I had to have it wrong.

"I like the new-age country thing you got going on, with the cowboy boots, skimpy sundresses, and big straw hat. You're really rocking it."

"Thanks," I said, feeling awkward.

"I can't get the sound of your voice and new look out of my mind. You're all I think about." Before his words even registered, he was on me, kissing me hard on the mouth, tongue thrusting.

I didn't know what to do. I was completely shocked. I did the only thing I could. I didn't kiss him back. I put both my hands on his chest and shoved him hard until he stopped. I thought I was going to be sick. Nate was Gavin's brother, and not to mention, my best friend's boyfriend.

"What the hell was that, Nate?" I said, wiping my mouth with the back of my hand. "I trusted you." I felt like bursting into tears. *How am I going to explain to Gavin that his own brother tried to get with me?*

Nate slid back into the driver's seat. "I'm sorry." He rubbed his hand across his forehead. "Your music is like a drug—it makes me think and do crazy things. It consumes me. I know it's not an excuse, but it's true. I've felt this way ever since you auditioned."

"Are you high?" I said. I'd never seen Nate do drugs, but right now, I thought he was experiencing a bad trip.

"No!" he said, anger in his voice.

"Then how could you do that to me? I'm dating your brother! Remember him? He's going to be pissed when he finds out that you kissed me." My hand was on the door handle and I was ready to bolt. I didn't even want to look at Nate again.

"You're not seriously planning on telling him, are you?" he said, looking like he finally regretted what he'd done.

"I have to tell him. Becca too. She's my best friend and I'd never keep something like this from her." I wasn't looking forward to either of those conversations. It was going to be difficult to find the words to explain something like this. "God, what were you thinking?" I let go of the handle as the enormity of the situation hit me. *What if they think it was my fault? Could I lose one of them? Or possibly both?* We sat in silence for a minute, my heart pounding loudly in my chest.

"Okay. How about this ... I'll tell them both, since it was my fault, but not until after the Summer Jam. It's only a week away and I don't want my fuck-up to get in the way of everything we've all worked so hard for. It wouldn't be fair to the guys."

"I think we should tell them now," I argued. I couldn't imagine living with this secret for a whole week. I'd be sick to my stomach. Plus, how was I supposed to look either of them in the eye, knowing I was keeping this from them?

"No. I'm taking you home. Gavin's not expecting you anyway. You should sleep on it. I'll call you tomorrow and you can let me know what you've decided. If you still want to tell them in the morning, you can. I won't stop you."

I couldn't really see any harm in thinking it over for the night. It would give me a chance to plan out what I would say. "Okay," I agreed, reluctantly.

As soon as Nate pulled into my driveway, I jumped out of the car. I ran up to my room and climbed into bed. I didn't even bother to wash my face or brush my teeth. I tossed and turned all night. I didn't know what to do. On one hand, I wanted to tell Gavin and Becca right away. But on the other hand, I could see putting it off. I really wanted to win the Summer Jam Contest. It was my one opportunity to prove to myself that I had changed, and that I could perform in front of a crowd without panicking. My voice was unique, strong, and the fiddle was a part of me like never before. I couldn't wait to show the world what I could do, what Karma could do. It wasn't my fault Nathan was a jackass.

By morning, I'd convinced myself to wait. I hadn't kissed him back and there was no way he'd ever try anything like that again. I shivered, remembering how awful it had been. It felt creepy, like being kissed by my own brother. I loved Gavin and I didn't like the idea of keeping this from him, even if it was only a week. I hoped he'd understand why we hadn't told him sooner. I refused to even consider the possibility that I might lose him. Becca and I had been friends forever, so I was sure if anyone would understand why we waited, it would be her.

Chapter Twenty

Gavin

I was in the passenger's seat of my mom's car, gazing out the window. We were on our way home from visiting the University of Buffalo and D'Youville College. They both had good pre-med programs, but were as different as day and night. The University at Buffalo was a huge campus with thousands of students. It was a public university and more affordable. D'Youville had an intimate setting and small class sizes. It had a price tag to match. Financial assistance may or may not be an option. Even though I wasn't about to take money from my parents, they made too much money for me to receive aid. I wasn't sure what I was going to do. I wanted the price of the public university with a private school setting.

"Gavin, you've been so quiet. Tell me what you thought of the schools. Which did you like better?"

"College is so fuckin' expensive."

"Gavin, watch your mouth." My mom looked pissed. She hated foul language.

"I thought it was appropriate in this situation."

"You don't need to worry about money." She reached over and patted my knee. "All you need to worry about is getting good grades. The rest is my job."

I faced my mom. "I'm paying, or I'm not going."

"Be serious, Gavin." My mom gripped the steering wheel tightly. "No one expects you to do it on your own. Your dad and I are more than willing to help out too."

"I'm not taking a dime from that bastard, and I'm not about to burden you. I'll take out loans if I need to." My voice filled with determination. I knew my dad could more than afford to send me anywhere. He was an orthopedic surgeon and was swimming in cash. And my mom was a pediatrician. She didn't make a ton of money, but she did okay. But I refused to take money from either of them.

She took her eyes off the road for a second and threw me a look. "I'm not going to argue with you about this right now. We're your parents and that's not going to change. Just because your dad and I aren't together doesn't mean we've stopped taking care of you. We'll figure this out. College is a big decision. It affects the rest of your life."

"I know." I wasn't about to carry guilt around if I let either of them help me, which is what would happen. I'd go to college, but it would be on my own terms and with my own money. My mind was made up.

"Don't forget these schools aren't your only choices," My mom's voice was upbeat. "Next week you're visiting University of Rochester and St. John Fisher. Both excellent schools right in town."

Living at home would save money. And there was Carly to consider. I'd heard her mention The Eastman School of Music. It would be great if were in the same city and not 60 miles from each other. I knew it would hurt to be far away from her. I planned to talk to her and see what she thought. College was a huge decision.

In the end, no matter what I decided, I wasn't going to accept my parent's help. This was my life, and I'd do it my way.

Chapter Twenty-One

Carly

Becca called to say that her body was still too crispy to hang out at the pool, so we made plans to go to lunch and start our back-to-school shopping. I couldn't believe summer was halfway over. It felt like just yesterday we'd finished our last final and were making our way to the pool, determined to make this summer the best one ever. And it was—right up until Nate kissed me last night.

I jumped in the shower, got ready, and threw on a blue sundress. I sat at the edge of my bed to put on my cowboy boots. I picked up one, and then let it drop to the floor. Becca bought these for me. She'd stood by my side through it all—my mom dying, my dad being gone all the time, my first crush, my first recital, my first kiss. I had to tell her the truth. I pulled the boots on, promising myself I'd tell her as soon as I got in the car. I could hear Becca honking in my driveway so I grabbed my purse and rushed out.

"Hey, how are you feeling?" I asked, getting into the car. I couldn't look Becca in the face. I kept my eyes on her shoulders and immediately noticed how red and painful they looked.

"It doesn't hurt as much today, but last night was terrible. My skin felt like it was on fire." She paused to hit a song on her iPod. "I felt better last night as soon as Nate sent me this song. Listen to the words. He's so sweet. No wonder I'm madly in love with him."

The song was "Beautiful Soul" by Jesse McCartney. It was about a boy who loved a girl because she was beautiful and promised that if she'd only give his love a chance, he'd be forever faithful and give her everything in return. I laughed inside at his ironic selection. Just last night, he kissed me. I watched her face as she listened to the words through the speakers; she really was in love with Nathan. Not the kind of love she fell in and out of, but the real kind. Her smile flooded her entire face and she seemed different. Happy. *Shit! How am I supposed to tell her now?*

We arrived at the mall and headed for our favorite stores. Becca noticed I was quieter than usual, but I used the excuse that I didn't have a lot of money to spend and was too busy raiding the sales racks to talk. She laughed and helped me find a few more sundresses to add to my growing collection. My anxiety grew when Becca came out of the dressing room wearing a pair of skinny jeans and asked me what I thought. Telling her the truth about Nathan was going to be harder than telling her the jeans she was trying on made her butt look big. I sighed. I would tell her when we took a break from shopping.

Finally, we wandered toward the food court. I ordered a chicken sandwich from my favorite sub shop, but once I sat down, I realized I wasn't hungry. I sat quietly at the table, picking at my lunch, hoping she wouldn't notice I wasn't actually eating it.

Becca sat across from me talking the entire time about Nathan. "I wonder if we'll see each other every day like we do now, or if he'll be too busy to hang out once his classes start?" She frowned, picking at her lunch. "I'll have to scour my magazines for advice on how to keep my man happy when we're apart."

"I'm sure you'll come up with something. You always do." *I should tell her now. This is my chance.* I took a deep breath.

"Becca?"

"Yeah?"

"I have to tell you—"

"Shit! Don't look now, but Gillian and Marlena are here. Are they stalking us? They always show up wherever we are," she grumbled. *Great. Just what I need—another interruption. I'm trying to tell Becca something really important here! They are the last two people on earth I want to see.* My stomach dropped to my feet.

Of course they spotted us and couldn't resist coming over to our table. I hadn't seen Gillian and Marlena since Drew and Gavin threw them out, and I knew they were waiting for the right moment to initiate payback. I hoped it wasn't going to be today. I already had enough on my plate.

"What have we here?" Gillian said. She glanced at my bags and snickered. "Back-to-school shopping at the Salvation Army, huh, Carly?" Gillian knew they were my bags because Becca was almost as rich as they were, although she didn't go rubbing it in other people's faces. Gillian would never be caught dead wearing clothes from the stores I shopped at.

"I like to keep an open mind," I said, not letting them get to me. I had bigger problems. This was the first time Becca had seen me speak up, and she looked pleasantly surprised.

Gillian turned to scrutinize Becca. "I see why you aren't at the pool." She stared at Becca's sunburn, smiling. "You might want to buy some sunscreen while you're out."

"Hilarious," retorted Becca.

I opened my mouth to defend my friend, but like always, Gillian got the last word. "We're off to the pool now. Guess we won't be seeing you." They spun on their heels, blatantly proud of who they were—obnoxious bitches who thought their shit didn't stink. I breathed a sigh of relief. Maybe Gillian wasn't going to try to get back at me. They'd taken two steps when Gillian called over her shoulder, "I've got my eye on you, Carly. I haven't forgotten it's your fault that I was publicly humiliated on Facebook. I'm going to get you back for that." She turned and walked away. I guess I was wrong. Gillian had no intentions of leaving me alone. She was just waiting until she could make the greatest impact.

I looked down at my half-eaten lunch. "I've lost my appetite." I pushed my plate away. Not that I had one to begin with. My appetite wasn't the only thing I'd lost. I'd also lost another opportunity to tell Becca the truth.

"Me too," Becca said.

Three hours later, Becca dropped me off at home. I'd tried several more times to tell her what happened with Nathan, but every time I got close, something or someone interrupted me. I was a horrible best friend. I walked slowly up the driveway carrying my shopping bags. How could I have spent the entire day with her and not told her that her boyfriend kissed me last night? I slammed the back door and let out a deep sigh. *Now what do I do? Try again tomorrow, or wait six more days?*

"What's up, little sis?" Drew said, walking into the kitchen. "Where have you been all day?"

I threw my bags on the table. "Shopping, obviously." I didn't even complain that he'd called me his little sis. I flopped into a chair and put my head in my hands.

"Is everything okay? Did you and Becca have a fight?" He walked over and placed his hand on my back.

I looked up. "No."

Sitting in the chair opposite me, he said, "What's wrong, then? You look upset."

I sighed, deciding I might feel better if I came clean. Drew might know what I should do. "Nathan kissed me last night."

Drew's forehead scrunched in confusion. "Nathan? I thought you were dating Gavin. Did you guys break up?"

"No." I wasn't sure I could continue. My stomach was in knots. If it was this hard to tell Drew, how was I going to tell Gavin and Becca?

"And I thought Becca was dating Nathan."

I took a deep breath. "She is," I said.

"I don't follow."

"When you didn't pick me up, Nathan offered me a ride to his house so Gavin could take me home after his mom got back. But as soon as we got in the car, he came onto me." I shivered.

"That bastard," exclaimed Drew. He looked me over and I could see the concern on his face and hear it in his voice. "Did he hurt you?"

"No, but he kissed me and stuck his tongue down my throat. It was disgusting." I wiped my hand across my mouth again, even though the kiss was long gone.

"What did you do?"

"I pushed him away."

"And did he stop?"

"Yeah." I saw Drew relax a little.

"Did you tell Becca? Is that why you're so upset?"

"I tried to tell her, but I didn't." Tears filled my eyes.

"Really?" Drew looked surprised. "Aren't you going to?"

"Of course." I was sobbing now. "But it's really hard."

"What about Gavin—does he know?"

"Not yet. Nathan wants to wait until after the Summer Jam to tell them." I sniffed loudly.

"What a prick. You have to tell them both, and now. The longer you put it off, the harder it's going to be. Gavin's already going to be mad as hell. And Becca deserves to know she's dating a bastard."

"I know. I'm going to tell them," I said with more confidence than I felt. Drew was right. If I waited, it would only make things worse.

Drew nodded. "Don't wait too long."

"I won't," I said, changing the subject. "I'm going to take this stuff upstairs."

"Let me know if you need anything." Drew grinned. "I'm more than happy to give Nathan the pounding he's got coming to him. Although for now, I'll let Gavin settle that score."

I climbed the stairs to my room and dumped the shopping bags on the floor. Talking with Drew had helped a little, but I still had to face Gavin and Becca. Since my attempt to tell Becca had failed so miserably, I decided it would be easier to tell Gavin first. I texted him to see if he could come over. He said he was back from visiting the campus, and was at work. He'd meet me at band practice tonight. *Shit! I can't wait that long.* I had to tell Gavin before I saw Nathan again. There was no way I could stand next to him on stage with this secret between us. It would be way too awkward, and the guys would know something was up. I could feel my chest tightening and the panic seep in. Thinking back to the first day of summer, I remembered taking one of Becca's quizzes and being asked which quality in a guy was the most important to me. I'd picked honesty. I refused to be a hypocrite. I took out my fiddle and began to play, knowing it would calm the war raging inside of me, and give me the strength I needed to tell Gavin the truth.

Chapter Twenty-Two

Gavin

I couldn't wait to see Carly tonight. I couldn't get the thought of her beautiful smile, soft, smooth skin, and dark, sexy eyes out of my head. I missed her. Hell, who was I kidding—I loved her.

"Hey, Nate," I called out, running down the stairs two at a time.

"Yeah?" he yelled from across the house.

I found him in the kitchen, sitting at the counter eating a giant sandwich. He didn't look up when I came in. "Can I catch a ride to band practice with you?" I'd finally saved enough to get my own car. This should be one of the last times I had to bum a ride from Nate or anyone else.

"Sure." He continued to stare at his plate.

"When are you leaving?"

"In ten," he replied.

"Cool. Thanks." I rummaged around in the fridge, looking for something I could devour quickly. I settled on the leftover Chinese. I didn't bother warming it up and sat down next to Nate, eating right out of the box. I took a deep breath, composed my thoughts, and asked, "Have you seen the baby yet?" I know my question seemed like it came from left field, and I wasn't up to meeting her, but since our last talk I couldn't help wondering what she was like. Maybe Nate was right. I haven't really given Dad or his new family a fair shake. I never did give my dad a chance to explain his side of things and lately, I've been thinking maybe I should.

Nate finally looked at me, surprise registered on his face. "Really? You're asking me about our sister?"

I shrugged, "Yeah, I guess I am."

"She's tiny." He chuckled. "And she cries a lot." I wasn't sure why, but hearing that made me feel better. "I'm not really into babies, but she's cute." I still wasn't sure how I felt about having a sister, but I was trying to accept it. He studied me closely. "Are you planning on going to see her?"

"No."

Nate went back to staring at his plate. He didn't give me a hard time about not making more of an effort like he always did. This was a constant source of tension between us, and I couldn't believe he let it go so easily. Normally, he'd question me about whether I'd returned Dad's phone calls. My dad left me three or four messages a week that I never bothered to listen to. Something was off.

"What's up?" I asked.

"Nothing. Why?" Nate stood and went over to the sink, rinsing his dish and putting it in the dishwasher.

"You're acting weird."

"Nah, sorry, man. I'm just getting nervous about the contest. It's in five days." He rubbed his chin.

"Are you sure that's it?" I felt like there was more to it than that.

"I'm sure." He nodded at my dinner. "Are you almost finished? We need to leave soon."

"Yup." I stood and threw the empty container in the garbage.

Even though we weren't late, we were the last ones to arrive. I guess Nate wasn't the only one getting nervous. Maybe he'd been telling the truth. The atmosphere in the garage was quieter than usual. Even Ed wasn't banging on his drums.

Carly rushed over to greet me when I walked in, throwing her arms around my waist. I squeezed her back. I wasn't normally a touchy-feely kind of guy, but I welcomed Carly's embrace any time. She must've missed me as much as I'd missed her. I inhaled deeply, breathing in her sweet summer scent.

"Hey, Gavin. I'm glad you're here."

"Me too," I whispered, lightly kissing her mouth. I let her go, standing back so I could sweep my gaze across her. It had only been two days since I'd seen her last, but it felt like more. I felt starved for her touch and her sweet lips. I wanted to kiss her again, but I knew the guys were anxious to begin rehearsal and if I let my lips press against hers, I'd never want to stop.

I kept thinking about what happened in my kitchen that night. We still hadn't made love. I was waiting for the right time. Maybe tonight? Her lips had seemed more urgent than normal. I'd have to make sure we had plenty of time alone later. I watched her ass shake in her hot little sundress as she climbed onto the makeshift stage.

The band didn't waste any time setting up. As I sat down to watch, I was amazed at how much they had improved. They sounded great. It was clear they had as good a chance as any at winning the contest. I could see the energy and excitement radiating off them, and it was clear as day that Carly's voice and fiddle were the secret weapons no other band had. I'd be pulling for them to win. I knew it meant a lot to all of them, especially Carly.

With my eyes glued to the stage and ears focused on the sound, I couldn't help but feel a little jealous. Nate had something with Carly that I'd never have. Their voices were the perfect complement to one another and they moved effortlessly around the stage. It was easy to see that they shared a special connection. My gut twisted when I saw how he looked at her. Then Carly turned in my direction and smiled as if she was singing directly for me. This gesture loosened the knot in my stomach. Carly and I might not have an onstage connection, but we had our own special bond, one that spanned beyond any stage. She continued to sing just for me for the remainder of the rehearsal.

"What do you want to do tonight?" Carly asked, as she put her fiddle away.

"Go to your place?" I suggested. I was desperate to make love to Carly. I knew she was ready and I believed the time was right. I wanted to hold Carly in my arms and please every part of her beautiful body. However, I couldn't announce my intentions with everyone listening to our conversation.

"My dad's home, and I really wanted to go somewhere private so we could—" My blood traveled south at her words, but before she finished her thought, Nate interrupted.

"We're going to Rosie's Ride and Slide. You should come. It's open until midnight tonight and it's only ten bucks to get in. Becca's coming, and Ed's girlfriend should be here soon," said Nate.

While the idea of spending time alone with Carly made my heart race, it didn't seem like it was going to be possible with her dad home and my mom checking on us every few minutes if we went to my house. It would be easier to restrain myself if we went out. Going to Rosie's sounded like a decent option. It was an old-school amusement park about twenty minutes from here, with wooden roller coasters, bumper cars, a wave pool, and water slides. I hadn't been there in ages. I gave Carly a look, hinting that I thought we should join them.

"What do you think? Want to go?"

She hesitated for a second, but nodded. "Sure."

It turned out to be a fun-filled night, even though I didn't have a moment alone with Carly. We laughed on the roller coasters and on the pirate ship, collided on the bumper cars, and held hands on the Ferris wheel. We joked while we waited in lines. I snuck kisses in here and there, but it wasn't the intimate session I'd originally been hoping for. When it was time to go, Becca and Nate caught a ride with us, so I didn't even get the chance to give Carly a proper kiss goodnight. I promised her that we would go on a picnic by the lake again soon.

Chapter Twenty-Three

Carly

It had been a long week and I was glad that the Summer Jam Contest was finally here. The excitement and possibility of winning was overshadowed by the fact that I still hadn't told Becca or Gavin about Nate kissing me. But regardless, they would know by the end of the day. Nate had promised me that as soon as the concert was over, we would tell them, together. I'd tried to tell them each a thousand different times, but in the end, I hadn't. Waiting a few more hours wasn't going to make a difference now.

I sighed. Becca was on her way over to help me get ready. She'd insisted on doing my hair and makeup. Things had been a little off between us, but she just thought it was because I was nervous of falling flat on my face again during the performance. Dressing me was her way of trying to soothe me, which only made the guilt worse.

I heard Becca downstairs talking to my dad, and a minute later, she was bouncing into my room carrying a huge bag. "What's in there?" I laughed nervously. It was getting harder and harder to act normal.

"Clothes, shoes, makeup, blow dryer, curling iron. You name it, I got it." She threw the overstuffed bag on my bed. "Let's see, where should we begin?" She looked me over from head to toe, then rummaged around inside her bag. "Here, take these." She handed me shampoo and conditioner; they looked expensive. "Go shower. I'll start organizing all the shit I brought. I'll do your hair when you get out."

I was like a robot, doing exactly what Becca said. In all honesty, it was the only way I knew how to get through this day.

As soon as I was out of the shower, Becca started working her magic on my hair. I couldn't even meet her eye in the mirror as she worked on me.

"What's wrong? Don't you like it?" she asked. She'd braided a small section of hair and pinned it back. The rest of my dark hair fell in waves down my back. It looked like a picture straight out of one of her magazines.

"It's beautiful." Tears filled my eyes.

"Don't cry. I believe you," she laughed.

"Thanks."

"Don't mention it. That's what friends are for, right?"

Pain stabbed my guilty heart. "Yes."

"Promise me no more tears. I'm doing your makeup next."

I sniffed loudly. "Promise."

Becca applied the makeup with soft, gentle strokes. I found it relaxing because I had my eyes closed most of the time. She'd instructed me not to move my lips or speak, which made things easier.

"Open your eyes. You look beautiful." It was true. I did. My makeup looked like a professional had done it. It was heavier than what I normally wore, but it would look light and natural from the stage.

"Thank you." I stood and gave Becca a hug, squeezing her tight. I didn't want our friendship to change once she learned the truth nor did I want her to be angry with me for not telling her sooner.

An hour later we were both ready. I was wearing a red sundress and the beloved boots Becca had bought for me. In my hand, I carried a jean jacket and a straw hat for later. Becca looked sexy in a pale blue eyelet tank top with a white cami underneath, and super-short jean shorts. She'd also bought herself a new pair of cowboy boots, which she rocked with her long legs.

"Damn, you two look good," whistled Drew as we made our way downstairs. He wasn't shy about checking out Becca from head to toe, and it was obvious he liked what he saw. She spun in a circle, reveling in the attention.

"Thanks. You're coming today, right?" I said.

"Of course," he nodded, staring at Becca the whole time. "I wouldn't miss it, but can I talk to you for a second?" He pulled me into the other room and kept his voice low. He hadn't approved of me waiting until after the concert to tell them, but he tried to be supportive anyway. "Are you okay?"

"Yeah. I just can't wait for this day to be over." The stress was wearing on me. I'd even lost weight.

"I know." He held my hands in his. "I'll be in the front row cheering you on. You're going to do great out there today, and then tonight, you're going to put all this other shit behind you once and for all."

I leaned my head against him, absorbing some of his strength. "Thanks."

"They're here," Becca called from the other room.

"It's show time," said Drew.

Nathan and Gavin were picking us up, which wouldn't make the ride to the concert awkward. Ha. My stomach flipped upside down at the thought. Drew was coming later with Lucas and a bunch of other friends. Becca and Gavin wanted to ride with us so they could get there early enough to score a spot in the front row.

"You can do this," said Drew.

I nodded. I hoped he was right. I followed him to the kitchen where they were all waiting.

"Hey, Girly, you look hot, " said Gavin. He squeezed me tight. I knew my heart would break if anything changed between us.

"Thanks," I said when he released me.

"Ready?" asked Nate. He was holding Becca's hand, acting

like nothing was the matter. He better not be wrong about believing it was the right thing to do to wait until tonight to tell them. I wish I had his confidence. I was quaking in my boots.

"I think so," I replied.

"Break a leg," said Drew.

Gavin helped me carry my things and we left.

The ride was quiet. Nerves were beginning to get the better of me. I had to pull it together. There was no way I was going to choke on stage again. I picked a favorite song and mentally ran through it. I felt the steady pressure of Gavin's hand in mine.

The four of us walked through the concert gates together, but then we had to go our separate ways. Only band members were allowed backstage. Becca wished me luck, and then it was Gavin's turn.

He pulled me tight against his chest. "The judges aren't going to know what hit 'em." He took off my hat and looked me in the eye. I could see how much he loved me. "I'm going to be right in the front row. Just pretend we're back in Ed's garage and you're singing directly to me."

I nodded, placing the hat back on my head, which Gavin immediately pulled over my face to protect us from all the wandering eyes while we kissed. At first, his lips moved slow and deliberate, but quickly became urgent and intense. I opened my mouth and welcomed his tongue. I poured my heart and soul into the kiss as my heart matched his, beating as one. I wanted this to be a kiss he'd never forget. I had never told Gavin I loved him, but I did. I loved him with my whole heart. It was the kind of love that songs were written about. Completely caught up in the moment, I forgot where we were until someone loudly cleared his throat.

Resting his forehead against mine, Gavin said, "That was different. More powerful than usual. Hopefully we can continue this, and more, later." He smiled, pensively. *Can he tell?*

"I needed something to occupy my thoughts while I wait backstage." I nervously chewed my bottom lip. I hoped he thought it was just nerves about the performance today, because I had kissed him as if it were our last kiss, and he seemed to have picked up on something. I didn't know what would happen after he knew the truth, and I wasn't taking anything for granted.

"Hmm." He licked his bottom lip. "Hope it works." He gave me another quick kiss, this time on my forehead, and disappeared as I went to join the others backstage.

There were fifteen bands entered into the competition, and each band had ten minutes to set up, sing their original song, and then exit the stage. We were performing tenth, so we had ninety long, agonizing minutes to wait before it was our turn to take the stage. I paced back and forth and went to the bathroom more times than I could count. The guys tried to reassure me that everything would be fine, but what they didn't know was that I wasn't just nervous about performing; I was also nervous about what was going to happen afterward.

It was finally our turn. As I walked on stage, the first person I saw was Gavin. Next I found Becca, standing right next to him. They were in the front row, just like they promised. All I had to do was get through this and then I'd be able to tell them. That thought made me feel better.

We quickly took our positions. We were going to perform one of Connor's songs, the one we believed was our best. If we made it to the final round, we would sing his other original piece.

Nate whispered to me, "You ready?" I nodded. Standing next to him still gave me the creeps, but I pushed it out of my mind.

Ed tapped out the beat. I took a deep breath and focused on Gavin. The noise settled around us as everyone stopped to listen. My voice sounded loud and clear, filling the entire arena. As I belted out the lyrics, Nathan joined in right on cue with Connor and Brady playing backup. In the middle of the song, I traded my voice for the fiddle. I broke eye contact with Gavin just long enough to notice that people were swaying along with our music. The crowd was totally into our sound.

The song ended with Ed doing his thing on the drums, while I brought in a fast-paced fiddle accompaniment on purplicious. We took our bows as screams filled our ears. It was our best performance yet. We had to be in the final round.

We waited anxiously backstage while the last five bands competed. Finally, the scores were tallied and we heard the emcee announce, "And the final three bands are Route 65, The Poison Apple, and Karma." The crowd went wild. I screamed as Nathan pulled me against him in excitement, making me cringe, until the rest of the guys wrapped their arms around me and it became a giant group hug.

The emcee called the three finalist bands back to the stage. This time, it was winner take all. We waited as the two other bands played their sets. Once they'd finished and cleared, we assumed our positions. We hadn't spent a lot of time practicing this particular song because Connor had only recently written it. Therefore, I was a little nervous. My only hope was that I wouldn't blow it for the group. I'd rocked the last song mainly because I'd been so busy obsessing over losing Gavin that I hadn't had time to feel stage fright.

I held the fiddle under my chin and looked into the crowd. Gavin was still there, smiling and waving. I didn't know if things would be okay beyond this moment, but for now, I knew they'd have to be. Gavin was mine and I was his. Ed gave us a beat and we played like we never had before. We brought the fucking house down. We had clearly won the crowd over.

The emcee held the microphone in his hands while we waited for the results. I tasted metal in my mouth because I had bitten my lower lip so many times it was bleeding.

"The winner of this year's Summer Jam Contest is ... drumroll, please!" Someone obliged and my heart rate sped up to match the beat. "Karma!" he shouted.

I couldn't believe we'd just won! I was so overwhelmed that I could barely take in enough oxygen. My whole body shook with excitement. We were jumping up and down, screaming. Karma was on cloud nine. We greeted the emcee who gave us our trophy and asked us to play an encore for the crowd.

We choose a popular cover song, switching it up to match our new sound. The crowd loved it. As the encore concluded, we ran offstage to celebrate with our friends and family.

Heading straight for Gavin, I leaped into his arms and he lifted me into the air. "I did it! We did it!" I gave him a huge kiss and he laughed.

"I'm so proud of you." He set me back down on the ground.

A small group had gathered to congratulate us. Drew waited patiently for his turn, and then clasped me tightly, spinning me around. "You really got it going on, little sis. You owned that stage. I wish Mom could've been here. Dad saw you. He said he'd congratulate you at home. He left so that you could celebrate with your friends. He had tears in his eyes, but don't tell him I told you."

That sounded like something my dad would do. He loved us and was always there for us, but he gave us our space too.

Holding out a Sharpie, Lucas and the guys from the basketball team asked me to sign their tickets. I laughed. They made me feel like a real celebrity. Other fans approached, raving about how much they loved our performance, complimenting me on my voice and fine fiddle playing. My heart fluttered in my chest.

I looked up and suddenly Gillian was standing directly in front of me, wearing a self-satisfied look. *What was she doing here?* Then it became clear to me that she was here to seek revenge. She wanted to ruin this moment for me. I straightened my back, determined to not let her get away with anything.

I'd stood up to her before, and I was prepared to do it again. Nothing she said could bring me down. I raised my eyebrows and waited.

Clearing her throat and speaking loudly, Gillian said, "You and Nathan sounded really good up there." Those closest to us turned to stare. No one had ever heard Gillian give a compliment to anyone who wasn't a member of her little clique. She continued, "I'm not surprised, though, because just last week I overheard Nate bragging to some of his buddies at the pool how he had a special connection with you." She made air quotes around the words "special connection."

In an instant, Becca was in Gillian's face, ready for a fight. "Of course he does. Carly is his brother's girlfriend."

Gillian's cynical laugh filled the air. I felt nauseated. I thought I might actually puke. "Are you sure?" Gillian knew I was with Gavin, and Becca was with Nathan. "Because Nathan said that one night after band practice, he and Carly were making out in his car, and by the tone of his voice, I could tell that he'd been totally into it. And from where I was standing during the concert, it was obvious to me that they've got a thing for each other."

"You lying bitch." Becca took a swing at Gillian, punching her right in the face. "Carly would never."

"Why don't you ask her?" Gillian wiped the blood off her mouth with her shirt, not seeming to care because she knew she'd won. She walked away and no one even noticed.

Quickly all eyes cut to me, and guilt was written all over my face. I stuttered, "It ... wasn't ... like that." I looked at Becca and Gavin, hating the hurt look I saw on their faces. I couldn't lose them, I couldn't. I rushed to explain. "Nathan kissed me. I didn't kiss him back." Standing next to me, Gavin stiffened but didn't say anything. Everyone around us fell quiet.

"What? When?" croaked Becca, her voice breaking up.

"The night you stayed home with a sunburn," I whispered. I watched Becca's face as she processed Gillian's words and their possible truth.

"You kissed my boyfriend, and you didn't tell me?" She screamed in my face, looking like she was going to punch me next.

"*He* kissed *me*. I wanted to tell you. I tried to tell you a million different times, but I just couldn't get the words out."

"It's easy. You say it like this—hey, Becca, I kissed your boyfriend. You know, the one you told me that you were in love with." Becca choked back a sob. "God, Carly. How could you do this to me?"

I glanced over at Nathan, hoping he'd step in and help me, but he didn't. He remained silent, letting me handle this on my own. He really was a bastard. I never should've let him talk me into waiting until after the concert. At the beginning of the summer, I'd promised to speak my mind and stand up for myself, but when it came to being honest with those closest to me, I'd failed. It might be too late, but I had to try and set things right.

I took a deep breath. I could do this. "I'm sorry. You're right. I should have told you. But I didn't kiss him. He kissed me."

"Same difference," she shouted, and took off running through the crowd. Tears streamed down my face.

"I'll go see what I can do," Drew said, running after her.

I turned to Gavin. A wide range of emotions played across his handsome face. "I'm sorry. I ..." I reached out to touch him and he recoiled. My heart ripped in half. The pressure in my chest was unbearable.

Ignoring me, he zeroed in on Nathan. "How could you kiss my girl? That is totally crossing the line, bro!" His voice rose with each word. His hands balled into fists at his sides, the dark and dangerous look in his eyes.

"I wasn't thinking," Nate said, rubbing his temple. "When she sings, she gets stuck in my head and I can't get her out. One night last week after rehearsal she needed a ride. Drew bailed on her and couldn't pick her up. She was going to call you, but I knew you didn't have a car, so I told her I'd give her a ride to our house since I was headed home anyway. That's when I kissed her, but she pushed me away. She loves you and wanted to tell you right away. But I wanted to wait. I said things to make her feel guilty. The plan was to tell you and Becca tonight after the concert."

"You selfish bastard!" Gavin yelled, throwing a punch. It was a one-sided fight. Nathan barely got a punch in as Gavin wailed away at his face and body. By the time the security guards intervened and pulled Gavin off his brother, Nathan was a bloody mess.

"Gavin!" I shouted, chasing after him. The guards had tossed him out onto the sidewalk and he continued to walk away. Catching up to him, I tugged on his arm.

"I have nothing to say to you," he said, shaking free of my hold. What was left of my heart crumbled into a million pieces.

I continued after him. I wasn't going to let him go without letting me explain. "Gavin, please," I cried.

He stopped walking and faced me. "As if my own brother kissing my girlfriend wasn't bad enough, but you not telling me, that's worse."

I opened my mouth to tell him that I tried, but nothing came out. Becca was right. I could've told him. It wouldn't have been easy, but I could have. Only I didn't. There was no excuse for the part I played in all of this. I understood that now.

"I'm sorry. Please forgive me," I sobbed. "Please ... are things going to be okay between us?"

"I can't be with you anymore. Every time I look at you, I'll see my brother—scratch that—my ex-brother sticking his tongue down your throat."

I gasped at his harsh words. They were like knives cutting me to my core. "It wasn't like that. I didn't kiss him back. I pushed him away. I didn't want him to kiss me. You have to believe me," I pleaded. "I love you." I finally spoke the words. It wasn't how I'd imagined I'd tell him, but it didn't make it any less true. I loved Gavin with my whole heart and I knew he loved me too.

"You have a funny way of showing it," he laughed darkly. "If you really loved me, you would've told me the truth. I can't be with someone who doesn't trust me enough to be honest with me."

I felt my world crash down around me. I was struggling to breathe. I didn't expect him to say, "I love you" in return, but I hadn't expected him to break up with me. I didn't know if I'd survive. My heart was broken beyond repair.

"I'm sorry, Carly, but I believe honesty is the most

important thing in a relationship. How will I know that you haven't kissed someone and just not bothered to tell me?"

"I would never do that. I would never kiss anyone. I love you, God damnit," I wailed. Gavin didn't respond. He simply walked away without saying another word. Hearing him call me Carly, and not Girly, had a final ring to it. I clutched my chest where I had a big gaping hole.

I'm not sure how much time passed, but Drew found me slumped against the fence near the exit. I couldn't believe I'd lost everything. Winning the contest had come at too high a price.

"You okay?" he asked.

"No," I said, through fresh tears.

"I talked to Becca and I think she'll come around. What about Gavin?"

"He hates me," I sobbed.

Drew reached out his hand and helped me up. "He doesn't hate you, believe me. I'm a guy, and I know these things." He was trying to cheer me up, but it didn't work. "Just give him time." Drew walked me to his car, supporting me the whole way.

"Thanks, Drew, for everything."

"No problem, little sis. That's what big brothers are for." I no longer had enough fight in me to remind him that I wasn't his little sister. It was time to let that one go.

All I could do was hope that he was right. I couldn't imagine beginning my senior year without my best friend by my side. Becca and I had been through a lot, and despite that my recent actions had hurt her, I was confident we'd get through this too. And Gavin—I would take Drew's advice and give him time, but then I was going to do whatever it took to win him back. I loved him and I wasn't going to give up.

Chapter Twenty-Four

Gavin

I didn't get home until the early hours of the morning. I'd stayed out all night trying to forget the shit that went down, but no amount of alcohol would do the trick. I was plowed and it still hurt like hell. My heart was shattered. I should've followed my gut and not gotten involved with Carly in the first place. I knew it would end like all relationships did. I slipped into bed, hoping sleep would bring me some peace.

I woke up a few hours later. I had a hard time sleeping when I was this drunk. I stumbled down the stairs in search of water and something to cure my throbbing headache.

"Gavin-" Nate said when I entered the kitchen. He was sitting at the counter, looking like hell. I didn't feel one bit bad about the damage I'd caused to face. He held an icepack over his eye.

"Don't talk to me. Ever."

"I was worried about you when you didn't come home."

I snickered. "You weren't worried about me when you were sticking your tongue down my girlfriend's throat."

"I'm sorry."

I pierced Nate with a look that could kill. I took two Tylenol and went back to bed.

When I finally got up, it was late afternoon. Carly had

called and left me numerous voice messages, but like I did with all of my dad's messages, I deleted them without listening to a single one.

The week passed in a blur. I simply went through the motions of getting up every day, going to work, or tutoring at the library. I spent the rest of the time in my room drawing, listening to heavy metal, or partying with Jack. The hole in heart was huge. I continued to ignore Carly's messages. I had nothing to say to her. By Friday she was starting to get the hint. She was calling me less and less.

Sitting on my bed, I felt her eyes boring into me. I rose and walked across the room to where I'd hung a drawing of her eyes months ago. I reached my hand out to tear it off the wall. I couldn't concentrate with reminders of her everywhere I looked. My hand shook and I found that even though I had never experienced such pain, I couldn't take it down. I shoved my hands in the pockets of my jeans and looked around the room. I had countless drawings of Carly scattered on the walls. I'd drawn her face, her wavy hair, her deep brown eyes, and her very kissable lips. I'd drawn her playing the fiddle, swimming in the nieghbor's forbidden pool, and watching a movie curled up in the crook of my arm. She'd been my first true love, and I knew I could never forget her.

I grabbed the basketball in my closet collecting dust and went out to the driveway to shoot hoops. I needed a distraction from thinking about Carly, and holing up in my room drawing wasn't working. I ran up and down the driveway, shooting baskets from every angle. At first, I missed more than I made. But it was only a matter of time before I was making more and more shots. I was loosening up, and it felt great to be playing. I'd forgotten how much I liked the sound of the ball dribbling and the swoosh of the net. Soon, I was dripping wet and my muscles ached from the inactivity and unfamiliarity of playing ball. Nevertheless, I felt better than I had in weeks.

"Hey, Gavin," my mom said, when I came back inside.

"Hey."

"I haven't seen you play in a long time."

"Yeah. I needed to work off some steam." She looked hopeful. She knew all about my broken heart and my dark mood. Playing didn't change anything, but it took the edge off.

"Did you talk to Nate?"

"Nope. And I'm not planning on it." Nate had moved out, renting a cheap apartment with some friends. He said it was because it'd be closer to campus when classes started up next week. But I knew it was to get away from me, and I didn't care. I didn't consider him my brother anymore. My mom was hurt, but I couldn't change what had happened.

"Carly?"

"No," I said forcibly, ending any further discussion.

Chapter Twenty-Five

Carly

I picked up my phone and dialed Gavin. It went straight to voicemail, just like the previous twenty times I'd called. My voice was laced with sadness and regret as I left a final message. "Gavin. I miss you so much. I know you probably haven't listened to a single message I've left, and you probably won't listen to this one either, but I have one more thing to say. I know I fucked up, and I should have told you the truth, but I didn't. I've accepted that you want nothing to do with me and I want you to know I'm going to let you go. I won't be bothering you any more. I'm sorry things ended, but I will never be sorry that I fell in love with you. I still love you. Thanks for the best summer ever." I hung up just as sob escaped.

Gavin hadn't returned my messages, and I doubted I'd ever hear from him again. I'd see him at school when it started in two weeks, but I knew he wouldn't talk to me then either. I'd spent the summer trying to speak my mind, and in the end, I hadn't been able to do it when it counted the most. I'd lost Gavin as a result.

I almost lost my best friend too. But Becca and I had been through a lot together and we'd gotten through this too. The day after the Summer Jam she surprised me by showing up at my house. She said there was no way she was letting some asshole come between us. She apologized for not believing me. And she forgave me for not telling her.

At least I had ensemble today to keep my mind busy. Then I was meeting Connor to work on the song for my senior recital. I was still going through with it. I'd learned to see things through to the end. I'd been so focused on preparing for the Summer Jam that I'd put my other commitments on hold. What a mistake.

Fame came at too high of a cost. Karma broke up because the tension between Nate and I was too great. We could never get passed what happened. The other members were disappointed, but were left with no choice but to move on. Brady and Ed were going back to college. Nate was staying in the area and taking classes. Connor and I were going back to high school. Reality settling in once again.

I grabbed my violin, purplicious was once again back with Mrs. Wang where she belonged, and left.

As I entered Finkbauer, I was bombarded by friends congratulating me on Karma's win. It made me feel depressed all over again.

"Do you think Karma will get a record deal? Last year's winner did," said Michael. He sat next to me. He was probably hoping that would mean I'd be giving up my chair.

"No. Definitely not. Karma broke up."

"Really?" He looked shocked.

"Yeah. Things didn't work out," I said, glancing around for the conductor. It

would be great if we started soon. I wasn't about to explain what happened.

"Too bad. I thought you guys had something," he shrugged.

"Me too," I said under my breath. And I wasn't talking just referring to Karma.

Ensemble passed slowly. Playing with the orchestra no longer held my interest like it once had. I missed the funky beat and sound of purplicious. I was glad when it was over and the younger kids took the stage. My heart still filled with happiness helping them on their journey. I just didn't know where my own was headed.

I knocked on Connor's front door. Ready to work on what really mattered. The song we were writing together.

"Hey, come in," said Connor, opening the door.

"How have you been?" I followed him to his room where his kept his keyboard, computer, and recording equipment.

"Shitty, but thanks for asking." I sat on the corner of his bed.

"Gavin hasn't called you yet?" Connor's eyes grew dark.

"No. And it doesn't look like he will."

"Dumb bastard," Connor whispered.

I didn't want to talk about Gavin.

And I had already apologized to Connor for my role in causing the band to break up. He'd had a lot vested. He accepted my apology, saying that with summer coming to end he had to concentrate on school and getting into college. Working on this song together was one of the ways I was trying to make it up to him. It would help both of us. Connor didn't know, but I was going to invite the top composition professor at the Eastman School of Music to my senior recital. He was a personal friend of Mr. Kinsler's and he assured me he'd get him to come.

"Let's get started," I said, pulling the guitar out of its case. "I've almost finished the lyrics. I'll show you what I've got."

"Great." Connor sat in a chair, giving me his full attention.

I didn't play the guitar well, but I knew enough to make it work, since I couldn't play the fiddle and sing at the same time. Connor and I had written the song to showcase the range of my voice. The guitar was simply an accompaniment. The lyrics were mine and still a work in progress.

Connor didn't interrupt while I sang. "Sounds good," he said, when I finished. "But I think it still needs some tweaking."

We worked on it for another two hours. Finally I put my guitar down. My brain fried. As soon as I stopped playing, my somber mood returned. I'd been depressed ever since Gavin broke up with me. Music was the only thing that brought me temporary relief. My heart would never be the same. I still loved Gavin and I always would.

"What's the matter? You look like hell all of a sudden," observed Connor.

"It just sucks. I miss him." I slumped onto the bed.

"You'll get him back."

Tears filled my eyes. The last time I saw Gavin he'd made it perfectly clear that he didn't want anything to do with me. "I doubt it."

Connor reached over and squeezed my knee. Right in my ticklish spot. I burst out laughing. It was crazy. One minute I was about to burst into tears and the next I was laughing. My emotions had been on a roller coater ride all week.

Connor took my laughing as a good sign and squeezed my knee again. I shrieked and tried to push his hand away.

"Do you have any other ticklish spots?" He moved his hand to my waist and tickled me. I cracked up. The truth was I was ticklish everywhere.

Suddenly, my laughter died. Gavin stood in the doorway. He looked pissed. His fists were clenched and his jaw was tight. *Shit!* This looked bad. What were the odds that he'd show up now?

Connor stood and immediately launched into an explanation. "Dude, it's not what it looks like?"

"What? You're not hanging out in you bedroom with my girlfriend?"

I wasn't his girlfriend any more, he hadn't talked to me in a week, but I didn't want to point that out. I considered him calling me that a good sign, or it would have been had he not found me here.

"I'm helping Carly with a song, that's all," said Connor.

I had told Gavin once that I'd enlisted Connor's help with my senior recital. Did he remember?

"Whatever, man. I thought we were friends. I came over here to see if you wanted to go car shopping with me, but I can see you're busy. Catch you later."

"Gavin, wait," I shouted. He stopped and faced me. There were so many things I wanted to say to him. "I've tried calling you."

"I know. I listened to your message today. Looks like I know why you've decided to let me go. Looks like you've already moved on."

I sucked in a breath. That wasn't what I meant. I had let him go because I loved him. I wanted him to be happy. I opened my mouth to explain, but he was already gone.

Chapter Twenty-Six

Gavin

That fucking hurt. Even though I was pretty sure nothing had been going on, pain filled my chest. I knew Connor was helping her with a song, but she didn't have to look so fucking happy about it. Especially when I'd been depressed as hell, drinking myself into a stupor every night. Relationships fucking sucked. I'd ignored her messages all week until today when I listened to her tell me that she was letting me go. Hearing her say that made my heart crack. And then seeing her for the first time since we broke up almost brought me to my knees. I'd even called her *"my girlfriend"*.

I stormed out. I couldn't look at her. I wasn't sure what I wanted any more. I hopped on my bike and rode around. For once I was glad I didn't have a car. It didn't clear my head like playing basketball, but the rush of the wind as I pedaled hard brought me some relief. For the first time in a week, I didn't go looking for Jack. I rode until I was exhausted, even taking a turn down Carly's street before going home. When I walked through my back door I still didn't have any answers.

"Did you find a car?" my mom asked. She was in the kitchen making dinner.

"No."

"I'll go with you over the weekend, if you want. I bet we

could find something. I know you had your heart set on having a car by the first day of school."

"Sure, Mom," I said with little enthusiasm.

"My pleasure. You're just in time. Dinner's ready."

We sat down at the counter to eat. It was only the two of us now. Gone were the days when we were a family eating dinner together at the table. It was too quiet. I hated it. After dinner I helped my mom clean up, and then I went to my room.

I checked my phone before going to bed. Carly hadn't called me even once. My heart ached. And I was angry. *Why do I care so much?*

I tossed and turned all night long, dreaming of the dark-haired angel.

Today was my last shift at Trader Joe's. I had enough money for my car, but I'd continue to tutor to save money for college. I'd look for a new job once school started. I was happy to kiss this job goodbye because ever since Julia heard I broke up with Carly, she'd been driving me crazy. She would follow me around the store like a lost puppy, and more than once I'd told her to get lost. Without fail, she kept coming back. She had even told her friends to come to the store when I was working to check me out. I told her repeatedly that I wasn't interested, but she didn't seem to get it.

My assignment was operating the cash register. It was better than restocking shelves because Julia couldn't come and talk to me whenever she felt like it. My shift ended in an hour. I handed the customer in front of me her change and then started checking out the next person without even looking up. Organic diapers. I always wondered who bought these. I'd restocked them just yesterday. I looked up and was startled to see eyes the same shade as mine staring at me. He looked older. I hadn't seen him in more than a year, but as I looked into his eyes, I noticed they were the same, yet different. They were brighter. *Is this what Nate had been talking about?* I considered the possibility that there was more to the story. Finally, I found my voice. "Dad?"

"Son." He smiled. "It's good to see you. You're looking well."

I brushed the shaggy hair out of my face. I was at a loss for words, and then I saw that he had a baby carrier in one of his hands. "Is that ... my sister?"

"Sure is." He held the carrier up and pushed back the light blanket that had been covering her. "Meet Hannah."

I came around from behind the cash register so I could get a good look at her. She was tiny. She had big eyes and a sweet face. I was surprised by how much dark, fuzzy hair she had. "She's cute," I admitted, returning to my post.

"Thanks," my dad beamed proudly. "Look at you, all grown up. I feel like I've missed out on so much," he frowned. "I would love to take you to dinner sometime. Catch up. You'll be heading off to college in a year."

"Maybe," I shrugged noncommittally. It wasn't much of an answer, but it was more than I'd ever given him.

He brushed his own graying hair back. "It was good to see you, Gavin. Don't be such a stranger. You have my number."

"Okay," I said, handing him his receipt. "Congratulations, Dad."

My dad's smile widened. He left, carrying my baby sister in one hand and the diapers in the other. When he got to the door, he looked over his shoulder at me.

I didn't go right home after work. I needed time to think. I had my mom's car, and I drove around, ending up at the park near Carly's house. A game was going on. I looked closely and saw that is was Drew and Lucas. I watched from my car for several minutes. Drew was good. I was itching to join them. Eventually, I reached around to the back seat and grabbed a T-shirt from the floor. I replaced my work shirt with the T-shirt. I inhaled and sighed. I forgot Carly was the last one to wear this shirt. She borrowed it one night. She gave it back to me when I drove her home, and I'd thrown it in the back, forgetting about it until now. It still had her summer scent and I felt my heart break all over again. Even though shooting hoops with Drew would be another reminder, I needed to play.

I took a deep breath and jogged over.

"Mind if I join you?"

Drew nodded. "Sure, man. It's good to see you again."

"Yeah," agreed Lucas.

We spent the next hour shooting around and playing a few games of twenty-one. Playing ball made me feel whole again. Drew never brought up Carly, but I could feel her with us the entire time. I thought about asking him how she was doing, but then I didn't. We played until I was so exhausted, I couldn't think anymore.

Drew gave me the speech again. "You're a solid player, man. You should try out for the team this year. We're looking for a good center. Our best one graduated last year."

"Thanks, I just might."

"Excellent." Drew slapped me on the back as we headed out. "Just so you know, she looks as miserable as you. And I know for a fact the dude helping her write a song, I forgot what she said his name was—"

"Connor?" I provided.

"Yeah, that's it. I know Connor has nothing on you. They really are only friends. She loves you, man. I might be wrong, but I had money on you loving her too."

His words hit me hard, and I almost stumbled. Did she still love me and want to get back together? The truth was, I loved her, and nothing was going to change that. Why was I letting Nate come between us? She should've told me that he kissed her, but maybe I was being too hard on her. If being apart caused us both this much pain, did it make sense to fight it? But what if I was too late? What if Carly had already moved on? Or was Drew right—her and Connor weren't anything more than friends. I had a lot to think about.

Chapter Twenty-Seven

Carly

I pulled the bow across the strings, trying hard to concentrate. I was working on the song that Connor and I had written together. It still wasn't quite right, but I didn't know how to fix it.

Suddenly the doorbell chimed. I knew my dad was downstairs, so I didn't run to answer it. It wasn't for me. Becca was out of town. It was probably Lucas or one of Drew's other friends. I closed the case and a wave of sadness rushed through me. It reminded me of how Gavin had closed the door on our relationship.

"Carly," my dad shouted from downstairs, interrupting my thoughts.

"What?" I yelled back.

"Come down here, please." I wasn't sure what he wanted, but I slowly made my way down the stairs.

My breath caught in my throat and my stomach felt queasy when I saw Gavin sitting on the edge of the couch, talking. I couldn't believe he was here. My palms began to sweat and my heart rate sped up in anticipation.

My dad stood. "I'll be in my office. I have some work to finish." My dad nodded at Gavin and then winked at me, walking out of the room.

Gavin came over to where I was standing, frozen at the bottom of the stairs. He reached out and grabbed my hands, holding them tightly against his chest. "I don't know why I'm here. I've never missed anyone as much as I've missed you. I don't want another day to go by without you by my side."

At first, I was confused; then it hit me, and the corners of my mouth turned up slightly. "Did you come here to play two truths and a lie?" He nodded, his blue eyes shining. "I've missed you terribly." I thought back to the sleepless nights and the long, dragged-out days. "The lie is the first one ... you don't know why you're here?"

"I've missed the hell outta you, and I can't imagine spending one more day without you. I've been a complete idiot. I know you didn't kiss my brother. I shouldn't have been so hard on you for not telling me sooner. I know you wanted to, but Nate talked you out of it. I'm sorry. Can you forgive me?"

Tears swam in my eyes. Happy tears. Emotion choked my throat, making it impossible to speak.

"It's okay. I understand. I'm too late." Gavin dropped my hands and turned to leave.

My eyes widened in horror. I grabbed his arm. I wasn't letting him walk away without explaining. "What?"

"I get it. You've moved on. You have more in common with Connor."

Relief spread through me. "I'm not with Connor. There's nothing going on between us. He told you the truth. He's helping me write a song." I placed my hands on either side of his face and looked into his deep blue eyes. "I love you," I said.

Gavin looked pleased. "Does that mean, you'll take me back?"

I threw my arms around his neck and kissed him with everything I had. It was like the last kiss we shared, but different. Hopeful.

"Is that a yes?" he asked.

"Yes! I'm yours and you're mine," I said, repeating the exact same words he said the first day we became more than just friends. Suddenly I knew what my song had been missing.

"I'm sorry it took me so long to get my shit together." We walked back to the couch and sat down. I felt a huge relief knowing that Gavin wasn't going anywhere. I felt happy again. Being curled up against his side felt familiar; I belonged here. "Hey, whatever happened with Becca? Did you make up yet?"

"Yeah. She came over the next day, shouting that Nathan was a dickhead for even thinking he could ruin our friendship." I laughed at hearing myself repeat Becca's words. "She decided she was never in love after all, and had already moved on. But I think my twin had something to do with her quick change of heart," I said with a wink.

"I'm glad everything worked out."

"Me too."

He leaned in and lightly brushed his lips along my neck until he found his way back to my mouth.

"Gavin," I whispered, pulling away and looking into his blue eyes, "I'm so glad you came back. I promise never to let anyone or anything come between us again. I'll always speak my mind even if it's difficult. I love you."

He stroked my cheek with his thumb and goose bumps broke out all over my body. "I love you too, Girly. I know I never told you, but I've loved you ever since our first date to the lake. And I plan on loving you for a long, long time."

My heart rate spiked at his words. It was all I needed to hear. I crushed my lips to his. I also planned on loving Gavin a long, long time.

Chapter Twenty-Eight

Gavin

It had been one hell of a summer. I'd sorted through some personal matters, grown as an individual, and most importantly, met the love of my life. With classes starting tomorrow, it was time to take the school by storm. Personally, I couldn't wait to start my senior year and experience all the bullshit that came with being the "kings and queens" of school. This year would be different than last. I'd have Carly on my arm. And I was ready to make new friends and try out for the basketball team. However, I didn't want to get ahead of myself—there were still a few precious hours of summer break left, and I planned on making the most of them.

Obviously, anything I planned on doing involved Carly and what better way to end the summer than to head back to Carrington Lake. Carrington Lake would always be our place. We'd built a special bond there and I wanted to continue the trend of creating all the memories we could, not to mention, we hadn't been back since our romantic picnic earlier in the summer.

With the intent of moving forward, I decided I needed to make a splash—no more borrowing Mommy's car. I'd saved up enough to purchase a car that ran—it wasn't a BMW, but it got the job done—which would only benefit mine and Carly's relationship. What made things even better was the fact that whenever I looked over at Carly in the passenger seat, I knew I was the luckiest man in the world. She was the most beautiful girl I'd ever laid eyes on. I know that sounds sappy, but when you're in love, there's no such thing as sappy.

As Carly and I headed down to the lake in my semi-new whip, she did what she always did—captivated me. The way she sang along to the radio drove me crazy. Maybe Nathan was on to something when he said the reason he'd kissed Carly was because he couldn't get her voice out of his head. On second thought, fuck him. He was still dead to me. These thoughts sort of contradicted the emphasis I'd put on growing up this summer. Nevertheless, the final few hours of sun-fueled freedom belonged to Carly, and I wasn't going to let a single negative thought ruin the evening.

When we arrived, the remnants of summer barbeques and weekend parties had been cleaned up, the place deserted. I was thankful for the fact that Carly and I had the place to ourselves for the evening. Carly packed the picnic this time and said she had a surprise for me. At this point, my imagination was running wild with what it could be. We still hadn't had sex, even though we'd talked about it and were both ready. I had a good feeling tonight might be the night.

Like last time, we took the canoe out for a quick trip to the middle of the lake and back. The amount of daylight was diminishing now that September had arrived, so we didn't linger as we did before. Making the most of the situation, I reveled in having Carly so close to me. With school starting and our schedules changing, I was going to miss these quiet moments. We were going to be in several of the same classes, but I knew we would be busy with homework, studying, and basketball. We wouldn't have as much time to enjoy each other's company like we did right now.

Carly spread out the blanket on the dock and unpacked the picnic.

"Is my surprise in the basket, Girly?" I asked, not able to contain my curiosity any longer.

"Nope, but I did make your favorite sandwich—ham and cheese," she said, handing me one.

"Thanks." I took a big bite. "Delicious."

We ate in silence for a few minutes and enjoyed the sounds of nature's beauty: fish jumping, crickets chirping, and the rustling of leaves on the trees. That was one of the things I'd grown to love most about our relationship. Through it all, we could still enjoy an easy silence. I thought about how lucky I was to have found this girl and how good it was going to feel walking down the halls with her on my arm.

"Are you worried about any of your classes this year?" I'd signed up for physics this semester and heard the teacher was a beast. What the fuck had I been thinking? It was my senior year and senioritis was a sure-fire bet.

"I'm a little nervous about physics," she said. "But we have it together, so it won't be that bad." She smiled. "What about you?"

"I was thinking the exact same thing."

"I visited another college," I said.

"Yeah?" I'd told Carly how I was thinking of going to a local college and living at home to save money. She wouldn't say how she felt about it because she didn't want to influence my decision.

"I'm going to apply to St John Fisher College. If I get accepted, I'll go. It's my top choice."

She grinned. "I hope we both get into the colleges that we want." She didn't come right out and say my decision made her happy, but I could tell by the look on her face and the sound of her voice that she was pleased. We'd get to see each other all the time if we both got accepted to our top schools. The Eastman School of Music and St John Fisher were both near our hometown.

We finished eating and packed away the leftovers. "I'll take this back to the car. I have to get something," she said, sprinting away like she was trying out for the track team.

"Is it my surprise?" I yelled.

"Maybe. If you're patient, you'll find out sooner rather

than later." Hadn't I been practicing that the entire summer?

To my surprise, she returned carrying a guitar. I didn't know Carly could play the guitar. This wasn't the surprise I had in mind, but I was curious to see what she was up to. If I knew Carly like I thought I did, she was going to sing for me. She knew her voice played tricks on my mind, which could very well lead to the surprise I was originally hoping for.

"Hey, how'd you get that in my car?" No sooner had I finished the question when the answer became clear.

"Drew," we said at the same time, laughing.

I remembered the day he slipped the fiddle into my car so that I could lead Carly back to Karma. Even though the band ended on a bad note, I know being a part of it was one of the happiest moments of Carly's life. Seeing her on stage, singing her heart out—it was a huge part of who she was. I knew she'd find her way to Nashville someday. I could easily picture her there, especially with her newly defined look—flowing sundress, jean jacket, cowgirl boots, and guitar in hand. Pure country. And sexy to boot.

"I didn't know you played the guitar. Is that the surprise?" I asked.

She laughed, and the cool evening air suddenly felt a little bit warmer. "No. That's not the surprise. I can't play the guitar very well, but I can play a few chords. I'm sort of self-taught. The surprise is that I wrote a song for you. Connor helped me compose it, but the lyrics are all mine." Her cheeks flamed bright and she chewed her bottom lip. Carly was nervous, and it was cute as hell. I was ready to make her mine, in every sense of the word, right now.

"You wrote me a song?"

"Yeah."

"Damn, girl ... that's hot." I was practically speechless. My girl wrote me a song.

She sat down on the dock next to me, and our feet dangled over the water. She strummed the guitar and made some minor adjustments. I turned so that I could see her better. I didn't want to miss a second of watching her play.

"I wrote this song about falling in love with you. It's called 'Love Could Last Forever.'"

Her rich, inviting voice flowed out of her very kissable mouth and it was all I could do to remember to breathe. The lyrics were powerful, passionate, and personal. My heart swelled.

From the first day ... you walked into the class,
I thought that we'd be friends, but nothing ever more.
I stole a glance or two, you didn't even know,
You were the mystery, the handsome mystery.
Hid all your qualities, couldn't penetrate the wall,
I often wondered why, just what I had to do,
So that we could join as two.
I finally had the chance, and I'm glad that you agreed,
For the double date, yeah, it must have been fate.
But you just weren't ready, ready to break the mold,
Fate pushed us together again. But we stumbled and fell,
But through the hardships, we'd always find a way.

We belong as one ... just look up at the stars,
Stars they never lie, and neither will I.
If we ... never change ... are true to ourselves,
Love could last forever.
I am truly yours, and you are truly mine.
We belong together, always and forever.
Ain't ever gonna change, that I know for sure.

I fell in love with you ... on this very dock.
You gave me the strength to speak my mind, do what I want.
Not always needing to talk, silence is strong.
Knowing we got each other, one heartbeat combined.
We're on top of the world, wasn't always that easy.
Sometimes there'll be stones that litter our path.
But heaven often knows, you gotta trip and fall.
Get right back up, slowly start again.

It's what we've always done ... finally found our way.
We trust in our love ... we'll be friends forever.
You will be you, and I will be me.
But as we grow together, let us not forget,
How this summer changed our lives.

We belong as one ... just look up at the stars,
Stars they never lie, and neither will I.
If we ... never change ... are true to ourselves,
Love could last forever.
I am truly yours, and you are truly mine.
We belong together, always and forever.
Ain't ever gonna change, that I know for sure.

She put everything out there, just like I did when I drew the picture of us now hanging in the center of my wall. That's how I thought of her, occupying the center of my universe. It was our love story, every last word. She was mine and I was hers, and it didn't get any more real than that.

The song ended and she put the guitar down and looked at me with wide eyes, waiting for my response. Words couldn't describe how I felt. I wanted to hold onto this girl forever.

"Fuck," I said, running my hands through my hair. "That was amazing."

"You liked it?"

"I loved it." I grabbed her and pulled her close, kissing her to prove how much it meant to me. With each day that passed, I fell deeper in love with Carly.

I brushed back a loose strand of hair from her face and carefully pushed her back onto the blanket. She'd brought two blankets, and I used the second one to cover us as my hands explored her body. I kissed her, nibbling and licking back and forth from neck to shoulder. I was precise and methodical with every kiss and stroke.

Carly whispered, "There is more to the surprise." She spoke with passion and confidence. Could this be the surprise

I'd been waiting for? Was it time to take our relationship to the next level?

"There is?" I said, barely able to control my excitement at the possibility of what was to come. Then, with as much confidence as she sang with onstage, she said, "I want to be with you in every way."

I'd been waiting for this moment since I'd first laid eyes on Carly. However, my decision to take things slow and get to know her as a person instead of a quick bang made this moment more memorable. I loved Carly and the physical attraction was undeniable. However, before I made the final move, I wanted to be sure she was 100 percent ready. "We don't have to have sex. I don't want to pressure you into anything you're not ready for," I said, placing my hands on either side of her face. "I mean that. I'll wait, forever, if that's what it takes."

"I know," she said. "And I love you even more for saying that, but I'm ready. I've been ready," she giggled. "You're in my heart and I want to feel you ... everywhere." Her eyes were dark and full of lust. It was clear to me that she wanted me every bit as much as I wanted her, so I didn't argue.

I kissed her again and didn't hold back. I had no doubt that what I felt for Carly was real, and I was ready to show her just how much I loved her.

We took our time. I wanted to savor every moment. The moon cast its silvery light. I wasn't worried that anyone was going to see us; it was as if we were the only ones on the planet. It was warm under the blanket, our bodies pressed tightly against one another. Although I'd had sex before, I'd never made love, and that was about to change. I wanted to show Carly how good it could feel when you loved someone. This was unchartered territory for me. I knew Carly was a virgin and I wanted her first time to be memorable and pain-free.

My tongue slowly crept down her torso and I made tiny circles around her clit. She quivered, her moans soft under my careful ministrations. I wanted to get her ready and wet, so that it wouldn't hurt when I entered her for the first time. Tonight was all about Carly.

When she began to tremble underneath me, I knew it was time. "I have a condom in my wallet," I said, reaching for my long-forgotten cargo shorts.

"You won't need one. I'm on the pill."

Holy shit! Now that was what I called a surprise. "Really?" I choked out. My voice was rough with passion.

"Yeah. I knew at some point we'd be ready and when Becca offered to go with me to get them, I went. I know you mentioned once how you got tested for STDs, so I'm not worried."

"Wow ..."

Our lips met again and our bodies came together like they never had before. I started out slow and gentle, making sure she was okay. I could tell by the look on her face that it initially hurt, but as her sweet spot moistened, the pain turned to ecstasy. We moved in rhythmic motions like we'd done it a million times. Her face filled with love, and she cast my name in her melodious voice. As our bodies climaxed and we finished our journey, I couldn't help but think that life didn't get any better than this. I lay down next to her with our legs still tangled and waited for our breathing to return to normal. There were no words for what just happened between us.

"Even though I wish we could stay here forever, it's getting late, and tomorrow is the first day of school. We should probably go," she said.

I gave her a quick squeeze and breathed in the scent that was uniquely Carly. "You're right."

Handing Carly her clothes, we quickly dressed. I folded the blankets, Carly grabbed her guitar, and we headed back to the car.

Before she could climb in, I backed her against the door and put my hands on either side, trapping her. "Originally I was sorry to see summer go, but now I'm actually looking forward to fall." I chuckled.

"Me too."

"I love you, Girly."

"I love you too."

Her voice uttering those three little words would forever be music to my ears.

###

Falling Into You (Senior Year #2) coming soon. Drew and Becca's story.

33387413R00148

Made in the USA
Charleston, SC
12 September 2014